runaway heart

a westward dreams novel

Books by Jane Peart

Brides of Montclair Series

Westward Dreams Series

The American Quilt Series

PART 1

To travel hopefully is better than to arrive.

R. S. Stevenson

Perhaps one day this, too, will be pleasant to remember.

Virgil

runaway heart

a westward dreams novel

BOOK 1

Jane Peart

ZONDERVAN®

ZONDERVAN.com/
AUTHORTRACKER
follow your favorite authors

ZONDERVAN®

Runaway Heart

Copyright © 1994 by Jane Peart

Value Edition 978-0-310-28802-2

Requests for information should be addressed to:
Zondervan, *Grand Rapids, Michigan* 49530

Library of Congress Cataloging-in-Publication Data

Peart, Jane.
      Runaway heart / Jane Peart.
          p. cm. — (The westward dreams series)
      ISBN 0-310-41271-4 (paper)
        1. Frontier and pioneer life—Oregon Fiction. 2. Man-woman
relationships—Oregon—Fiction. 3. Women pioneers—Oregon—Fiction. 4. Women
teachers—Oregon—Fiction. I. Title. II. Series: Peart, Jane. Westward dreams series.
PS3566.E238R86 1994
813'.54—dc20   94-20318
                                                         CIP

Printed in the United States of America

08 09 10 11 12 13 14 15 16 • 21 20 19 18 17 16 15 14 13 12 11 10 9 8 7 6 5 4 3 2 1

Chapter 1

*J*ust before sundown a stagecoach, rattling and swaying precariously, lurched down the rutted road into the small Oregon town, sending up cartwheels of dust in its wake.

Inside, its only remaining passenger, Holly Lambeth, clinging desperately to the hand strap, slid from side to side on the tattered leather seat, terrified that the vehicle might pitch over at any minute.

At last with a bone-jarring jolt it came to a stop. Drawing a deep sigh of relief, Holly wiped the small mud-spattered window and peered out hopefully. Before she could get a good look, the coach door was yanked open by the grizzle-bearded driver who stuck his head inside and, displaying tobacco-stained teeth, announced, "This here's Riverbend, lady. This is where you get off. End of the line."

Ignoring her qualms of the probable truth of his statement, she gathered the tiered skirt of her peacock-blue traveling suit, crisp and smart three days ago but now quite the worse for wear, and prepared to get out. Lifting it carefully over two layers of ruffled petticoats, she stepped gingerly down the rickety steps onto the wooden sidewalk.

It felt good to stretch her stiff muscles after the long, cramped journey over rough winding roads. For a moment she stood straightening her snug braid-trimmed jacket, then slowly pivoted to look about her. Just then a gust of wind caught her tiny feathered bonnet, tugging the pins that held it, loosening strands of her russet-brown hair from its coil, and blowing dust and grit into her face. Grabbing her hat brim with one kid-gloved hand, she fumbled into her purse for a handkerchief, then lifted her veil to dab her eyes.

Since it was close to six o'clock and therefore supper hour for most of Riverbend's citizens, there were only a few people on hand as the stage arrived; otherwise, the appearance of a fashionably dressed young woman might have received more than one or two curious glances.

Holly Lambeth was used to drawing admiring looks. In spite of having a peach-bloom complexion, long-lashed hazel eyes, and a dimpled smile, Holly would never be considered beautiful. What made her so attractive was her vivacity and sparkle.

That sparkle, however, was sadly missing now. As she gazed around with mounting dismay, Holly's conviction grew that she had made the *second* worst mistake of her twenty-three years. The first and worst, of course, was to have kept Jim Mercer dangling for over a year in an "on-again, off-again" engagement.

The sun began slowly slipping behind a rim of purple hills. Overhead dark clouds gathered.

This must be the center of town. Holly glanced down the long unpaved road where the signpost read "Main Street." It was lined with an odd assortment of buildings. Some were old weather-beaten wooden ones with sagging balconies, others of raw brick, some uncompleted. Wheelbarrows of bricks stood abandoned as if left by workers.

So *this* was Riverbend, Oregon.

Numb with fatigue, Holly bit her lower lip and fought back the tears that threatened, tightening her throat. There was no use telling herself it was her own fault she was here. Her family and friends had all been quick to tell her that.

But at the time, "*any* port in a storm" had seemed the answer to her problem, the "storm" being the gossip whirling around her when the fact that she had been jilted became known. Anything had seemed better than facing the curious looks, the whispers, the pitying glances that had followed her. Even harder to bear were the smugly spiteful looks of those who made it no secret that they thought it was high time Holly Lambeth got her "come-uppance."

Now that it was too late, she realized she had been vain and foolish in recklessly risking Jim's love and patience with all her silly flirtations, her careless disregard for his pride. If only . . .

But it was too late for "if only." She had nobody to blame but herself that she was here in a forsaken Oregon frontier town instead of planning a fairy-tale wedding, with a white lace gown and veil, walking arm-in-arm with her army-lieutenant husband beneath an arch of crossed sabers held by his West Point classmates.

As if it had just happened, Holly felt the shock of that morning when she had read in the local paper, along with the rest of Willow Springs, the announcement of Lt. Jim Mercer's marriage to the daughter of his commanding officer at his first army post.

"This all yours, miss?" The whiskey voice of the driver cut through her remorseful memory. With a start, Holly turned to follow his dirty index finger pointing to his helper on top of the stagecoach, straddling her trunk and unstrapping it.

"Yes, and please be careful—," she began, but her voice was lost in the noise of the tumbling luggage. Holly was forced to jump back as her trunk catapulted down and landed at her feet. She gasped and was about to reprimand the fellow sharply when he hollered down, "Anything else?"

"Yes, my valise and hatbox, and please—," she started to caution again when the valise and hatbox, containing her very best bonnet, came hurtling down in the same manner as her trunk.

"Well!" she gasped indignantly. But whatever else she might have said was checked by the surly expression on the driver's face. She realized he was expecting a gratuity, highly undeserved in her opinion. Under his glare she dug into her purse and handed him a coin. Acknowledging it with only a pull on the soiled brim of his battered felt hat, the man turned and shuffled down the street.

It came as no surprise to Holly to see him push his way through the doors of the nearby saloon, the Nugget. She had observed that this was his custom at every stagecoach station en route, a practice that had not done much to lessen her anxiety, traveling the treacherous mountain roads on the way to Riverbend.

The one he now entered was one of several other such establishments along Main Street with names like Last Chance and the Doggoned Best. Most of Holly's information about the far West had been gained from the covers on the pulp magazines confiscated by her cousin Willy's mother from his hidden horde. These depicted lurid scenes of cowboy shoot-outs, Indian attacks, and barroom brawls. Looking down the unpaved street lined with saloons, she felt as if she might have stepped right into the pages of one.

Before being hit by her next attack of second thoughts on her fateful decision to come West, she heard a familiar male voice behind her say, "Cousin Holly?" Holly whirled around to find herself face-to-face with Ned Thornton.

"Oh, Ned! It's so wonderful to see you!" she exclaimed holding out both hands to him.

When his kind, homely face turned crimson, Holly realized she may have greeted him too effusively. Belatedly she remembered that Ned had been one of the many young men flocking around her at Willow Springs parties, hoping to add his name to her dance card. He'd had quite a case on her then—now, of course, he was married to her cousin Hetty Granville. The same Hetty who was providing her "a port in the storm."

"Welcome to Riverbend, Holly," Ned stammered.

Trying to allay any embarrassment Ned's own memories might be causing him, Holly rushed on, "Is Hetty with you? Where are the children? I can't wait to see them."

"They're all at home. They're so excited about their cousin's coming all the way from Kentucky that they've run Hetty crazy with questions all day. Hetty's fixed a real special supper so we best get along home or else she'll be might—" Ned stopped abruptly and pointed to her three pieces of luggage. "Are these yours?"

"Yes, but I can carry my hatbox and valise," Holly said.

Shouldering Holly's small trunk, Ned told her, "It's not very far. It's only a short walk. We live just at the end of town so I

10

can be near the store. You knew, didn't you, I have the General Store? That's it right over there." There was a note of pride in Ned's voice as he nodded his head to a neat-looking building across the street.

"Yes, I do know, Ned. I've heard you've done very well. Of course Hetty has written to her folks, Aunt Dolly and Uncle Sid. We all think it's fine you and Hetty have made such a good life for yourselves. Although it does seem awfully far from home." How far, Holly was just beginning to realize.

"It's a good place and it's growing. The railroad's going to be coming in here before long—branch line through here between Portland and Sacramento. That's going to bring a lot more people and more business here. Everyone's counting on that. Thirty years ago this was just a raw gold-mining camp, but the vein ran out within a few years. Then homesteaders came here and brought their families. Farmers came and prospered. This is fine orchard country; Riverbend's becoming famous for its pear crop. Yes, indeed, Riverbend's turned into a solid township. One day folks think it will become the county seat," Ned said with conviction. "It's home now to me—to us."

Good for Ned, Holly thought as they walked along. Ned had been wise to leave Willow Springs, move out from under the shadow of his critical father, a prominent judge, and his older brother, a brilliant lawyer. Evidently here Ned had become his own man, made a place for himself. And, Holly reminded herself a bit ruefully, Hetty had been smart enough to see his potential and marry him.

Holly doubted her cousin's welcome would be as genuine as Ned's. The truth was she and Hetty had never been friends. In spite of the facts their mothers were sisters and throughout childhood the girls were constantly thrown together at family gatherings of the Lambeth and Granville clans, they had always clashed. Holly considered Hetty a prig, a tattle-tale, a goodie-goodie, and Hetty accused her of being a showoff, a tomboy, and a tease. Both of them were right.

As they grew up it was worse, and the differences between them became more pronounced. Holly developed into a young lady of natural charm and gaiety that was enormously appealing. Unfortunately Hetty inherited her father's plain looks and prickly personality instead of her pretty mother's sociability. While Holly's fun-loving vivaciousness attracted many beaux, Hetty became a typical wallflower. Of course, now the shoe was on the other foot. Hetty was married to a prosperous man, had children and a home, while Holly remained unmarried and possibly on the brink of becoming an old maid!

Well, whatever their past differences, Holly determined to try to get along with Hetty. Surely they were beyond all their old squabbles. She would do her best to make herself useful, helpful, and be cheerful, making sure Hetty wasn't sorry she'd offered her cousin a temporary haven.

These mental resolutions were interrupted when a tall man stepped out of the door of one of the buildings in front of them. "Evenin' Ned."

"Evenin', Adam," Ned replied. Putting down Holly's trunk on the wooden sidewalk, he turned to her saying, "Holly, this is Adam Corcoran, the editor of our local newspaper, the *Riverbend Monitor.* Adam, I'd like you to meet Hetty's cousin, Miss Hollis Lambeth."

Holly set down her valise, gratefully. It was heavier than she thought, jammed with last-minute things she'd forgotten to put in her trunk.

At Ned's introduction Adam Corcoran removed his broad-brimmed hat, bowed slightly. "Delighted, Miss Lambeth." The fast-fading light cast shadows upon an angular face. Although the high-bridged nose gave a look of arrogance, that was offset by the humor in his eyes and his mouth under the well-trimmed mustache. "I take it you have just arrived? Then you have not yet had a chance to get much of an impression of Riverbend." He smiled. "And just how long to you plan to stay in *our fair city?*"

Holly thought she detected a hint of irony in his tone and had the feeling he might be baiting her. It made her uncomfortable, and she replied coolly, "I've not any definite plans as yet, but I'm sure I'll enjoy my visit however long."

"Ad, here, runs the newspaper practically single-handed. Besides writing all the articles and doing all the reporting, he

12

helps Tom Simmons set type and gives young Mike Flannery a hand with the press."

"You didn't mention my editorials, Ned, and the fact that they are often controversial and not always well received. We also print some pretty outraged letters to the editor and have had a few smashed windows—mainly on Saturday night!" Looking directly at Holly, Adam said, "What Ned's too polite to tell you, Miss Lambeth, is that I'm not the most popular man in town."

"I wouldn't say that." Ned shook his head. "You give folks a lot to talk about. Debate never hurt anything."

Adam threw back his head and laughed a rich, full laugh. "Ned, you should have been a diplomat instead of a storekeeper. Or maybe, better still, a politician. Let me know if you ever want to run for mayor or—"

"Not me, not ever." Ned joined in the laughter, then said, "Well, we best be getting on home. Hetty'll be wondering what's keeping us. I'm sure she probably saw the stage arrive, and the children will be driving her crazy. Even when I went home at noon for dinner, they were already asking if it was time yet and running to the window to see if their cousin Holly had arrived."

"I wish you a very pleasant stay in Riverbend, Miss Lambeth, and I'm sure we'll meet again."

Adam Corcoran's voice held a confidence that annoyed Holly, so she merely nodded, then picked up her valise again, and moved on with Ned.

They had gone only a few more steps along the uneven boardwalk when a small, shabby, black buggy pulled to a stop on the road beside them. A man called out, "Howdy, Ned! Did my box of medical supplies come in on the stage?"

The man leaned farther out, took off his hat, ran his hand through a shock of thick hair, and greeted Holly.

"Howdy, Doc!" Ned responded. "Not unless it was on this last one. I haven't had a chance to check the freight yet. I had to meet my wife's cousin from Kentucky who came in this evening." Ned indicated Holly, saying, "Miss Hollis Lambeth."

To her he said, "Holly, I'd like you to meet the most important man in town, our doctor, Blaine Stevens."

The man in the buggy took off his hat, leaned farther out, and greeted Holly, "Good evening, Miss Lambeth, welcome to Riverbend. I hope you had a pleasant journey."

While Holly hesitated between truth and exaggeration, Ned answered for her. "Well, that kind of depends what you mean by pleasant, I guess." He chuckled. "It was Joe Rossiter's run—"

"Oh, no! Not *Joe Rossiter!*" the doctor affected a look of horror. Even as he shook his head, he laughed. "What an introduction to Riverbend! I've ridden with Joe a time or two myself. It's like being with one of those circus stunt riders! I sure hope it didn't ruin your impression of Oregon!"

"Well, not completely," Holly retorted, dimples appearing at his accurate description, adding saucily, "*—but* my fondness for stagecoach travel has been severely impaired!"

A boyish grin showed that he appreciated her humor. For the next few minutes they conducted a lively exchange on the dangers of stagecoach travel and tipsy drivers while Ned looked on with indulgent amusement. Then, almost mid-sentence, Holly checked herself. This was just the sort of unconscious flirtatiousness Jim had resented in her. He had accused her of flirting with any man in sight. It was just this kind of behavior that had landed her in her present situation, she reminded herself. Hadn't she promised herself she was cured of it forever? No matter how attractive the man was—and she had to admit Dr. Blaine Stevens certainly was—

Abruptly Holly suppressed a jesting remark, the dimples vanished, and she tried compressing her mouth into a prim line. Her sudden withdrawal from the conversation seemed to puzzle both men, and an awkward pause followed. Finally Blaine said, "Well, at least you made it here safely. I'm sure Hetty's delighted that she'll have someone from her hometown for a visit."

Holly, who was not at all sure of that, made no comment. But Ned did. "And speaking of Hetty, if we don't get home, she'll be sending out a posse to find us. The stage being late won't be enough excuse if supper's spoiled—"

"You *married* men have it rough all right, having to hurry

home to a good, hot, home-cooked meal after a hard day's work!" the doctor scoffed jovially.

"And you *bachelors* don't have to worry about a tongue-lashing if you're late!" was Ned's good-natured retort.

"Well, so long," Blaine said. "My regards to Hetty, and I hope to see you again, Miss Lambeth."

As they started walking again, Holly couldn't help wondering if all that emphasis on who was married and who was a bachelor in that joking exchange had been for *her* benefit. Was Ned setting her up with his good friend the doctor? But Holly dismissed the idea. She had other more immediate things on her mind. The closer they got to her cousin's home the more anxious she began to feel about her meeting with Hetty. After all it had been almost six years since they had seen each other.

"This is it, home sweet home," Ned declared, opening the gate of a picket fence in front of a neat board-and-batten house. They went up the path edged with familiar flowers that Holly guessed Hetty must have grown from seeds Aunt Dolly sent her. Just as they reached the porch steps, the front door was flung open and there stood Hetty.

The light from an oil lamp she was holding in one upraised hand fell on her face, making harsh shadows on her high cheekbones and strong jawline. Her hair was pulled straight back, and her narrowed eyes, glittering like jet beads, moved over Holly—not missing a single button, bow, or feather. She could not see the accumulated dust and stain of travel, only the stylish outfit her cousin was wearing, and Holly saw the expression on Hetty's face—a mixture of envy and dislike.

A chilling wave of certainty froze Holly. On Hetty's face she read the truth, the confirmation of all her doubts—that her cousin resented her coming—and that she was unwelcome.

Chapter 2

"You're late," Hetty said tersely to Ned before Holly even had a chance to speak.

"The stage was late, and then I had to close up the store and walk over to the hotel—," Ned began apologizing.

Holly chimed in, trying to smooth things over, "And then we met some friends of Ned's and stopped to chat—" When Hetty's face did not lose its stony expression, Holly attempted a quick change of subject and greeted her cousin cheerfully, "Well, Hetty! Hello! It was so nice of you to have me come."

Hetty's glacial gaze came back to rest on Holly. "It's the least I could do for kin," she replied stiffly.

More than a little taken aback by this "uncousinly" reception—a far cry from the kind the word "kin" she had used would ordinarily imply, at least in Willow Springs—Holly glanced at Ned as if seeking some explanation of Hetty's attitude, but Ned couldn't seem to meet Holly's eyes.

"Well, come in, don't stand there letting all the night air in," Hetty said sharply to Ned, then turned her back on both of them.

"You first, Holly," Ned murmured in a low voice.

Holly stepped inside while he followed with her trunk. She looked around at the large room and got a fleeting impression of starched calico curtains, a round table and chairs in the middle, and at the other end a big, shiny black stove.

16

"The parlor is in there," Hetty said, gesturing to a closed door to the right.

"We don't use it except on Sundays or when company's comin'," piped up a clear high voice.

"Mind your tongue, Aurelia."

When Hetty spoke, Holly turned to see a little girl wearing a starched pinafore, her coppery brown hair in tight braids bristling with bows, staring at her.

"Why, hello there!" Holly exclaimed.

"I'm Aurelia." The little girl took a step forward, smiling, then pointed a chubby finger at a small boy who was peering from behind one of the chairs drawn up to the table. "And that's Teddy."

"Well, Aurelia, come and give me a kiss! What a pretty name!" With her plump rosy cheeks, tiny turned-up nose, cornflower blue eyes sparkling with curiosity, the child seemed to Holly more like a miniature Aunt Dolly than like her mother. "And how pretty you are, too!"

"Don't talk nonsense," Hetty cut in sharply. "I don't want her getting silly notions about herself, her looks, or anything else."

Surprised to be chastised for such a spontaneous remark, Holly looked at her cousin. What she saw in Hetty's eyes was unveiled hostility. In a moment, Holly realized Hetty did not like her, never had, and nothing had changed. What she could do about *that*, at the moment, Holly had no idea.

Seemingly undaunted by her mother's curtness, Aurelia held up her hand, spreading her fingers, and announced, "I'm five. And Teddy's nearly four."

"Stop chattering, Aurelia," her mother reprimanded, then she turned to Holly, and pointedly eyeing the quantity of Holly's luggage, said, "I don't have a spare room. When we built this house we didn't count on having house guests, so you'll have to sleep in with the children." Her mouth pursed.

"Oh, don't worry about it, Hetty. I'll be just fine." Holly assured her quickly, stung by Hetty's use of the words "house guests." In Willow Springs *family* were never considered *guests*. Relatives were always welcomed warmly whether for one night or a week and were usually urged to stay longer. Hetty was making it no secret that she considered having Holly here an imposition.

Hetty's chin jutted out defensively as if she knew how she had sounded. "Come along, I'll show you where to put your things."

"Let *me* show her, Mama!" begged Aurelia, coming over to Holly's side and slipping a tiny hand into hers.

Holly squeezed it gratefully. "Yes, *do* let Aurelia."

Frowning, Hetty looked at Aurelia then back to Holly, and then said, "Well, all right, go on. But don't be all day back there. Supper's ready to serve if it hasn't been ruined what with Ned's dawdling with his men friends—"

"I'll carry something," Aurelia offered, and Holly let her take the hatbox.

As they went hand in hand down the short hall, Holly could hear Hetty haranguing Ned about something.

"Here we are," Aurelia announced, pulling a little ahead of Holly and opening the door to the bedroom they were to share.

Holly entered, set down her valise, and looked around. There was a pine chest of drawers, a large bed with low posters, covered with a sunburst quilt in indigo-and-orange colors. Pushed against the wall on the other side of the room was a smaller cot.

"That's Teddy's," Aurelia told her. "He hid under the table when he heard you and Pa coming. He's shy."

Obviously *she* wasn't. Holly had the feeling that she and Aurelia would get along just fine.

While Holly took off her bonnet and rummaged through her valise for her hairbrush to remedy the havoc the long trip and the wind had done to her hair, Aurelia climbed up on the bed ready to chat. There was a narrow mirror hanging over the chest, and Holly went over to it and began taking out her hairpins. Watching her from her vantage point on the bed, Aurelia said, "When we knowed you was comin', Mama had Pa order that looking glass special to hang up there. Mama said we better have one because you liked to primp."

Holly was half-amused, half-annoyed at the remark. Of course, she realized the little girl spoke with the sublime innocence of childhood, just repeating what she'd heard. She wondered what else Hetty had said about her, and she asked casually, "Did your mama talk a lot about me before I came?"

"Oh, yes, after Grammum's letter came, she and Pa talked about it all the time. Then Pa said, 'That's enough, Hetty, she's comin', and that's all there is to it,'" Aurelia gave a little bounce after quoting her father.

Holly's cheeks flamed with humiliation at the thought that she had been discussed and almost refused the haven her aunt and mother had sought for her. In the aftershock of Jim's surprise engagement to another girl, Holly had been dazed and vulnerable to suggestion. She should never have succumbed to Aunt Dolly's persuasion to get out of town for awhile, away from all the gossip, to go on a long visit to her cousin in Oregon. *I should have known better.* Holly fumed inwardly, thinking of Hetty's cold greeting. *Well what did I expect? Hetty's still the sour little girl she always was. I should have remembered.*

Holly shook out her hair and brushed it vigorously until it made a crackling sound.

"Your hair is just *be-yootiful!*" Aurelia sighed. "You are *so* pretty! You're about the prettiest lady I've ever seen. Prettier than any of the ladies in this town, I think." She paused and for a long moment regarded Holly, her brow wrinkled, her curly head to one side, then asked, "So why aren't you married? Mama says you're an old maid, but you don't look old to me. And she said you were jilted. What's jilted, Holly?"

Resentment flared up in Holly. Hetty had certainly not hesitated to detail her private story even to her children! Was it just to Ned? Or did unknown listening "little pitchers have big ears"? And if Hetty had told her friends, how many other people in Riverbend knew Holly's personal disaster? Maybe the whole town knew! Maybe Adam Corcoran would feel it was newsworthy enough to print in the *Riverbend Monitor*. Holly flung down her brush in irritation.

Then realizing Aurelia was still observing her, waiting for an answer to her question, Holly went over to her, took the puzzled little face in both her hands, and kissed her cheeks. "Actually, Aurelia, being an 'old maid' means you just haven't been lucky enough yet to find a man to make happy."

19

"Oh, I see." Aurelia grinned, the answer seeming to satisfy her.

"Now, Aurelia, could you tell me—is there a—?"

Aurelia jumped off the bed. "Yes, I'll show you." She ran and opened the bedroom door saying over her shoulder, "I'd go with you, but I don't like going out there when it's dark."

Holly followed the little girl through the hall, out through a back door, and onto a porch. "That's it," Aurelia told her, pointing to a shedlike structure at the end of a large garden.

"I'll wait 'till you're done and walk back with you," Aurelia offered as Holly hurried along the flagstone path. When she rejoined the little girl, Holly said, "Thank you, Aurelia. Now I'll just wash up a bit and tidy myself then we'll go in for supper, all right?"

"Oh, yes. We're having roast chicken and dumplings, and peach pie for dessert. Do you like peach pie? Umhmm. I do! I think it's my favorite kind, 'less it's rhubarb and strawberry, but we only have that in the summertime—"

Aurelia went right on talking, not waiting for Holly to comment or make any reply. This gave Holly a chance to think while she poured water from the ironstone pitcher into the washbowl, getting ready to scrub some of the gritty grime of stagecoach travel from her face and hands. Taking her toilette case from the valise, she got out her small cake of rose-scented glycerin soap from its shell box. She wished she had time to wash all over and put on a fresh chemise, but she was afraid to delay too long and keep Hetty's supper waiting. Causing Hetty any more upset than she had caused by her arrival was something Holly did not relish.

The image of herself she saw in the mirror revealed that she was more tired than she realized. She looked pale, and there were purple smudges under her eyes. She hadn't had a really good night's sleep in weeks! Not on the transcontinental train coming cross country nor in any of the places that passed for hotels in which she had spent a night or two as she made connections to California then Oregon!

Holly made quick work of her wash-up and redid her hair. Then whirling around, she held out her hand to Aurelia and with an effort at gaiety, asked, "So, shall we go in to supper?"

When they came out into the big kitchen, Hetty was standing at the stove, stirring something and did not turn around at their entrance. Ned was sitting in the big Boston rocker reading a newspaper, but when he saw Holly, he got to his feet and stood there uncertainly. The table was spread with a crisp white cloth and set with the Blue Delft dinnerware, which Holly recognized as Aunt Dolly's second-best, probably given to Hetty to bring west with her.

"Everything looks so nice, Hetty," Holly remarked to Hetty's back.

Hetty turned, and Holly was shocked to see she she still wore the same "mad-at-the-world" expression she had often seen on her in childhood. Hetty said with a shrug, "It's not as fancy as you're used to, I'm sure. But I like to do things proper even if this isn't Kentucky!"

At this Holly nearly choked. As if Hetty had not been brought up in the very same environment as Holly! They had the same grandparents, and their mothers were sisters, for goodness' sake! What was Hetty trying to prove? And how could *she* not have remembered what Hetty was like? Hetty had sat glum-faced through too many family celebrations for Holly to have forgotten.

Holly sat down without another word. Aurelia wiggled up into the chair beside Holly. Teddy, still with his head burrowed almost to his chin, climbed up into the chair opposite. Ned took his seat at the end of the table.

Hetty brought a large tureen over from the stove, set it down before Ned's place at the table, nodded brusquely to Ned, and said, "We'll have the blessing now, Ned."

All heads bowed reverently while Ned mumbled something in so low a voice Holly had to strain to hear. *Poor Ned,* was her reaction. Had he escaped from under the shadow of his father, the pontifical judge, and his brother only to be brought under Hetty's less benevolent domination? She certainly hoped not. She had caught a glimpse of the "new" Ned in his encounters with Adam Corcoran and Dr. Stevens, and she liked what she saw.

For all Holly's valiant efforts, supper was a strain. Even though Ned did his best by asking her about mutual friends in Willow Springs and Holly cooperated by bringing up news of events and people they all knew and might be interested in hearing about, Hetty's determined nonparticipation hung over the table like a pall. She spent most of the time correcting the children's table manners and once in awhile giving a sniff of disdain at some of Holly's remarks.

Teddy held Holly in a steady stare throughout the meal, but everytime she tried to make eye contact with him, he would duck his head into his plate. If it had not been for Aurelia, who alternately gazed at Holly adoringly or smiled at whatever she said, the meal would have been intolerable. As it was, Holly found she could hardly eat a bite. By the time it ended, she felt as if her neck were in a brace from stress and her face stretched from maintaining as pleasant an expression as possible.

Finally it was over. Hetty ignored Holly's compliments on the delicious supper and turned down her offer to help clear away or do the dishes. So, in desperation, using weariness from the long trip as an excuse, Holly said she believed she would retire early.

"I'll fix your lamp then, Holly," Ned said. While he trimmed the wick, lighted it, adjusted the flame, and replaced the glass globe, Hetty banged pots and pans. Holly darted a quick look at her cousin. Did Hetty even resent Ned's attending to her needs?

As he handed her the lamp, Holly said, "Thank you, Ned—," then added hesitantly, "Well, good night, Hetty—good night, everyone." Hetty acknowledged her with a brief nod; Aurelia waved and smiled. Teddy had disappeared again under the table.

Holly left the kitchen and went down the hall to the bedroom. The discomfort she felt during this first evening was unbelievable. With a sense of relief she closed the door, leaned against it, and shut her eyes for a full minute. Placing the lamp on the bureau, she sat down on the edge of the bed. She would have loved nothing better than to take a hot bath, but she hadn't dared risk asking Hetty to boil water or for the use of the copper tub she had seen hanging on the porch when she went out back.

She felt exhausted not only from the long day of travel but from the emotional stress. What weighed her down most heavily was the knowledge that she had done the wrong thing by coming. Hetty's feelings were plain. She hadn't wanted her to come, didn't want her here. But at the time, taking her aunt's and mother's advice had seemed reasonable enough. She herself had been anxious to escape, so it was easy enough to believe that by the time she came back to Willow Springs some other topic of gossip would have replaced the one that everyone was enjoying about her and Jim Mercer.

Back home it wouldn't have mattered. Holly hadn't cared about Hetty's opinion of her. Although, to her credit, Holly *had* tried to include Hetty in the parties and picnics and fun she herself was enjoying. Even though it *was* at her mother's prompting, to be sure, Holly *had* tried to encourage some of the young men who had clustered around *her* to dance with her cousin. Truthfully, Holly had to admit, for the most part she had lived in her own world, surrounded by admirers, basking in the sunshine of doting parents and dazzled beaux.

Now that the tables were turned, *Holly* was the needy one, Hetty had the upper hand. Their roles were going to be reversed. Now that it was too late, she deeply regretted having come. How could she possibly put up with Hetty's insufferable attitude until it was safe to go home? Or would it ever be safe? What if Jim decided finally to do what he had often promised to do when *they* were "courting"? Many times he had talked of resigning his Army commission and going into business with his father. What if Jim brought his bride home to Willow Springs?

I can't think about all that now, Holly told herself firmly. *I've got to make the best of it, even if it was a mistake to come.*

She started undressing, undoing the tiny satin-covered buttons of her Basque jacket, unfastening the tiered skirt, loosening the strings of her petticoats, and letting them drop to the floor. She unlaced the stays of her little corset, and took off her stockings and high-heeled bronze boots.

From her purse she got out the key to her trunk and unlocked it. As she lifted the lid, the faint fragrance of roses recalled the day she was packing to come to Oregon. A picture of her mother tucking the little net sachet bags of crushed, dried rose petals from their garden in among her freshly washed and ironed chemises and nighties floated into her mind, and she was over-come with a wave of homesickness.

Quickly she checked the urge to cry and determinedly took out a white cambric nightgown, frilled and edged with tatting. For a moment she held it to her breast, closing her eyes, relish-ing its scent. Then she put it on, slipped into her pink-flowered flannel wrapper, took the lamp, and went down the hall and outside to the "necessary."

The summer darkness was velvety; a starless, dense blue sky enveloped her; the grass between the flagstone path was wet with evening dew; the air spicy with the smell of cedar and ever-greens. In a breath, Holly was swept back thousands of miles to where a soft Kentucky twilight lingered and fireflies darted among the wisteria—suddenly, although it wasn't cold, Holly shivered.

When Holly went back inside, Aurelia was in her nightie sit-ting up in the big bed. "If I crowd you, Holly, just give me a shove, all right?" she said. Stifling a yawn, she slid down into the covers. Holly blew out the lamp and got in beside the little girl. She smiled in the darkness.

In spite of Hetty's attitude, *at least* she had *one* ally in this house. Of course, Ned was kindness itself, but he had to be cau-tious for fear of provoking Hetty. Holly was sure she could soon win over little Teddy. She had always loved children, and they loved her.

But what was she to do about Hetty? Hetty was the real chal-lenge. She yawned, sighed; tomorrow she'd figure out some way to win over Hetty, she decided drowsily. She had always been able to make friends easily, hadn't she?

She turned, spoon-fashion, around Aurelia's small warm body. Immediately Aurelia cuddled close.

Holly began drifting off to sleep when suddenly something jerked her awake again—it was the memory of the stage driver's voice shouting "end of the line"—

Chapter 3

*H*olly opened her eyes slowly, then snuggled deeper into the quilts, delaying until the last possible minute getting up and facing another day of Hetty's questionable hospitality.

From the kitchen she could hear movement, voices. She knew Hetty was already bustling about, frying bacon, whisking a pan of biscuits out of the oven, while at the same time fussing at the children and nagging Ned about something or other. In the two weeks Holly had been here, she'd been appalled at Hetty's constant picking at Ned. She should be grateful she had such a kind, patient, caring husband. Ned was also a wonderful father. Hetty was luckier than she seemed to realize. But, of course, there was no way she could tell her cousin that.

Holly lay there a little longer, dreading the moment when she would have to toss the covers aside, knowing, since there was no stove in the bedroom, how cold it would be. She would have loved a cup of coffee and dreamily remembered how her mother sometimes brought her one in the morning—especially if she had been out at a party or dance the night before. Holly sighed; those days were certainly gone forever.

She also knew if she went out to the kitchen now, Hetty would make her feel she was just in the way. Her offers to help were usually turned down, brushed aside curtly, making her feel generally useless and inadequate. If it hadn't seemed so deliberate, it would be almost funny. Whenever Holly had insisted that there *must* be *something* she could do to help, Hetty always seemed to pick the worst and most menial of tasks.

Like the day Hetty handed her the wire brush and said she could beat the rugs. With the best of intentions Holly had gone outside where the rugs were hung on a clothes line stretched between two poles in the backyard and started beating them. Dust flew out at once, enveloping her and causing her to sneeze and cough. Teddy, who had slipped out of the house and was sitting on the steps of the back porch watching her, started to giggle. Catching him, Holly began to play "peek-a-boo" with her shy little cousin behind the flapping rugs. It ended up in riotous hilarity. When Aurelia heard the laughter she, too, came outside to join the fun. Of course, Hetty quickly followed and put a stop to the game. Marching over to Holly, she snatched the beater out of her hand, saying curtly, "If you can't do it right, don't bother doing it at all."

Covered with dust, Holly stood aghast watching her stiff-shouldered cousin go back inside the house, holding on to the protesting Teddy with one hand and pushing Aurelia in front of her.

There was just no pleasing Hetty! Smothering a groan, Holly burrowed her head into the pillow, remembering another unpleasant incident that had happened the very same day.

Not having thought to cover her head while in the process of rug-beating, Holly had decided to wash her hair to get rid of the dust. While Hetty had gone to the store, Holly heated her own water and got out her shampoo. Aurelia, as usual, was her interested audience.

Impulsively Holly had asked the little girl if she wanted her hair done, too. Of course Aurelia did. She also wanted it put up in curling rags. They were in the process of doing that, sitting out in the warm September sunshine, when Hetty returned. With one look she took in the scene and halted it.

"I thought I told you I don't want Aurelia growing up vain and silly. Her hair's worn in plaits, and that's that."

"Oh, just this once, Hetty? Just for fun?" Holly persisted, not believing Hetty really meant to prevent the little girl's pleasure.

"I wish you would *just for once* realize that *I'm* in charge here, not *you*, Holly." Hetty's voice was edged with sarcasm. "Come along, Aurelia, I'll braid your hair proper," she said, brushing past Holly and marching into the house.

Holly had repressed a natural urge to argue with her. It was so stupid of Hetty to get into a tug of wills over something so harmless. She also kept herself from doing the spontaneous thing of hugging Aurelia, who was struggling not to burst into tears at her mother's dictum.

That night when they were in bed together, Holly cuddled Aurelia and told her a long story to make up for her disappointment of no curls.

Shortly after that, another incident occurred that put Holly even more at her wit's end. Again she had asked Hetty how she could help, and Hetty had pointed to the stove and said shortly, "It needs blacking." Then she added sarcastically, "But of course, you wouldn't want to get your hands dirty."

At this, Holly had simply smiled. "Where's the polish?"

Hetty looked startled but got out some rags and a jar of Queen's Mirror-black and set them down on the kitchen table before leaving for her Sewing Circle.

Holly had never in her life before cleaned or shined a stove, but she was stubborn enough not to give Hetty the satisfaction of a job not well done. She was down on her knees, having already skinned two knuckles, when the children woke up from their naps and came out to the kitchen.

"Your face is all smudge, Holly!" gasped Aurelia.

"Just call me 'Cinderella'!" Holly laughed at the two stunned little faces as she blew some strands of hair that had fallen over her eyes. While she finished up on the stove, she regaled them with a fine dramatic version of the fairy tale while they sat cross-legged on the floor beside her. When Hetty got home, she was not only astonished, but Holly could see she even resented the fact that the stove shone with new brilliance.

Recalling the uncomfortable moment, Holly thumped her pillow behind her head and stared gloomily out the window. She wished desperately she had never come to Oregon. If it weren't for the children—

At least the children accepted and loved her. It had taken some time for Teddy to get over his first shyness, but now he followed her around like a puppy. Aurelia would have become her shadow if Hetty allowed it. However, Hetty seemed to resent the little girl's uninhibited affection for Holly and restricted it as much as possible.

Holly found this hard. One would think any busy mother would be grateful to someone who could entertain children. Both children were entranced by Holly's talent for storytelling. Aurelia would ask her questions like, "What did you do when you were a little girl?" and Holly would spin out stories from her vivid childhood memories. Although always within hearing during these times, Hetty kept a stony silence.

But one day when Holly was holding them spellbound about her Shetland pony and describing her tree house in the big oak in the backyard, where her friends climbed up the little ladder to have tea parties, Hetty had cut in crossly, "I don't want you filling up my children with all those make-believe stories."

Astonished, Holly exclaimed. *"Make-believe!* What do you mean, Hetty? Surely you remember the tree house Papa built— and Rags, the pony? Why, we all used to take turns riding him."

Hetty's expression tightened. "It was a make-believe life. Not like life is out here in the West. My children have to learn to live in the real world; they aren't being reared pampered and sheltered and no good to anyone," she snapped. "Out here folks don't set much stock on silly birthday parties and making a fuss about things." To the children she said, "Come on, you two, instead of listening to a bunch of silly stories, you can help me get in the laundry." With that she picked up the oak-chip clothes basket and started toward the back door.

Holly was too startled by Hetty's outburst to say anything. Was Hetty trying to erase everything about the life they both had lived in Willow Springs? And if so, why?

With a sorrowful glance at Holly, Aurelia obeyed. Teddy started to howl saying he wanted to hear more about the pony, and Hetty gave him a smack on his bottom.

Holly longed to give Hetty a piece of her mind. But, of course, she didn't. After all Aurelia and Teddy *were* Hetty's children, and she had no right to argue about any rules Hetty laid down for them.

After that incident, Holly confined her storytelling to when she and Aurelia were in bed at night or other times when they happened to be alone—which wasn't often. Hetty kept both children busily occupied with little chores most of the day, so there wasn't much time for Holly to invent games or tell them stories.

Holly could not help wondering if such enforced "busyness" was all that good. Shouldn't there be time for playing? Even for dreaming? Aurelia was bright and creative, loved pretending and make-believe. She loved it when Holly would leave off a story midway and let her finish it. Holly just hoped that when *she* left to go back to Willow Springs, Aurelia's active imagination wouldn't be stunted.

Holly bunched up the pillow, flipped over onto her back, and stared moodily at the ceiling. She knew she should get up. She thought she knew exactly how the French aristocrats must have felt mounting to the guillotine, or even the early Christians going into the lions' den. Of course, that was an exaggeration, but Hetty *was* a formidable adversary. Nothing Holly did or said met with Hetty's approval.

Hetty maintained a constant distance. She never initiated a conversation. Often she did not even reply to Holly's comments or concerted efforts to be companionable. But there was still another way Hetty made Holly feel unwelcome. She consistently excluded Holly from any of the social life that *she* had made for herself in Riverbend. Hetty had never invited any of her friends to meet her cousin, nor had she asked Holly to accompany *her* when she went to visit any of them.

On several occasions after Ned returned to the store following the noon dinner, without a word to Holly, Hetty would simply gather up her sewing basket, put on her bonnet and shawl, button Aurelia and Teddy into their outdoor garments, and start to the front door. Then, as if an afterthought, she would call over her shoulder the brief announcement, "I'm going over to Selma Peterson's. She's got a pattern I want to trace," or "I'm

29

going to my quilting group, something I know you wouldn't be interested in since you never enjoyed handiwork."

Sometimes Aurelia would plead, "Can't Holly come with us?" but Hetty would ignore her and, without a backward look, leave.

After the door closed behind them, Holly vented her indignation. True, she never *had* enjoyed needlework nor embroidery, but she might have enjoyed meeting some of the young women in town even if she did not share their interest in *handiwork!* Who knows, she might even enjoy learning how to quilt. What in the world did Hetty expect her to do with her time?

Holly would have to be blind not to see. Hetty did not care if Holly was happy here or not. She was not going to lift a finger to introduce her to anyone, or try to make her life in Riverbend interesting. This was such a contrast to the way newcomers were treated in Willow Springs that Holly could not believe it.

I must have been out of my mind to come here! In self-disgust Holly threw back the covers and got up. The day ahead held nothing but gloomy prospects. Back in Willow Springs she might be going shopping, making visits with her mother, having "gentlemen callers," or looking forward to an afternoon party. In the evening there may have been a play or a concert to attend or perhaps a buffet supper and dance. Well, thinking about all those things was like Alice's following the Red Queen's instructions and "imagining six impossible things before breakfast!" Holly thought with a sigh, *I can't go back. Not now. Not until spring at least. I have to somehow make the best of things here.*

Holly had started taking long walks. Within days after her arrival in Riverbend she had discovered that the slightest thing seemed to cause Hetty to fly off the handle. Holly began watching her every word, remark, and gesture. Sometimes the only alternative to avoid an argument with her cousin was to get out of the house. On these walks Holly found that Riverbend was a pleasant enough little town with a wealth of natural beauty. Now in early September the weather was sunny, and along the roadside a profusion of wildflowers, golden poppies, and delicate purple-blue wild asters delighted the eye. Beautiful trees, tall firs, sweeping-boughed hemlocks, dark green cedars grew right to the edge of town. One day she had found a path that led right down to the river, and this became a favorite place for her to go when tension with Hetty became unbearable.

In the town itself quite a lot of building was going on in anticipation, she supposed, of the coming of the new branch line of the railroad, which was to catapult Riverbend into unprecedented prosperity. There was a fine brick courthouse being constructed at one end of Main Street, and on some of the new roads fanning out from the center of town some houses were being built. Somewhat to her surprise, she saw several churches as well as saloons; the saloons, however, were winning about three to one.

There were more settled areas of town; tree-lined streets forming small neighborhoods, nicely painted frame houses with neat fences, deep yards, and flower and vegetable gardens around the side. Wistfully she wondered if there might be people in those houses who could be acquaintances, perhaps even friends.

One house she passed often and found particularly appealing was nestled under large trees at the end of a winding lane. It was a doll-sized yellow clapboard with a slanting roof and lacy white fretwork on the little porch. There was a painted sign on the gatepost, V. DODD, DRESSMAKING, FINE NEEDLEWORK.

Often Holly had stood at the gate of that house, half-tempted to go up and knock on the blue-painted door, perhaps on the pretext of asking about alterations or to look at patterns or to discuss a new outfit?—to see for herself if "V. Dodd" matched the charm of the exterior. But, of course, she couldn't do that. Holly had always had girlfriends to go shopping with or simply to visit—she sadly missed the companionship, the camaraderie and fun. Of all her many Lambeth and Granville cousins, Hetty was the only one with whom she was not congenial.

Holly got dressed slowly, unconsciously steeling herself for another prickly encounter with Hetty. *No matter what, I must try to be cheerful and pleasant,* Holly lectured her reflection in the mirror sternly. *Maybe, today will be different. Maybe Hetty will be in a better mood. Maybe . . .*

But, of course, Hetty wasn't. Ned had already departed for the

31

store when Holly came out to the kitchen. Hetty, who was stirring something in a big pot on the stove, turned her head and gave Holly a swift glance, then turned her back again. Holly gritted her teeth. Why couldn't Hetty at least be civil? With determined brightness Holly said, "Good morning."

Aurelia, sitting at one end of the table cutting out little squares of calico from a huge pile of scraps beside her, looked up and smiled, "Morning, Holly. See what I'm doing? I'm cutting out patches for Mama." She held one up with pride.

"That's wonderful," Holly nodded encouragingly.

Teddy was sitting on the floor, struggling to get his high-topped shoes buttoned, his small pink tongue moving from one side of his mouth to the other as he concentrated, his chubby little hands fumbling at the task.

On impulse, Holly asked him, "Want some help?" and dropped to her knees beside him.

The words were hardly out of her mouth when Hetty swung around from the stove ordering, "No! You're not to help him. He's got to learn to do it himself. He's a big boy. I won't have you babying him!"

Startled at the harsh command, Holly stared at Hetty whose face had turned red and mottled. Ugly. Slowly, Holly rose from the floor, but not before she saw tears well up in Teddy's eyes. She didn't say anything, just looked at Hetty speechlessly. Hetty's face got redder, but she didn't apologize. She turned back to the stove and started stirring again.

"There's coffee still in the pot if you want some," she said in a muffled voice, "and biscuits."

But Holly was too shaken by the anger bristling through her. Aurelia looked up at the sudden stillness in the room, a deadly quiet tingling with tension. Her eyes widened as she looked anxiously from Holly to her mother.

Holly knew she had to control her fury for the children's sake. She managed a reassuring smile for Aurelia, then said in a tight voice, "No, thank you, I'm not hungry. I think I'll go for a walk. I need some fresh air." That was all she allowed herself to say to indicate her reaction to Hetty.

Back in the bedroom, Holly put on her bonnet, carefully

anchoring it with two long hatpins, trying to calm herself. Her hands were actually shaking.

"If it were possible, I'd take the first stagecoach out of here!" she declared to her reflection. But where could she go? She was trapped. "I must get hold of myself. I must not lose my temper. Whatever happens I won't let her break me." Maybe she could walk off her seething anger. Whatever, Holly was determined not to stoop to Hetty's level.

Returning to the kitchen, she halted at the door and, in the most even tone she could muster, asked Hetty if she needed her to stop at the store for anything.

Still at the stove, her back to Holly, Hetty merely shook her head. But as Holly turned the doorknob and started out, Hetty's voice followed her, warning, "Don't bother Ned at the store, Holly. He's got customers to look out for; he don't have time to waste gabbing."

"I had no intention of doing that, Hetty," Holly could not resist calling back. It was all she could do not to slam the door after her.

She went down the porch steps and out of the yard, so angry she had no idea in what direction she headed.

Chapter 4

*H*olly's heart was beating like a metronome; her pulses raced. She was angrier than she could ever remember being. She walked so fast that before long she was quite warm and breathless.

Without realizing it, she took the path off the road onto the trail leading down to the river. She had come quite a way before she calmed down enough to notice what a beautiful day it was. Under the ponderosa pines and the red-barked manzanita, clusters of wildflowers sprinkled with early morning frost, glistened like gems in the sunlight streaming down between the trees. Through the heavy brush she caught a glimpse of the sparkling water below.

She found a sun-warmed rock to sit upon. This close to the river, the sound of water rushing over the rocks was loud but in a way rhythmically soothing. A few leaves from the aspens and birch trees on the bank had fallen and drifted onto the shining surface. She watched them dancing and drifting with the rippling flow.

As the silence of the woods settled around her like a peaceful cloak, from high up in one tree came the fluting sound of a bird. But the peace of it all—instead of soothing her—only seemed to accentuate her sense of isolation and loneliness. Eventually, she began to think about the dilemma of her situation. Her walks had become a palliative but no solution. Yes, the woods *were* beautiful and the weather lovely and these walks *did* help, but what was she to do when the legendary Oregon winter rains began? What would she do then to escape? Her every attempt with Hetty met with resistance. She was at the end of her rope.

It wasn't only the problem with her cousin, it was everything else! Losing Jim had been a dreadful blow. Nothing like that had ever happened to her before. Life had always been so easy and pleasant for her that she had never dreamed it wouldn't go on being that way forever. It was even more painful to know she had brought the whole terrible thing on herself!

Holly had never been introspective, never explored her feelings nor thought much about her life; she had been too busy living it. Rarely had she thought beyond the next dance or party, what she should wear, or which invitation to accept. Life in Willow Springs, in the large white clapboard house with its deep porch and green shutters had been, in retrospect, serene and blissful!

Before Jim's "betrayal" nothing really bad had ever happened to her. It had left her dazed and bewildered. In that state, she had let others make up her mind for her, suggest to her what was the "best thing" for her to do. Now she realized the "*best*" thing may not have been the "*right*" thing for her to do at all!

Suddenly Holly felt very young and sad and childishly like crying. She put her head in her hands and let the pent-up tears come. After awhile, she lifted her head and sniffled. What good would crying do? She couldn't sit here moping all day. She wasn't ready yet to go back to the house. She still had things to sort out, to think about. She was now hungry and could have used a cup of coffee and something to eat.

She would go by the store, which she had not had a chance to see yet, being careful not to "bother Ned" as Hetty had cautioned her. Perhaps she could amuse herself looking around.

Wiping her eyes, she dug into her reticule for a hanky to blow her nose. As she drew out one of the fine lawn, lace-edged ones that her great-aunt Ancilla had made and given her at Christmas, a small, rectangular, printed paper fell from it onto the ground. Curious, Holly picked it up. As soon as she saw what it was, she started to smile. *Of all things!* she thought. Great-Aunt Ancilla up to her usual "tricks." A tract!

Her mother's aunt was known in the family as "the Evangelist." Passing along tracts was the dear old soul's "ministry," as she told everyone. She was forever giving them out to family, friends, and perfect strangers. She slipped them into books, put them under dinner plates, folded them into freshly ironed laundry, tucked them under bed pillows.

Even as the tears dried on her cheeks, Holly laughed. She had been asking for help with her problem, and here like a message from home came one of her fey little auntie's tracts.

Great-Aunt Ancilla held staunchly to the belief that no matter what your problem, whenever you need guidance of any kind, go to the Word. To her mind, the Bible had all the answers. Well, if ever Holly needed guidance it was *now*. She read the bold line of type at the top of the little booklet: "WHATSOEVER YOUR HAND FINDS TO DO, DO IT WITH ALL YOUR MIGHT" ECC. 9:10. On down the page there were further exhortations to be cheerful, patient whatever your path in life happened to be, to trust in God and He would make "straight your path."

Oh, if I could only believe that is true, Holly sighed, and her shoulders drooped a little. But as she continued reading, oddly enough, some of the anger, some of the lostness she had felt began to fade. There *was* "comfort in the Word" as Great-Auntie Ancilla declared so positively.

The wind off the river had risen, and the sun shifted and moved up behind the towering trees. Involuntarily Holly shivered and, feeling chilly, got to her feet and started walking down toward the edge of the river where it was warmer. But as she did, a stone caught in the tiny heel of one of her dainty boots causing her to twist her ankle. As she did, the heel broke off.

Drat it! Holly picked up the narrow little heel and held it in the palm of her hand frowning. The fragile nails were bent and loose. She could not possibly reattach it. It would have to be fixed by a shoemaker—if there were such a thing in Riverbend!

Stepping on the toe of one foot, she hobbled awkwardly back toward the road and turned in the direction of Hetty's. In her anger after leaving the house, she had walked very fast and come much farther than she realized. Now, thus handicapped, she would have to retrace her steps. *This is a fine kettle of fish!* she complained glumly to herself as she limped along.

She had to stop to rest every few minutes, and her lopsided gait made her very tired. Holly wasn't sure how long she had hobbled, although it seemed like forever when she heard the clopping sound of horses' hooves approaching. She halted and turned to see a small, black-hooded buggy rounding the curve of the road. As it came nearer, it slowed then pulled alongside her. With a mixture of embarrassment and relief she saw that it was Riverbend's doctor, Blaine Stevens.

"Miss Lambeth!" he tipped his hat and leaned toward her. "You're limping! Have you injured yourself?"

"Well, no, not exactly—I've—" She held out her hand, opening the palm and showed him the dainty broken heel.

"Well, thank goodness, it's nothing serious. You don't need a doctor; you need a ride, right?" He smiled and in a flash jumped down and helped her into the buggy.

"Would you like me to take you back to the Thorntons' or to town, where you can get your shoe fixed?"

"I guess to town, if it wouldn't be too much trouble."

"Right! And it's not any trouble at all. Luckily, I'm on my way from a house call, not on my way *to* one." He looked over at her and smiled.

Once settled in, Holly glanced over at the doctor. "I can't thank you enough for rescuing me! I don't know how much longer I'd have lasted, hobbling like that."

"That's my role in life!" he laughed. "Rescuing people."

"Lucky for me!" she joined in his laughter. At close range, Dr. Stevens did not appear as young as she had thought at their first meeting. Of course, that had been in the evening, when it was fast growing dark. Now she guessed him to be in his early thirties. His was a face that was both young and old, the skin of his cheeks was taut and tan, his eyes remarkably clear and blue, but there were fine lines around them. There were deeper lines around his mouth, etched there, perhaps, by the suffering and pain he had witnessed in his profession. It was a face that Holly instinctively felt that one could trust.

As he looked over at her, smiling, his eyes held both laughter and interest. "So, other than today's mishap, I hope you've been enjoying your stay in Riverbend. I'm sure you and Hetty have had lots of things to catch up on—I know how most folks enjoy hearing about things back home. It must be even better to have a visitor."

Holly was at a loss as to how to reply. Blaine's natural assumption about her and her cousin was one that anyone would make. But nothing could be further from the truth. He was looking at her expectantly, so she hedged her answer carefully. "Well, of course, it's been six years since I've seen Hetty or Ned, and—to be honest, we never were very close. I mean our lives were—*are* quite different. I mean, she's busy with her home and children and I—"

Holly halted. Why on earth was she rattling on like this, and to a perfect stranger? She felt her cheeks get hot.

"Of course. I understand. Life in the East is much different—takes some adjustments and getting used to the West isn't all that easy, either—" Blaine stopped, then tactfully switched the subject, saying, "Here we are, and I'll take you right by Hedrick's, the shoesmith; he'll have your heel back on in a jiffy."

"Thank you, Dr. Stevens, you've been very kind."

Blaine drew up in front of a small storefront, secured the buggy brake, and got out. He came around the other side and helped Holly down.

"I'd be happy to wait for you, then drive you home, Miss Lambeth."

"Oh, that won't be necessary, but thank you," Holly said. "I'm very grateful you came along when you did."

"It's no trouble at all. I'd be delighted, in fact. I have a house call to make out in the direction of the Thorntons' and can drop you off there on my way."

Holly hesitated, then seeing no reason to refuse the offer, smiled and said, "Very well, thank you."

Blaine spun the hat he held in his hand for a second before saying shyly, "I'd suggest you ask Jake about some sturdier boots if you're going to do much more walking, Miss Lambeth." He smiled shyly. "There's some awfully pretty country around here, but some of it's kind of rugged."

"As I have just found out!" Holly laughed. "Thank you for the advice. I'll do that."

When the heel was replaced, Blaine was waiting outside. He helped her back into his buggy for the short distance back to the Thorntons' house.

Blaine assisted her from the buggy and escorted her to the gate. Before opening it for her, he said, "There's some very nice country around Riverbend, not all within walking distance. If you'd like, Miss Lambeth, I'd like to show you some of it. Maybe some Sunday? After church? That's my day off—well, at least—I cannot always be certain of attending the service. A doctor's life is not exactly his own, Miss Lambeth. Sometimes there are emergencies—so far, I'm reasonably sure of next Sunday." Little lines crinkled around his intensely blue eyes as he smiled.

He went on to quickly to explain that he could not always be certain of attending the service. "A doctor's life is not exactly his own, Miss Lambeth. Sometimes there are emergencies—I do like to try to make church. But I'm reasonably sure of next Sunday." He smiled; little lines crinkled around his intensely blue eyes as they looked down at her.

For a moment Holly debated whether it was wise to accept the young doctor's invitation, then she became conscious of the movement of the curtain at one of the windows and realized Hetty must be watching. She felt a flare of indignation. Somehow she knew it would irritate Hetty if she made plans to drive out with Blaine Stevens. Defiantly, she thought, *Why not?* "Why, yes, Dr. Stevens, that sounds very nice indeed. I would enjoy that." Here was a chance to break the awful monotony of Sunday at Hetty's.

Smiling demurely, she put out her hand and said sweetly, "and thank you again for rescuing me."

The following Sunday, Holly came out of her room, ready for church, dressed in a bronze poplin "promenade" dress. Her bonnet beribboned with brown grosgrain sported a cluster of golden daisies, and she carried a silk, flounced parasol. Aurelia, seated on a high stool while Hetty finished braiding her hair, saw her and exclaimed, "Oooh, Holly, you look so-o pretty!" Hetty turned to look at her cousin, and her expression made Holly draw in her breath. What she saw on Hetty's face was ugly. For a minute, Holly was stunned. It was devastating to be the target of such raw dislike. Nervously she drew on her gloves, trying to think of something to say to ease the tension. But none came. Then Hetty said to Aurelia, "You're done now. Go out to the wagon. Your pa's waiting."

Holly stood there uncertainly. Hetty had turned away, presenting only her back, with its rigidly held shoulders, shutting out any possibility for any words. Silently Holly went out the door, feeling sad that she had caused her cousin such distress. But what could she do? A few minutes later, Hetty came out wearing a Quaker plain shovel bonnet and gray bombazine. Without saying anything, she got up into the driver's seat of the wagon beside Ned.

Seated with the children, Holly sought for something she might do to scale the barrier between her and her cousin. If somehow Hetty envied her outfits, the way she dressed or looked, why didn't she do something about her *own* appearance? There was much she could do! A less severe hairstyle would soften her sharp-featured face. She could certainly wear brighter colors. Surely she had the pick of the yards of fabric at Ned's store, many colors to choose from and more becoming patterns from which to make her clothes. Holly would have easily made such suggestions to any of her other cousins—but not to Hetty! Never Hetty. By this time they had reached the church, and without a word, Hetty marched the children off to the Sunday school rooms, leaving Holly to walk into church with Ned.

The Thorntons' pew was at the front of the church. It took all of Holly's willpower not to look around to check the congregation for Dr. Stevens. She hoped he had not forgotten or that there had not been an unexpected emergency this morning. That possibility kept her preoccupied during what turned out to be a rather dull sermon. After the service she stood with Ned outside on the church steps, searching for him. But there was still no sign of Dr. Stevens. Holly began to get worried. What if he didn't show up?

Holly had intended to tell Hetty about Blaine's invitation, but after the scene in the kitchen that morning there had been no chance. Now it was awkward. It would appear that she had purposely withheld the information. Which is exactly the reaction she got when Hetty returned with the children.

Ned was in conversation with some of the men when Hetty said, "Come along, Holly, we'll wait for Ned in the wagon." Hetty's voice had its perpetual impatience.

"I'll not be going home with you, Hetty," Holly replied coolly. "Dr. Stevens is meeting me here; he has asked me to go for a drive."

Hetty's eyes popped wide then squinted suspiciously. "Oh?" she said, then pointedly glanced around the quickly emptying churchyard. Neither Blaine nor his small black buggy were anywhere to be seen. A sly smile twisted her mouth, and she asked "You sure about that? Maybe you misunderstood Dr. Stevens' intentions?"

Because she was having her own misgivings, the snideness in Hetty's voice brought Holly's own anxiety into sharp focus. *Could* she have been mistaken? Unwilling to give Hetty a chance to gloat, Holly lifted her chin, saying with more assurance than she felt, "He's possibly delayed by a patient's sudden illness or—he told me this was always a possibility—"

Ned finished his conversation with the man he'd been talking with and joined them. "Ready?" he asked innocent of the building tension between the cousins.

"Holly isn't going home with us, Ned. She has an appointment with a gentleman," Hetty told him with a toss of her head. "Come on, children." Hetty grabbed Aurelia and Teddy by the hand and marched down the church steps without a backward glance. Ned stood for a minute looking after his wife, then doubtfully at Holly.

"You go ahead, Ned. Blaine Stevens invited me to go driving. I'll be home later," Holly said with all the poise she could gather.

"Oh, Blaine? Well, that's nice, Holly. He's a prince of a fellow." Ned looked both ways down the road then back at Holly. "You sure? He could have been called out, you know—"

"Yes, I know, he said there's always that chance." Holly nodded her head wishing Ned would go. If Blaine *didn't* show up for some reason, she didn't want any witnesses to her embarrassment.

Ned hesitated. He looked up at the sky where some shadowy clouds moved ominously. "It looks like it might rain—I don't like to leave you here by yourself in case—," he halted, flushing, and amended, "what I mean to say is, you know how it is with doctors—Blaine may have got called out on an emergency—"

"I understand that, Ned. He told me he might be late. Please go on, don't keep Hetty and the children waiting. Something must have delayed Dr. Stevens, he'll be along soon," she assured him.

Reluctantly Ned left. The children waved as the wagon went by; Hetty looked straight ahead.

Now, I've done it again, Holly thought grimly. *Oh, well, it wouldn't have mattered what I said or did, Hetty just doesn't want to be friends with me, no matter what! It probably riles her that someone as attractive as Blaine Stevens has asked me out.*

As the minutes passed and there was still no sign of Blaine, Holly experienced a whole gamut of emotions, reciting to herself all the reasons why he hadn't come. The grayness of the day was disheartening as well. Then to her dismay a few drops of rain began to fall. Startled, she stepped back under the eaves of the narrow church porch. But soon they increased in rapidity and force, and before long it was raining hard.

Well! What now! The church doors had been locked; there was not a soul in sight. Should she wait here any longer or, horror of horrors, walk back to Hetty's house and face her derisive scorn?

Resolutely, Holly decided that would probably be easier than being stranded here indefinitely. She had a dainty parasol with her, which was no bigger than an upside-down thimble and was only carried as a fashion accessory. For some reason she had brought it with her this morning, thinking it would shield her from the sun as the day had promised to be fair. With a sigh of resignation she slipped it from her wrist, where it hung by a wide ribbon, unfurled it, and, picking up her skirt, went down the church steps, out of the churchyard, and started along the road toward the Thorntons'.

Immediately the skies opened up, and a strong wind sent leaves scuttling from the trees and the rain tugging her tiny umbrella. Holly could feel it spattering the back of her jacket and moaned at the damage it must be doing to her best velour bonnet.

Over the insidious patter of the rain on the small circle of silk she was barely managing to hold over her head, Holly heard her name shouted, "Miss Lambeth!"

A moment of indecision. Having recognized Dr. Stevens' voice, should she walk haughtily on, soundly snubbing him in order to show him that one didn't stand up Holly Lambeth and get away with it, or should expediency take precedence here and avoid ruining her best outfit and shoes?

She whirled around and saw the little buggy weaving and wobbling down the lane with a red-faced doctor driving it with one hand and wildly waving the other. He reined up beside her, jumped out, and, thrusting a huge black umbrella over her, stammered out a profuse apology. "Tom Haskins' boy jumped on a haystack and onto a pitchfork, Miss Lambeth, and sparing you the details—I had to rush out to their farm, take care of him. I hope you'll forgive me and I'm sorry about the rain—"

At his evident genuine distress, Holly couldn't help melting. At the same time the rain seemed suddenly to diminish and turn into a gentle patter. As they stood there, unexpected sunshine seemed to push through the clouds and envelope the abject doctor in a beatific light.

"Am I forgiven?" he asked.

The alternative being an ignominious return to Hetty's house, Holly chose to be magnanimous.

"Well, of course, you're not responsible for the rain, Dr. Stevens, and certainly such an emergency has to be met, so, yes, of course."

"We could still take a drive, if you like," he suggested tentatively.

The rest of the afternoon proved fair enough with pale sunshine alternating with sporadic showers. But Holly hardly minded. It turned out to be the pleasantest afternoon she had yet spent in Riverbend.

She found Blaine Stevens to be charming and intelligent and also blessed with a lively sense of humor. He was not only interesting but easy to talk to as well. They found that, although they were from different regions of the country, both had come from small towns, close families. They shared common interests in books and music and enjoyed the beauties of nature.

It was late afternoon when they started back toward town and, without warning, Blaine reined up sharply in the middle of the road. Pointing, he said in an awed voice, "Look, Miss Lambeth, a rainbow!"

Before them a delicate arch of yellow, lavender, green, blue, and orange formed a bridge in the pale blue sky against the purple hills.

"How beautiful!" Holly sighed.

They both sat motionless for a long while until the glorious vision faded away. Without a word, Blaine gave the reins a flick and they drove on silently, still caught in the beauty of the moment they had shared.

"I would say a day that ends with a rainbow has to be a good omen for a friendship, wouldn't you, Miss Lambeth?" he asked her as they reached town and turned down the road to the Thorntons' house.

"I agree, Dr. Stevens, it would certainly seem so," replied Holly thinking that seeing Blaine again presented a very pleasant prospect.

By the time they reached the Thorntons' it had started raining again. Blaine said, "Although there's a chance we still might have some good weather, this is what I'm afraid you've got to expect, Miss Lambeth, as we head into an Oregon winter."

"That's what I've heard."

"I hope you're not easily depressed by weather?"

"Oh, I don't think so," Holly assured him as he walked with her up to the door under the shelter of his big umbrella.

But Holly was wrong. That Sunday began a week of incessant rain.

"Doesn't it ever stop?" Holly asked the third morning as she stood at the kitchen window staring out at the steady drizzle.

Confined to the house where she was either ignored by Hetty or annoyed by her, Holly spent most of her time in the bedroom she shared with the children. She decided to finish taking her things out of her trunk, which for some reason she had left partially packed.

As she brushed and hung up her clothes with clove-studded orange balls to prevent the chance of mildew from all the dampness Hetty had warned her about, Aurelia crept in and deposited herself on the bed to watch.

"What's this, Holly?" the little girl asked smoothing the thick, velvet cover of Holly's photograph album.

"Would you like to see?" Holly asked and sat down beside her and opened it for the child to look through the pages of pictures.

"That's my house in Willow Springs," Holly told her with a tiny lump in her throat as she placed her finger on a photo of the Lambeth homestead. "And there's my Grandma Vinny and Grampa Granville sitting on the porch, and there's my mama and papa, and that's our collie, Tamas, lying on the steps . . . ," and Holly began to turn the pages slowly pointing out each picture and telling Aurelia who was in it.

Then they came upon the page with Jim Mercer's picture, his handsome face trying to look brave and stalwart in his West Point cadet uniform, the cape folded back, the glittering double row of brass buttons, the epaulets and shoulder cord, the gauntleted hand on the saber hilt.

"Ohhhh-ummm," breathed Aurelia, "Is this a prince?"

In spite of the sudden clutch in her heart, Holly had to laugh.

"No, honey, not a prince—but he *is* a soldier, a lieutenant in the United States Army." She went on, "His name is Jim Mercer, and I was supposed to marry him."

"You *were?*" Aurelia sounded awed.

"Yes."

"Then why didn't you?"

"Because I was a very vain and foolish young lady," Holly told her. "He married someone else instead."

"Oh, Holly, I'm sorry!" Aurelia looked at her with sorrowful eyes.

Holly gave her a hug. "Oh, honey, that's sweet of you, but it was my own fault."

"Did he marry a princess?" Aurelia was still interested in the story, sad as it was.

45

"Not exactly. She was a colonel's daughter, and I guess a sort of princess," Holly said. "Let's turn the page."

On the next page there was a full-length picture of Holly in the lovely ball gown she had worn at her coming out party. She had camellias in her hair and was holding a bouquet in a frilled lace ruff.

"Oh, Holly, that's *you*, isn't it? And *you do* look like a princess. Tell me about the dress—," Aurelia begged.

"Well—," began Holly, "it was sky blue and had a tulle over-skirt caught up with tiny blue velvet bows and—"

They were both so occupied that they didn't hear the short knock, if there was one. Suddenly the bedroom door burst open. She stood on the threshold; her voice was shrill. "Aurelia, get down off that bed this instant. You know I don't like you lolling around wasting time."

Startled and still holding the album, Holly stared at her cousin.

"But Mama, Holly's showing me pictures of the town you both grew up in and pictures of Great-Gramma and your mama and Holly's party and—"

"That's enough, Aurelia, go on out to the kitchen. You've got chores to do."

As the little girl slid obediently down from the bed, her eyes glistened as she bit her lower lip to keep back the unshed tears.

Holly rushed to defend her. "Hetty, it was *my* fault, I was just showing her pictures of Willow Springs and—"

Hetty went white. "I said I don't want you filling my child's head with a lot of nonsense—"

"Hetty, I was showing her pictures of *our* grandparents, *your* parents—surely you shouldn't mind—"

"Since when did you give a fig what anyone minds?" demanded Hetty. Then she went out and shut the door.

After Hetty left, Holly sat rigidly on the edge of the bed. Outside, the rain drummed relentlessly. Appalled by Hetty's reaction, Holly asked herself why Hetty should object to this harmless pastime?

Staring out the window, where the rain beat monotonously

46

against the panes, Holly felt trapped. A prisoner! She must find a means of escape. But how?

She looked down at the album she was still holding in her lap, turned the rest of the pages stiffly, the images of the people, the events, the places that had made up her life before, reminding her of what she had left. Willow Springs and all the gaiety and sunny memories it evoked had disappeared in the rain and fog of Oregon. To tell herself it would be only a year didn't help. A year could seem like forever.

At the end of the week the heavy rain had slowed to a steady drizzle. For days Holly's sense of desperation had deepened. Finally, she felt she could not possibly stand being cooped up in the house with Hetty's punishing coldness and intractable hostility any longer.

The children were both napping, and Hetty, tight-lipped, was mending. Without explaining, Holly flung on her warm cape and, defying the weather, went out for a walk.

By the time she reached town, it had stopped raining. Wet leaves plastered the board walkways, and puddles were everywhere, making navigating the streets hazardous. But Holly didn't care. It was so good to be out, with the cool wind in her face, the feeling of being free surging through her.

At the *Riverbend Monitor* Adam Corcoran sat with his long legs and booted feet up on the editor's desk. Leaning back in the swivel oak chair, he stared gloomily out the window onto Main Street. He was alone in the office. It was Friday, and the weekly edition of the paper had been "put to bed" yesterday. Old Tom was probably parting with most of his paycheck over at the Nugget, and young Mike had gone squirrel hunting.

Ad squinted his eyes and surveyed the street scene in front of him. Not much going on this noon. Not that there ever was in this isolated "neck of the woods." It was a far cry from San Francisco with its busy streets crowded with all sorts of colorfully dressed people on the go, filled with purpose and activity. Only a few short months ago, he had been part of it. Blazes, he missed it!

My own blasted fault, Ad thought grimly. Maybe he should

have curbed his instinct about O'Herir, reined in that powerful reportorial drive, but it was too much a part of him. He had caught the scent, and the hunt had been on, and Ad had had to follow it. His dogged probing and investigative reporting of the shenanigans of a popular and powerful politician had landed him here. A series of articles delineating the number of payoffs and kickbacks had cost him his job.

With a rush of adrenaline, Ad remembered the intense excitement of working on the big-city daily newspaper from which he'd been fired. The firing came from the top, the ownership, management. It had been final. There had been no recourse. Privately his editor, sorry to lose one of his best men, told him to "lie low" for a couple of months, maybe only until the next election, and he'd see if he could get him his job back.

Ad hadn't wanted to leave San Francisco; he loved the city, the life he lived there. His job was one he enjoyed, had worked hard to get, but after he was fired, no other newspaper would hire him. At least until the flurry his series had caused died down.

So Ad had been forced to leave the city and seek employment elsewhere. Eventually he landed the editorship of this small weekly, off the beaten track, in this remote part of Oregon, a town only a few years past its "gold rush" days, now settling in as a community of farm families, timber fellers, small lumber mills, a twenty-minute stop on the stagecoach line.

A temporary "stop-gap," he reassured himself when he came nearly seven months ago. But the dreary exile had dragged on, and from what he heard from friends in San Francisco, the situation there was still chancy. The politician he had been investigating was reelected and it looked as if it would be a long time before Ad could safely return and expect to be reinstated.

He keenly missed the camaraderie of his fellow reporters; he missed San Francisco, the theaters and fine restaurants, the amusing conversation of attractive women, and the sophisticated pleasures a city offered.

In Riverbend there wasn't much for a man like Ad, little to stimulate him intellectually, few people well-read enough to argue or debate with him on many subjects he liked to explore, little to do for a man who had never enjoyed hunting or fishing. Nights were spent reading until, bored with himself, he flung the book aside and sauntered over to the Golden Slipper in search of company, only to stay too long and drink too much. He'd had no feminine companionship for months, unless you counted the poor, painted saloon girls with whom the miners in from the hills and the ranch hands in from nearby spreads drank, danced, and had a few laughs. But it wasn't Ad's style and he often left feeling depressed and deeply lonely. Something he'd never experienced before.

He had made no close friends here. At first he'd received a few Sunday dinner invitations from some of the families, but he soon found if you didn't attend church regularly or fit neatly into the category of prospective husband for marriageable daughters, the invitations stopped coming.

After he'd written a few editorials that were considered "downright radical," Ad was thought too controversial for most of the town folk. But since there was no one else to print the weather reports, the cattle stock prices, the church socials and bake sales, announce the births, accept the eulogies to go along with the obituaries, publish the preacher's weekly sermons or the times of the Town Council meetings, Ad was tolerated as a "necessary evil" for Riverbend.

He liked Blaine Stevens, but as the only doctor in the vicinity the man was so conscientious about his patients, he rarely had any time to call his own. There was always a baby to deliver, a child with colic, or an old woman, alone and ill, he had to ride out to see. Ad also liked Ned Thornton, but he was totally henpecked, and that kind of nonsense disgusted Ad. A confirmed bachelor, Ad was thankful he had escaped a similar fate, having survived several near-lapses and thus far successfully dodged matrimony.

But thinking of Ned brought instantly to mind the young woman Ned had introduced as his cousin. Hollis Lambeth. Unconsciously, Ad shook his head. How such a lovely creature had appeared so unexpectedly in Riverbend, of all places, went beyond Ad's powers of imagination. It was as if she had been dropped from Mt. Olympus.

Ad closed his eyes for a moment, willing her image back onto the screen of his mind. Tall, slender, with creamy skin and wide, heavily lashed eyes. Dressed simply in a peacock-blue suit, everything about her was neat and trim. She looked unrumpled, without too many flounces and furbelows that can make a woman traveler look frumpy. She wore little jewelry, no dangling earrings, only a small fob watch pinned to her jacket lapel. She wore dark-blue kid gloves, and a tiny, pert bonnet with a veil barely covering the cinnamon-brown hair. A veil and gloves were two things you didn't often see on Riverbend ladies. There was a coolness about her, a reserve, that Ad immediately admired.

What was she doing here visiting a couple like Ned and Hetty? And why had she come to a place with so little to offer in the way of social life a young lady of her apparent grace should enjoy? Ad's investigative reporter instincts stirred. There was some mystery about this new arrival. What it was triggered his curiosity.

As if he had willed his thoughts into reality, he looked out the window and saw Holly coming up on the other side of the street opposite the *Monitor* building. Ad swung his feet down and leaned forward to watch her. Unconsciously he smiled. She had such a graceful walk, erect yet natural, not mincing nor stiff. Still there was something purposeful in her stride. Where was she going? Where was she headed?

He saw her pause at the corner, close her umbrella, look for a long time down either side of the street. Would it be too obvious if he strolled out and met her apparently by chance?

But Ad was a man who figured one should always take whatever opportunity Fate graciously presented. This seemed to be one that had landed happily right in his lap. Ad decided to seize the moment. He swiveled his chair around, slipped on his jacket coat, grabbed his hat, and made it out the door just as Holly came directly across the road.

Chapter 5

*I*n a few long strides Ad crossed the road and approached Holly casually as if he had been leisurely sauntering down the street and had come upon her quite accidentally. Giving no hint of the mad dash he had made from his office into the street, he swept off his hat. "Good afternoon, Miss Lambeth."

Holly stopped short. She had been so engrossed in her own troubling thoughts that hearing her name startled her. Adam Corcoran's greeting took her quite by surprise and brought color like twin blushing roses into her cheeks.

"Good day, Mr. Corcoran," she replied, acknowledging with a nod that they had been previously introduced, then started to move on.

But Adam was standing right in front of her, making that impossible. To sweep past him would have been rude, and, after all, he *was* a friend of Ned's. Besides, it seemed clear he intended to exchange more than merely a polite greeting as he asked, "I hope you're having a pleasant stay in Riverbend, Miss Lambeth?"

Innate honesty tempted Holly to blurt out a truthful "No!" But her ingrained good manners and social grace compelled her to give the obligatory although somewhat ambiguous response. "Indeed, thank you, Mr. Corcoran. I am finding it most interesting."

Almost as if he had discerned the subtle evasion in her answer, looking amused, he pursued the subject. "However, I assume you find it a great deal different from the East?"

"Oh, well, yes. Very," Holly countered and again attempted to pass him. But all six feet and at least three inches of him were blocking her way.

"Especially this weather, I presume," Adam said as if determined to continue the conversation he had initiated. "It will take some time to get used to; I can tell you that from my own experience." Ad paused, then seeing he had aroused her curiosity, he went on, "I must admit I had a few qualms when I arrived here a few months ago from San Francisco."

He let the name "San Francisco" sink in for a minute, watching what her reaction might be. Ad knew that Eastern periodicals gave their readers rhapsodic descriptions of San Francisco, calling it the "Paris of the West Coast." Such padded verbiage attributed more ambiance than it really had—or deserved, for that matter. But it tended to lend a certain aura to anyone lucky enough to be able to say he knew the city.

Holly looked at Adam Corcoran with a new interest. Obviously he was a gentleman, well-dressed. The gray broadcloth coat, spotless linen, and silk cravat spoke of good taste and certainly not the kind she had seen worn by other Riverbend men. He was certainly well-groomed, clean-shaven except for his mustache; his olive skin was smooth and clear; his eyes held both intelligence and humor. His speech was that of an educated man with a southern courtliness of manner that made her feel a bit homesick and prone to be friendly.

While Holly was making this calculated survey of him, Adam's practiced eye was reaffirming his first impression of her. Miss Hollis Lambeth, he decided, was the most attractive young woman he had seen in a very long time, especially in Riverbend. The cool air had brought the bloom of roses to her skin, several strands of hair loosened by the moisture clung in fetching tendrils to the side of her cheek, and there was surely a suspicion of dimples around her very tempting mouth.

Holly was as curious about Adam Corcoran as he was about her. What might have brought such a man to this remote

Oregon border town? Why had he buried himself here? Was he running away from something, someone? Did he have a past he was trying to forget? Even that possibility did not frighten her; rather, it intrigued her. It made her think that maybe she had more in common with Adam Corcoran than anyone else in Riverbend.

All this went through Holly's mind in a second. Now she listened with a new spark of interest as Adam said, "However, in case you may be a bit concerned by the exterior of the town—" Ad made a sweeping gesture to encompass the "down and out" look of Main Street "—I hasten to assure you, it is not completely without some of the cultural amenities one hopes to find in a new place. There are traveling theatrical troupes who come up from San Francisco regularly, with a good repertoire of plays, ones that have received good reviews in the East. Often the players are well-known in Europe and are making American tours. Some are even stars of Shakespearean drama and comedy."

Ad saw he had hit the mark. Holly's eyes suddenly sparkled. He played his advantage quickly. "I would consider it a real pleasure if, on one of these occasions, you would do me the honor of accompanying me to such a production should one happen while you are here."

Holly loved going to plays, and the possibility of such a diversion gave her the needed "light at the end of the tunnel" she had not thought to find in Riverbend. She gave Ad a delighted smile. "Why, thank you, Mr. Corcoran, I surely would."

Gratified by his success in achieving her acceptance, Adam was about to suggest he walk on with her wherever she was going, when Ned Thornton came out onto the porch of the General Store, waved, and called, "Holly! Your box came on the morning stage!"

Holly returned the wave and called back, "Oh, good! I'll be right over, Ned, thank you." To Ad she explained, "I've been expecting a package from my mother, and it's come. So, if you'll excuse me—"

"What a coincidence! I was going over to check on the very same thing myself."

"A package from your mother?" Holly's eyebrows arched in surprise.

Ad chuckled, "No, not a package from my mother, but a friend in San Francisco sends me a bundle of the daily newspapers each week. Of course, the news is a week late, but it's a feast I look forward to, I can tell you. So may I escort you?" he offered.

With only a split-second's hesitation, Holly took his arm, and they crossed the street together, Ad skillfully manipulating them around the potholes and mud puddles.

A bell over the door jangled as they entered the store. Ned, in his shirtsleeves and wearing a blue cotton storekeeper's apron, greeted them both. "Holly, I was going to bring your box with me when I came home for supper."

"Well, I'm here now, so I can carry it myself."

Ned shook his head, "'Fraid not, Holly. It's real heavy. Don't know what your mother must have put in it! Bricks?"

Holly laughed while Ad quickly offered, "I'll be happy to carry Miss Lambeth's box for her and see her home."

Ned looked from one to the other; a smile played around the corner of his mouth. He glanced at Holly as if to say, "Another male admirer, ready to do your bidding, eh, Holly, just like in Willow Springs?" But there was no maliciousness in Ned's eyes, just an indulgent twinkle. "Why don't I just open up the box for you, Holly? It's over there in the corner, and you can take your time looking through it, decide what you want now, and I can bring the rest later."

"Good idea," Holly agreed, and she and Ad followed him to the back of the store.

Ned cut the cords binding the sturdy box; then, taking the pronged end of a hammer, he pried out the nails and with a wrenching sound pulled up the lid. Pushing aside some layers of excelsior, they all peered inside.

"Books!" they said in unison.

"*That* should keep you busy all winter, Holly," Ad remarked dryly.

"Oh, I hoped it was books," Holly sighed happily. "Mama promised to send me some."

Just then the bell over the door jangled, and a woman came into the store. "I better go wait on my customer," Ned told them in a low voice and left Holly and Ad bending over the box of books.

"So you like to read, Miss Lambeth? Better watch out, you'll ruin your 'Southern belle' image. Unless you're not afraid of being considered a 'blue stocking'!"

"I despise labels!" she retorted icily. "Educated women—*even in the South*—enjoy good literature. I grew up on Lamb's *Tales of Shakespeare*."

"You consider *these* books *literature*, do you?" Ad asked, picking a book up at random and reading the title out loud, "*Wherever the True Heart Leads* by Marcella Valencourt?" He looked at her with an amused expression.

Holly had the grace to blush and half-indignantly snatched it out of his hands. One special thing she shared with her mother was a love of romantic novels. She was glad some were mixed in with other favorites, Dickens' novels and George Eliot's, too. They had both wept over *The Mill on the Floss*. She was ready to defend her mother's choices when Ad apologized. "I didn't mean to offend, Miss Lambeth. Variety, as they say, is the spice of life, in reading material as in everything else."

"Books?" a woman's voice behind them asked. "I didn't know you carried books, Mr. Thornton."

Holly turned around to see a woman. She was dressed in a beautifully cut buff poplin walking suit, trimmed with brown cording, standing with Ned at the counter but peering in their direction.

"I didn't order them, Mrs. Dodd; they belong to Hetty's cousin. They just arrived for her by stage," Ned explained. "Come over, I'd like you to meet her. Holly, I'd like you to meet Viola Dodd, Riverbend's finest seamstress. Hollis Lambeth." *Viola Dodd, Seamstress!* The resident of the charming little yellow house she had wondered about and now at last had the chance to meet.

The woman was very small, slight with a delicate almost fragile appearance. Under a tastefully trimmed bonnet, her face was a pale oval. Her features were refined; her mouth was rather compressed; her nose was delicate and aristocratic. Holly always particularly noticed noses probably because her own was short and tended to tilt at the tip.

"I'm pleased to meet you," Holly said. Knowing that Mrs. Dodd was a seamstress, Holly realized that she must have made the stylish outfit herself. Holly was duly impressed.

"And I you," Mrs. Dodd murmured politely at the introduction, then her eyes wandered back to the pile of books.

Recognizing the longing in Viola Dodd's eyes, impulsively Holly offered, "Would you like to borrow one?"

A look of surprise broke through the woman's composed expression. Flushed with pleasure, she exclaimed, "Oh, may I? How very generous of you. I do enjoy relaxing with a good book after sewing all day!"

"Of course," Holly said. "Do choose any one you like," and she stepped back to make room for Mrs. Dodd at the edge of the box.

With one gloved hand she reached into the neatly packed contents of the box, slowly examining the books one by one. Her deliberateness in making her selection made Holly aware that Viola Dodd would be careful about any choice. She also had the instant longing to know her better.

"I believe this one will do nicely," Mrs. Dodd said as she picked up *Silas Marner*. "I hope this wasn't one you were planning to read yourself, Miss Lambeth?"

"No, not at all, not at the moment," Holly assured her.

"I will take very good care of it and return it promptly. I suppose here at the store with Mr. Thornton?"

Holly hesitated, wishing she could invite Viola Dodd to bring it to the house, stay for a visit, but of course, she knew that was out of the question. As if reading her thoughts, Viola spoke softly, rather shyly, "Unless," a slight hesitation, "—unless you might care to come to my house some afternoon for tea? Perhaps then we could discuss our shared interest in books?"

Holly nodded eagerly, and Mrs. Dodd continued, "Very well, then, thank you again." Mrs. Dodd slipped the small volume into a large reticule. "I shall send you a note when I finish the book, and we can set a time and day."

"Oh, yes, that would be lovely. Thank you very much."

Suddenly Holly felt lighthearted. At last something to look forward to, the promise of an invitation, the prospect of a friendship!

Chapter 6

*H*olly's mother had thoughtfully packed some children's books along with the novels. There was a large book of fairy tales that Holly could read to Aurelia and a book illustrated with pictures of all kinds of carriages any little boy would love. Holly knew Teddy would be thrilled. Ned gave them a smaller box, and Ad helped her put those in along with a number of the novels, including one she thought Hetty might like to read.

"I guess that's enough for now since Ned will bring the rest home later," Holly said.

"I hope you don't intend to read during your entire time here, Miss Lambeth," Ad commented.

Holly responded with pretended shock. "Certainly not, Mr. Corcoran. Besides books, I intend to read the editorials in the *Riverbend Monitor* as well. I understand they are educational as well as entertaining!"

"Well put and well taken." Adam smiled. Bending to pick up the box, he gave a mock groan. "Are you sure you don't want to take one or two *more?*"

Amused at his clowning, Holly laughed and shook her head.

On their way out, they stopped to speak to Ned who was busily stocking shelves. "We're going now, Ned," Holly said; then seeing glass jars of peppermint sticks, molasses chunks, and licorice twists, she asked, "Would it be all right if I took the children some candy?"

For a minute Ned seemed about to say no; then giving Holly a conspiratorial wink and leaning toward her, he said in a stage whisper, "Why not? As long as we keep it a secret," and filled two small paper bags with a mixture of the candies.

"I'll bring the rest of the books home with me this evening," Ned promised as she left.

Outside the store they turned in the direction of the Thorntons' house. Holly was feeling a great deal better than earlier when she had rushed out in anger. Being with Adam Corcoran had restored some of her natural good humor. The frank admiration in his eyes and his light, teasing manner had been beneficial as well.

She was even feeling optimistic about Hetty. Maybe Hetty would be so pleased with the books, especially those for the children, she would get over whatever was making her so unreasonable. Holly's mind was filled with possible ways she could soften up her cousin and reach some kind of amicable relationship. After all, they weren't children anymore but two grown-up women who should be able to get along. Otherwise—well, otherwise, Holly still didn't know what to do.

Suddenly Ad put out a warning hand on her arm to hold her back. "Let's cross the street," he suggested.

"Why?" asked Holly, puzzled.

"Because—" Ad never got to finish the sentence because the sound of loud voices shouting, punctuated with swear words, made hearing anything momentarily impossible. A moment later the double doors of the Doggone Best saloon swung open, and a figure lunged out.

"Uh-oh, too late. I wanted to avoid this—," Ad said and drew Holly quickly off the sidewalk onto the street. "That's poor Cliff Larkin," he told her, adding, "I only hope nobody on the Town Council sees him."

"Who is he?" asked Holly. As Ad steered her to the other side of the street, she looked back over her shoulder at the man staggering down the opposite sidewalk, weaving from post to post, hanging on each trying to get his balance.

"Believe it or not, he's the town schoolteacher. School's due to start in another week, and he's probably having a last fling

59

before having to face all those bright little faces early every morning."

"*He* teaches *school?*" Holly's tone matched the look of astonishment on her face. All she could think of was her own schoolteachers—prim Miss Rebecca Burns who had taught her in grammar school; Louisa McGill, the severe headmistress at the Blue Ridge Female Academy she had attended after sixth grade. And Mr. Bradley, the principal at Willow Springs Secondary, had also been a church elder and taught Sunday school. All the teachers she had ever known were a far cry from this poor wretch stumbling down the street.

"Shouldn't someone help him?" she asked anxiously, twisting her head around to watch the man's unsteady progress.

"Someone will," Ad assured her. "Yes, see, there he comes now. The town's good Samaritan. The doctor."

Holly saw Blaine emerge from the door of one of the buildings along the path the drunk was taking. With a few steps he caught Larkin in time to keep him from falling.

"That's Blaine Stevens, better known as Doc," Ad said, unaware that Holly knew him. "He'll take care of him, take him upstairs to his own place above his office, let him sleep it off, then sober him up."

"What a shame!"

"He'll be all right. That is, until the next time. Blaine tells me the man has a brilliant mind—or did before it got soaked with alcohol. Comes from a good family back east, too. Although they've disowned him now," Ad said; then he placed Holly's hand on his arm. "Don't worry your pretty little head about it. Doc knows what to do, and Larkin will be at his blackboard with his pointer, teaching all those eager little scholars when the schoolhouse bell rings come next Monday."

Holly watched the two men entering the door over which was a neatly lettered sign: "Blaine Stevens, Physician and Surgeon." Blaine had not seen either Holly or Ad; he had seemed totally concerned with helping that sadly in-need human being.

"Doc's an enigma." Adam shook his head. "I'll never understand why someone of his caliber has buried himself here. I've seen his diploma. He graduated from one of the best medical colleges in the country and studied in Scotland and Germany. He could probably get a post in any hospital in America or teach in a university. He's a fine doctor and—" Ad halted "—well, it's none of my business, I guess, everyone who comes to Riverbend has his own reasons." He glanced at Holly as if daring her to tell him why *she* had come.

By this time they had reached the Thorntons'. Ad opened the gate for Holly to pass through. As they walked up onto the porch, the front door flew open and Hetty stood there glaring at them both.

Ad whipped off his hat, held it to his chest, and bowed slightly. "Good day, Mrs. Thornton. I'm bringing your cousin home safely after piloting her through some hazardous obstacles."

His speech was designed to be amusing, but Hetty didn't smile. Indeed she was looking very unamused. Quickly Holly explained, "My box from Mama arrived by stage and was at the store, Hetty, but it was too heavy for me, so Mr. Corcoran kindly offered to carry it here for me."

"Ned could have brought it home," Hetty replied shortly.

Holly felt embarrassed at Hetty's unfriendliness. What on earth could Mr. Corcoran think? However, Ad seemed not at all disturbed by Hetty's lack of cordiality. He simply smiled and suggested courteously, "Shall I put it inside?"

Hetty was forced to step back and hold the door open for him to place the box inside by the door.

He then tipped his hat to her. "Nice to see you again, Mrs. Thornton; have a pleasant day." Turning to Holly, he bowed over the hand she extended, saying, "Good day, Miss Lambeth, and I hope I may have the pleasure of calling on you soon."

Conscious of Hetty's eyes boring into her like two sharp knives, Holly murmured. "Thank you for your help, Mr. Corcoran."

With an enigmatic smile Ad went down the porch steps, nonchalantly strolled down the path, went out the gate, and turned back toward town.

Holly stepped inside the house. The door had barely closed behind her when Hetty confronted her, demanding, "What are

61

you trying to do, Holly? Have every available man in Riverbend dancing to your tune? Don't you know how it looks? Flirting and flitting all over town, attracting attention? This isn't Willow Springs, you know. It doesn't take much here in this town to give a woman the tag of 'fast.' Ned and I have a good name here, and I don't appreciate your damaging it by being seen with anyone you can find to fetch and carry for you. Especially someone like Adam Corcoran whose reputation in this community is questionable, to say the least!"

Stunned at the vicious attack, Holly stared back at her. Anger welled up hotly, then seeing Hetty's flushed face, bulging eyes, the heat turned to ice.

"Are you quite finished, Hetty?" she asked coldly. "If you are, I have something to say. I doubt that you care about *my* reputation. And for your information, Mr. Corcoran is as perfect a gentleman as I have ever met here or anywhere else. Furthermore, I like to make up my own mind about people, not be told whom I should speak or walk with. It was *your* husband who introduced me to Mr. Corcoran in the first place, and *Ned* seems to have high regard for him. Now if you'll excuse me, I'm going to take off my bonnet and open my box from my mother!"

Holly brushed past Hetty, biting her lip to avoid saying anything more she might regret. Without another glance in her cousin's direction, Holly shoved the heavy box with her foot across the floor, down the hall. She went into the bedroom, letting the door bang behind her.

She was angry. Angry for losing her temper. Even angrier that Hetty could make her *this* upset. Worse still, it spoiled what Holly had hoped would be a happy, conciliatory occasion. Hetty's outburst had prevented her from sharing the books her mother had sent for all of them to enjoy, to perhaps bridge the gap that separated them.

The longer she was here, the more impossible it got. Was there no solution? Was there no escape?

Chapter 7

*H*olly had no sooner reached the haven of the bedroom when there was a sharp rat-a-tat-tat on the door. Whirling around, she yanked it open to face a flushed Hetty.

"I don't want you to start giving Aurelia the notion that she can loll around looking at books all day. I'm trying to teach her to do her fair share of chores, and there's plenty for her to do to help around here, so I'd suggest you put those books out of sight."

Holly stared at her cousin in disbelief. "You don't want Aurelia to enjoy books?" she gasped.

"People out here have more to do than daydream and live make-believe lives. Things out here don't come easy. People work hard and don't have time for nonsense."

"But Hetty, our family always loved to read. You and I both were given books when we were little girls," Holly protested, and leaning into the box, she pulled an *Alice* volume out to show her. "Look, see what Mama sent? Don't you remember how we loved *Alice in Wonderland?*"

Hetty's expression just got grimmer. "I guess you didn't hear what I said—I want Aurelia to fit in; I don't want my daughter to grow up any different, with high-falutin' ideas, thinking she's better than anybody else," and she turned around to leave.

Still, Holly made one last try. "Can't I even give this to the children as a gift from my mother, Hetty?"

"I've said what I meant and I meant what I said," was Hetty's rejoinder as she marched back down the hall to the kitchen.

Totally bewildered, Holly shut the door again and sat down on the edge of the bed, Hetty's words echoing in her head. They brought back the hilarious discussion that Alice had had with the Duchess that, as children, they had repeated endlessly, always dissolving into helpless laughter afterward. Holly, now recalling that ridiculous dialogue when Alice says, "I say what I mean and I mean what I say," to which the Duchess replies, "Nonsense! That's like saying that I see what I eat is the same as I eat what I see"—and on and on wondered if Hetty had inadvertently mouthed the same words without realizing the source? Were there, after all, some happy memories of their shared childhood that Hetty couldn't suppress?

What was behind all that fury? What did Hetty *really* mean by saying she didn't want Aurelia to be "different"? Would reading, enjoying good books, make Aurelia grow up dissatisfied, discontent, unhappy in this environment? What was Hetty really saying? Was she talking about Aurelia or herself? It seemed that everything she tried to do, every time she turned around, she met Hetty's opposition. How could she possibly go on here with Hetty?

Frustrated, she shoved the box of books under the bed, took off her bonnet, and pondered the bleak prospect of the year ahead. If there were any place she could go, Holly would have packed up and left on the spot. There seemed no way to get along with Hetty. But with no viable alternative until she could figure out what to do next she would just have to accept it. Only a miracle could change the situation. And were miracles a common commodity in 1882?

Out of the blue, or so it seemed, help came from an unexpected source. One evening a few days later, when Ned came home from the store, he handed Holly a note. "Mrs. Dodd left this for you."

Surprised, Holly opened it and read it eagerly. True to her promise, Mrs. Dodd had written,

My dear Miss Lambeth, I cannot tell you what pleasure reading *Silas Marner* afforded me. I am indebted to you for the enjoyable hours I spent with the book you so graciously lent me. I would like to return my thanks by having you to tea, Wednesday next at three o'clock if you are free to come? I always take Wednesday afternoon off, and so look forward to entertaining you. You may send word by Mr. Thornton, as I plan to be in the store on Tuesday to pick up some material he ordered for me due to arrive that day.

With kind regards,
Viola Dodd.

On Wednesday afternoon Holly dressed with special care, aware that she would be viewed by a professional who would notice every detail. She chose a simple but stylish ensemble, a jade-green velvet hat trimmed with a cluster of feathers. When she emerged from the bedroom and came into the kitchen, ready to leave for Mrs. Dodd's, Aurelia looked up from the floor where she and Teddy were building with blocks and asked, "Oh, Holly, are you going to a party?"

Hetty was at the ironing board, but at that she looked up. Her narrowed glance at Holly revealed her curiosity, but her tightly pursed lips said she would rather be tortured than ask Holly where she was going.

Determined not to let Hetty's manner bother her, Holly spoke pleasantly, "I'm going over to Mrs. Dodd's; she's invited me to tea."

"Viola Dodd may put on fine manners, but after all, all she does is sew for other people!"

Although usually Holly made a point of not getting into arguments with her cousin in front of the children, this, however, was too much. This mean-spirited remark shocked Holly into responding, "What an unkind thing to say, Hetty!"

Hetty turned crimson.

Afraid that this could escalate into a full-blown argument or worse, deliberately, Holly controlled herself. Smiling at the children, she went to the door. "Good-bye, then, I'll see you later." Aurelia's sweet little voice followed her—"Have a nice time, Holly!"

In Viola Dodd's parlor there was none of the clutter of the popular decorating style, influenced by the English Queen Victoria, found in most houses of the time. It was not overloaded with the prevalent trend for crocheted antimacassars, China dogs, painted seashells, artificial flowers under glass domes. Instead it had the quiet taste of its owner.

When Holly remarked on a silver-framed photograph on top of the piano, showing a lovely young girl, Mrs. Dodd said simply, without further explanation, "My daughter, Avesta; she's away at boarding school."

Mrs. Dodd—"Please call me Vi,"—served a delightful tea consisting of egg salad sandwiches cut in triangles and a moist lemon sponge cake. Holly relaxed at once in her hostess's warmth. Soon they were chatting as if they had known each other a long time. Holly had spent many hours in her bedroom reading to avoid Hetty during the day without Ned's presence as a buffer. So, books were a natural topic of their conversation. Holly discovered Vi loved the novels of Sir Walter Scott and that they shared a very favorite author in Charlotte Brontë.

All too soon the melodious chiming of Vi's mantel clock reminded Holly that she had stayed past the acceptable time for a first-time call. However, it had been such a pleasant respite from her tension-filled existence at Hetty's that she hated to leave.

"Oh, do you have to go?" her hostess said, seeming almost as reluctant to have her leave. "There are so few ladies here in Riverbend I find I have enough in common with, although I'm sure there must be others who enjoy books and reading as much as we two, but most are married with small children which puts me—*and* you—out of their circumstances, doesn't it?"

"But does it have to?" Holly demanded. "At home, back in Willow Springs, I know my mother and aunts have friends in their Garden Club, for instance, who are all ages and in different walks of life—some of them are spinsters like me and—" She halted suddenly saying, "Oh, I'm sorry. Of course, *you're* not a spinster, I forgot you have a daughter."

Vi only smiled and went on to say, "You're quite right. I'm sure that's the best way to look for friendships. Not age nor situation but common interests." She paused as though thinking for a minute. They were now standing in the little hallway. Then Vi said slowly, "I don't know whether you'd be interested or not but just suppose—"

"Suppose what?"

"Suppose—we had some sort of book club. Invite some ladies to get together maybe once a month to discuss books, exchange them, and so on?" Vi suggested.

"Why, yes! But whom would we ask to join?"

"We'd first have to find out who in Riverbend likes to read. Sadly enough, there is no library. . . ."

Just then Holly thought of the box brimming with books under her bed. Hetty's disdain of having them around, the letter from Mama saying she was sending *more*—

"I'm getting an idea!" she exclaimed. "But I guess I better think it through a little bit."

"If it's on the line of a book club, I'm all for it." Vi smiled as she opened the front door for her, "I'm so happy you could come today, Holly. I haven't enjoyed an afternoon so much in—I couldn't tell you how long. Please come again soon."

"As soon as I get my idea figured out better, I'll talk it over with you," Holly promised as they walked out onto the porch.

"Pray about it!" was Vi's surprising suggestion.

"You sound just like my Great-Aunt Ancilla!" Holly laughed as she went down the steps.

"I hope that's a compliment?"

"It *is*!" Holly assured her.

The afternoon was well along, and Holly hurried through the gathering autumn dusk, filled with enthusiasm about her new friendship and excited about the plan stirring in her mind. But when she stepped inside Hetty's house, she was greeted by a smoldering look from Hetty and her announcement, "You're late. I'm serving supper now. Ned's been home a half-hour."

Holly started to apologize but Hetty's next words chilled. "Ned brought *another* box from your mother. If it's books . . ." the implied threat was in Hetty's voice, but Holly did not wait to hear it. She went back to the bedroom to take off her hat and jacket and saw the large carton at the door. *Oh, dear Lord, what now?* Holly murmured to herself, not knowing it was a prayer.

Later that evening, upon opening the box, she found a note from her mother inside: "Dear Holly, I trust by this time you are settled in at Hetty's and things are going smoothly." *Oh, Mama, if you only knew,* Holly sighed, then read on: "I hope it won't upset you to know that Jim Mercer and his bride are here visiting his parents. . . ." Reading this, Holly felt a dart of pain. Surprised by it she wondered if it was wounded pride she felt or regret? Would any mention of Jim always hurt her in some way? She read on: "—and I heard she was going to remain here since his next post is in some unsuitable place for wives."

Her mother had written something more, then scratched it out heavily. Curious, Holly held it up to the light so she could read through it. "Jim's mother introduced me to her after church on Sunday, and she is quite pretty."

She would be! Holly thought miserably, then continued with the letter: "Well, your father wants to take this box to the post office, so I shall close now. Hoping you are in fine spirit and good health, everyone sends love."

Squeezed at the bottom of the closely written page was a post-script: "Great-Aunt Ancilla just came by and wanted me to enclose these for you." Several small tracts fell out of the envelope. Holly fanned them out in her hand seeing a picture of the dear little old lady in her mind. Across the top of the first one in bold black type was the Biblical instruction: "Whatever your hand finds to do, do it with all your might." Slowly she reread it; wasn't this the same tract she had found in her hanky that day in the woods?

Her one hand was resting on the top of the new box of books, and she repeated the quotation to herself: "Whatever your hand finds to do, do it with all your might. . . ."

The half-formed idea that had come to her as she left Viola Dodd's burst into full possibility. Vi had said, "Pray about it." Great-Aunt Ancilla had sent the tracts! Maybe this was the answer to her unspoken prayer? Why not? This might well be the guidance she had been seeking, the direction she was looking for. *Could* it *actually* be? It *did* seem more than coincidental that this tract with the same message had come to her *twice*.

Feeling that Ned would know how such a project would be received, a few evenings later Holly decided to tell her idea at supper and find out his reaction. She had hardly finished speaking when Hetty let out a sound suspiciously like a snort. "A lending library!" her tone was derisive. "Who in Riverbend has time to read silly novels?"

Holly held on to her temper. "They wouldn't be *all* novels, Hetty. Mama sent a variety of books—and she's sending more—"

"My land! Where does she think you're going to put them, for pity's sake?" Hetty demanded. "Does she think we have a house as big as the Lambeths'?"

"That's just it, Hetty. I *know* you don't have room here. That's why I thought, perhaps . . . ," and Holly glanced hopefully at Ned who was listening intently, ". . . that Ned might have a small corn . at the store where we could keep the books and I could be there certain hours to take care of lending out books. I would think some of the mothers would particularly like the nice selection of children's books Mama sent—"

Before Hetty could interrupt again, Ned spoke up, "I think that's a really good idea, Holly. I could put up a few shelves for you. I think people might be very interested. As long as they're in the store anyway. I know the copies I get of the *Farmers' Almanac* go almost as soon as I put them out. With no town library here, I think we'd be providing a great service for people."

Hetty's mouth pressed into a straight line. If Ned was for the idea, she wasn't about to contradict him no matter how much she opposed it.

Chapter 8

*A*lmost from the first week after Holly put up her carefully lettered sign, LENDING LIBRARY, the venture was a success. Contrary to Hetty's dire predictions and confirming Holly's hope, the women in Riverbend were starved for books and welcomed the project.

The first day the women who had come into the store to purchase flour, sugar, and salt, and other staples, to finger the bolts of bright cloth or leaf through one of the mail order catalogs Ned kept on hand, only eyed Holly's corner curiously. Initially, most seemed too shy to investigate.

As the hours passed with no customers, Holly tried to act busy, dusting the shelves, rearranging the books. Then she got the idea to make an attractive display of some of the books with illustrated covers and print out brief plot summaries to place beside them. The next day one or two women wandered over, and Holly immediately engaged them in conversation, telling about the lending plan and encouraging them to browse and select a book if they liked.

From then on, probably by word of mouth, awareness of the library spread and grew rapidly. In two weeks' time, Holly was doing a thriving business and meeting quite a few Riverbend women.

One of the early and most enthusiastic borrowers was Geneva Healy, a plump, rosy-cheeked woman with a snub nose, bright blue eyes, and an endearing smile, who came into the store about once a week. She was the wife of a prosperous dairy farmer, Holly learned from Ned. She was usually accompanied by two small curly-headed little boys, ages eight and nine, and one about three at her heels.

The first morning she spied Holly arranging books behind the low counter Ned had built for the library, she came right over. After they had exchanged "Good mornings," she hoisted the smiling cherub onto her hip and declared, "Oh, I love to read! I've read the few books I have over and over, and here you are with a good dozen or more I've never even heard of!"

"You're welcome to take one if you like. Just pick out what you want, then sign this little card, and I'll mark the date and give you three weeks to return it. If you haven't finished it then, you can take it out for another two weeks. Does that sound fair?" Holly asked. She was rather unsure if she should bend the rules of the three-week "borrowing time" for a woman with small children and a household to keep. Hetty just *might* be right, Holly worried, maybe none of the Riverbend women *did* have the time or inclination to read.

But Geneva seemed delighted. She introduced herself, and when Holly did the same, Geneva looked astounded. "You're Hetty's cousin? I'd never have guessed. There's no family resemblance, not a bit! Not that I know her well. Not well at all, as a matter of fact. I've just seen her at church, and before she had her little boy she used to help out here in the store once in awhile." Geneva put her head to one side, regarding Holly again. "Well, well—"

Geneva must have told her friends because within the next few days Holly did, according to Ned, "a land-office business" in books. She always greeted the tentative customers pleasantly and asked them what type of story they liked, then suggested titles they might want to borrow, explaining they were allowed to keep them three weeks before returning them.

The response to the library was gratifying. Hetty had implied that many of the women, isolated on remote farms, burdened with endless chores, felt they didn't have time to indulge in reading. Holly found that most of the women had come to

Oregon, leaving family and friends in the east and midwest, and experienced real loneliness. But with Holly's encouragement they now discovered that reading gave them a welcome outlet and provided an interesting break in their otherwise lonely routines.

It was Geneva Healy who actually organized the Riverbend Literary Society, confirming Vi's original idea. "We can have the first meeting at my house," Geneva offered. "We'll keep it simple, just cake and tea so the hostess won't have to fuss; we can just have a good time talking books! What do you think?"

"I think it's a wonderful idea!" Holly agreed enthusiastically, and so the Riverbend Literary Society was formed. That day Holly came home excited about the idea and in her elation shared Geneva's suggestion with Hetty. "Won't that be lovely? A real chance to get together and talk about something other than recipes and babies!"

Hetty's response was caustic. "*Most* women think *those* are the most important things, *more* important than *books,* and *enjoy* talking about their children and exchanging recipes! But, *of course,* someone like *you* couldn't possibly understand that."

Whoops! thought Holly, *that was a mistake.* Another black mark against her in Hetty's book inadvertently made. Trying to make amends, Holly tried again, "I didn't mean that the way it sounded, Hetty; I meant it would give women something *different* not *better.* Remember how your mother and mine used to enjoy the Garden Club, which wasn't about gardening much at all, but gave them a chance to gossip and giggle and be girls again . . ." Seeing Hetty's frown she added lamely, ". . . at least that's what Papa used to say."

Hetty sniffed and went on folding laundry.

"Wouldn't you like to join, Hetty? The first meeting will be at Geneva Healy's on Monday afternoon."

"No thank you," Hetty said emphatically, and that ended the matter. Holly knew there was no use trying to persuade her. Hetty was not going to enter into any project or idea that Holly came up with, so she might as well accept that.

Ned had allowed Holly to put up a small poster with an invitation about the time and place of the first meeting. To everyone's surprise not only ladies showed up. Besides the Bodine sisters, who ran Riverbend's bakery, Mr. Clegg, the church organist, came, as did Mr. and Mrs. Phillips, the town watchmaker and his wife. Mrs. Phillips explained that she read to him while he worked; they both loved good books. It was a lively meeting with much discussion, and they all decided that at each meeting someone would give a book report to the group of the book they had just read.

The biggest surprise of all was that both Ad and Blaine showed up. Adam declared that he wanted to write an article about it for the *Monitor*, and Blaine came during the last half-hour when refreshments were being served, then offered to take Holly home.

So in spite of Hetty's reaction to the idea, the Riverbend Literary Society flourished. Viola Dodd was one of its most supportive members. She closed shop on the meeting days and was particularly insightful when critiquing the books under discussion. Through the Literary Society, she and Holly became real friends.

One meeting day, after the other ladies had left, Holly stayed behind and offered to help Vi clear away the tea things. What she really wanted to do was talk to her, ask the older woman's advice about the situation with Hetty, which seemed to get more intolerable with each passing day. Vi's warmth made it easy for Holly to confide. "I don't think she wanted me to come out here in the first place. She just did it to please her mother, my Aunt Dolly. I think she's always resented me for some reason. I'm not sure why," sighed Holly.

Vi regarded her over the rim of her teacup but didn't say anything.

Holly went on, "What could I have done to make her so—so unfriendly?"

"You really don't know, do you?" Vi asked, then set her cup down carefully, wiped her mouth daintily on the small white embroidered napkin. "It's nothing you've done, Holly. Don't you understand that?"

"Then why?"

"Jealousy."

73

"Jealousy? Why should Hetty be jealous of *me? She* has everything I don't: a husband, a home, children." Holly was genuinely astonished at such a suggestion.

A silence fell, and Vi calmly poured them each more tea, then asked, "Have you prayed about this, Holly?"

"Yes, of course I have. Well, a little, I guess. I've worried about it more than I've prayed, to be truthful. And especially because I love the children so much and I'd love to spend more time with them, but . . . I just don't know how to deal with Hetty."

On the way home from Vi's that afternoon Holly thought hard about what Vi had said. Was it really possible that Hetty was jealous? Back in Willow Springs when Hetty sat at home while Holly went out dancing, it might have been true. But here in Riverbend, where Hetty was the wife of a respected, prominent citizen, and she, Holly, was a stranger, an outsider? But Vi was the most sincere, truthful person Holly had ever met and had wisdom as well. If *she* believed that was the reason for Hetty's coldness, Holly should at least consider it a possibility.

She felt somewhat ashamed when Vi had asked her if she'd prayed about her relationship with her cousin. To be honest, she had mostly resented it, thought it unfair, and felt herself to be the injured party.

Slowing her step, Holly probed the situation more deeply. If Hetty had always been jealous of her and had finally made a new life for herself in Oregon and had thereby escaped the family's constant comparisons of the two cousins—and then that same cousin suddenly appeared on the scene—wouldn't *you* feel upset? Holly's conscience demanded. If all this was true, what could she do about it? Unless she packed up and went back home, Holly had to stay in Riverbend and make the best of it, and Hetty had to put up with her.

Chapter 9

To Holly's amusement Adam Corcoran became one of the lending library borrowers.

"I thought those bundles of San Francisco newspapers you pick up at the post office every week kept you supplied with enough reading material," she teased him one day as he looked over her titles.

"Well, you can get an overdose of murders, mayhem, and political skullduggery, which is what seems to be the content of most of the city rags these days."

She pretended to be shocked. "I thought you missed the big city."

"I do. Maybe I'm getting soft in the head. Maybe the bucolic life is getting to me. Or maybe, it's just possible, that Riverbend has grown more interesting since some *new* people arrived in town."

She was checking out Dickens' *A Tale of Two Cities* to Adam just as Blaine Stevens came into the store and started over to the library. At his approach, Ad placed his hand on his chest as if suffering a heart attack and gasped, "Don't tell me our dedicated physician has time to read books!"

"It's good medicine; I recommend it to all my patients. A good book occasionally takes them out of their pain and away from their worry for a few hours." His grin included Holly. "I write dozens of prescriptions for a good book to be taken regularly."

"I can understand your giving that advice to sick people or someone who's laid up with a broken limb and worrying about who's going to do his plowing, but what are *you* doing here?" Adam kept up the ragging.

"Haven't you ever heard the saying, 'Physician, heal thyself'?" asked Blaine. Holly was observing the two men, apparently good friends ribbing each other.

At length, Adam said, "Well, check this out for me, if you will, Miss Lambeth, and I'll be on my way. I've got a paper to put to bed."

When he had sauntered off, Holly, assuming her role of librarian, asked Blaine, "So, what kind of leisure reading do you enjoy, doctor?"

"Believe it or not, I enjoy poetry," Blaine told her, leaning his folded arms on the counter and surveying her pleasantly.

"Poetry?" She *was* surprised. Science and poetry seemed a strange combination. "What kind of poetry?"

"Narrative, heroic. Byron, Browning," he replied.

Holly frowned. "I'm sorry, I don't believe we have either of those. Mama doesn't approve of Byron and well—we *do* have the collected sonnets of Elizabeth Barrett Browning—but they're mostly love poems and . . ." For some reason Holly felt her face flush under Blaine's interested gaze. Trying to reshelve the book, she dropped it and thought crossly, *What is the matter with me to be so clumsy?*

Blaine did not seem to notice her fumbling and went on talking. "Actually, I own several volumes of both Byron and Browning—and to be truthful, I came here under false pretenses. I wanted to ask you to go for a drive with me this Sunday after church—if the weather's still fine, and I thought maybe I could show you some more of the countryside."

Holly's head, which was bent to retrieve a dropped book, popped up in surprise. "Why, thank you, Dr. Stevens, I would enjoy that very much."

"Fine." Blaine's smile broadened. "Unless there's an emergency, and I can never be sure of that, and there are no sick calls, I'll attend service and meet you afterward."

Holly reshelved the book, smiling. "See you on Sunday then, Dr. Stevens."

Watching as Blaine departed whistling, Holly was amazed at herself for being so pleased at such an ordinary event as being invited for a drive. But at least it offered an escape from a long, stifling day, trapped at Hetty's. To be honest, Holly had to admit she had missed the company of young men, which she had always enjoyed. Of course, Adam Corcoran had shown some interest in her. But he tended to be sarcastic, which sometimes wore a little thin. So what harm could spending an afternoon with Dr. Stevens do? He was interesting and amusing. She most certainly had no intentions of becoming involved in any romantic way with anyone in Riverbend, whatever Hetty might think!

The rest of the afternoon passed quickly. Holly's spirits had lifted immeasurably at the prospect of an outing with Blaine. The Bodine sisters, Miss Eva and Miss Emmeline, who ran the local bakery and who had become regular lending library devotees, came in to chat and brought a little basket of cupcakes for her. Mr. Clegg, the church organist, also came by to return his book and take out another. Holly helped two new ladies who were interested in selecting books, and by the time Ned was ready to close the store, Holly realized that the day had flown by and had been especially pleasant.

Sunday morning, Holly was standing in front of her mirror, critically checking her appearance. She was wearing an outfit that she had not worn before in Riverbend. Now she wondered if it mighty be too dressy for a country drive. While she wavered about changing into something simpler, an impatient knock came at the bedroom door, followed by Hetty's querulous voice, "What's keeping you, Holly? Are you coming with us to church or not?"

Opening the door, Hetty peered around it. Her gaze swept over Holly from the bonnet trimmed with tiny blueberries down the scalloped bodice and flounced skirt of her blue faille walking suit. "My, my!" was all she said, but acid dripped from her voice. Then she quickly withdrew, saying, "We're in the wagon, waiting. Hurry up if you're coming."

Holly gathered up her gloves and handbag and hurried out, wondering why Hetty always somehow managed to make her feel guilty. When she got into the wagon beside the children, Aurelia gave her an awed compliment. She squeezed the little girl's hand appreciatively and smiled, but it only made Holly feel worse. Hettty's unspoken but obvious criticism had done its damage. At least she'd be gone for the day and out from under it for a few hours, she thought gratefully.

It wasn't until they were going up the steps of the church that Holly informed Hetty in a whisper about her invitation from Blaine. Hetty's startled look was her only reply. Holly had not wanted to make too much of it by telling her beforehand, because Hetty always managed to spoil things by her sarcasm. Holly did not want this day to be ruined by one of Hetty's disparaging remarks.

After the service, Blaine was waiting for her at the bottom of the church steps when they came outside. "Sorry, I couldn't make the service," her told her as he took her arm and led her over to his small buggy. "Just as I was leaving, I got a message that one of the Findley children was running a high fever, so I had to make a sick call there. Did I miss a good sermon?"

Truthfully, sitting next to Hetty, Holly was too distracted by her cold disapproval to have paid much attention. So she fibbed guiltily.

"Oh, yes, it was very good."

Blaine glanced at her with mischievous eyes. "Care to give me a summary? What was the Scripture the text was taken from?"

Caught unawares by his question, Holly's eyes widened, then seeing that he was teasing her, she attempted to sound contrite, "I'm afraid I don't remember enough of it to tell you."

"Maybe it was something like 'This is the day the Lord hath made, let us rejoice and be glad'?" prompted Blaine.

"That sounds just right," Holly laughed.

Soon they were out from town, riding through some of the loveliest country Holly had ever seen. The woodland on either side of the winding road was glorious with autumn color, lush and green, and the river that ran parallel sparkled like silver in the sunlight.

Holly found Blaine thoroughly enjoyable. He was totally natural as he spoke of growing up back in Connecticut, of his family consisting of a mother, a stepfather whom he admired, and two married sisters. His own father had been killed in the Civil War, he told her, when Blaine was only nine years old.

"Regrettably, as so many of the War casualties, his was unnecessary. He bled to death on the battlefield because they didn't get him to a field hospital in time. My uncle was an Army doctor, and he told me that. Maybe it was the thing that motivated me to become a doctor myself. I wanted to know how to keep things like that from happening to people. My uncle said he saw so many soldiers die for lack of knowledge and the right treatment during the war." Blaine stopped. "Pardon me, Holly, I didn't mean to get on to an unpleasant subject like that on such a beautiful day. So, tell me, how do you like Oregon by this time?"

Holly wondered how she could possibly tell him. On this lovely fall day she almost thought that she could learn to love living out here, but then there was Hetty. How could she explain *that* situation?

Lately Holly had been debating whether it might not be better to leave Riverbend and go back to Willow Springs, even if Jim's bride was now there, to face whatever she had to face in the way of snide gossip. Would that be any worse than to go on living in that strained atmosphere at Hetty's? Since Holly had started the lending library and made some friends of her own, Hetty seemed to resent her even more. Was it worth it to remain under these circumstances?

Before Holly could tactfully answer Blaine's question, he suddenly jerked the reins and pulled the small vehicle to an abrupt stop.

"What's the matter? What is it?" Holly exclaimed in alarm, grabbing the seat handles.

"I don't know, I'm not sure, but look over there!" Blaine pointed to a figure slumped against a tree at the side of the road.

"Who is it?"

"It's Larkin!" Blaine said grimly. At that name Holly recalled the scene on the street when she was with Adam Corcoran and they had seen him reeling drunk.

"You mean the schoolteacher?"

"Yes. Poor devil."

"Is he—?"

"Dead? No, but dead drunk." Blaine threw the reins about the brake handle, sat for a moment as if trying to make a decision. Then he turned to Holly saying, "We can't leave him here like that. At least *I* can't," his mouth tightened. He gave Holly a long, evaluating look. "If someone else finds him, it will mean his job for sure. I've got to get him back to his place where he can sleep it off."

Holly felt an inner trembling. She had rarely seen anyone intoxicated. A few times at some public event or at an occasion like Fourth of July celebration she had seen someone slightly tipsy. Then, somebody always escorted the inebriated person off the premises with a minimum of fuss. But Larkin was something very different indeed. However, her reservation was fleeting. Hesitating only a second, she asked, "How can I help?"

"Good girl," he commented briefly. "I'll see if I can convince him that he needs to go home. Maybe he can make it on his own. Unless he's too far gone. Then I may need you to help prop him up."

Blaine got out of the buggy, and Holly followed him. Larkin was sitting on the ground, leaning against the tree trunk, his disheveled head sunk onto his chest. His horse had wandered a few yards and was grazing on the meadow grass. Probably this was not the first time he had been left to his own devices.

Blaine crouched down beside the man. Speaking in a low voice, he gently shook his shoulder. "Larkin, it's Doc. Come on, fella, wake up. Time to go . . ."

The man groaned, raised his hand, and moved it limply as if brushing away an annoying fly. "Lemme alone—go 'way," he mumbled.

Blaine looked up at Holly. "Looks like it's going to take more than persuasion." He stood up, plunged his hands into his pockets, tilted his head back and skyward as if for inspiration.

Then, sighing, said, "I guess the only thing to do is try to get him into the buggy. I think, between us, we can manage. He doesn't weigh much." He looked at Holly questioningly. "I know it's a lot to ask—a lady." She shook her head vigorously.

"Of course not. What about his horse?"

Blaine glanced at the placidly grazing animal. "We'll tie his reins to the back of the buggy," Blaine said and went over to the horse. Rubbing his nose and speaking to him softly, Blaine led him back and secured him. He then brought his own horse and buggy around closer to the tree where Larkin was slouched.

"Now, if you can get his arm over your shoulder, Holly, we'll get him on his feet, I think we can drag him over and into the buggy."

Drawing up her skirt with one hand, Holly leaned down and with some effort pulled Larkin's arm across her back and over her shoulder, grasping his wrist with her hand. On the other side Blaine was doing the same thing.

"All right now, slowly straighten up," Blaine directed. I'll take most of the weight; now grab him around the waist; let him fall toward me—I don't want you hurting yourself, Holly."

Larkin was a small man, almost skin and bones. Even so, Holly was breathing hard by the time she and Blaine half-dragged, half-carried him over to the buggy. He was mumbling and protesting by then. Finally, with Blaine pulling and Holly pushing, they got him into the buggy seat.

"Hurry and get on the other side, Holly," ordered Blaine. Holly obeyed, running around to catch Larkin before he slipped down. By the time Blaine got in and picked up the reins, Larkin was coming to, slightly. Gradually he seemed to become aware of his situation but just barely.

"It's not far to the schoolhouse," Blaine told Holly as he skillfully got the buggy turned with the added encumbrance of Larkin's horse behind and moved back onto the road. "I just hope we don't meet anyone on the way—especially a member of the Town Council or School Board."

They rode the short distance in tense silence, with Larkin mumbling and eventually snoring, lurching heavily from one to the other. The smell of liquor was so strong that Holly wrinkled her nostrils distastefully and felt almost nauseous.

As they pulled into the schoolyard Blaine said, "I'll go around to the back where his living quarters are in case anyone riding by should see us."

When at last they halted, Blaine had to rouse Larkin again. When that proved impossible Blaine rummaged in Larkin's pocket, located his keys and tossed them over to Holly. "Would you please go unlock the door? I guess there's only one way to settle him safely." With that Blaine simply slung the man over his shoulder in the famous "fireman's carry."

Holly hopped down from the buggy and ran ahead to the back of the building. Fitting a key into the lock, she opened the door, holding it for Blaine to walk through with his inert burden. She stood there on the threshold, then heard the creak of mattress springs as Blaine must have dumped Larkin onto his bed, the clump of boots being dropped. A few minutes later Blaine reappeared.

"This binge must have started here, possibly as early as Friday afternoon after school." He pushed back his hat, rubbed his brow with one hand, frowning. "Couple of empty bottles around. When he ran out of booze he must have decided to go into town. . . ." He paused, pressing his lips together. Then he said thoughtfully, "I think I should try to straighten up some of this mess before leaving. Be sure to get rid of any unopened bottles there may still be around before he wakes up enough to start drinking again. On the other hand—" Blaine halted mid-sentence. "I probably should take you home, Holly. This has all been a pretty sordid spectacle for you to see. I know that poor Larkin would be humiliated if he thought that you—or anyone, for that matter—but particularly a *lady* like yourself had not only seen him like this but—"

"Oh, Blaine, don't! I understand. I *do*, really," Holly assured him, recalling the times she had seen Mr. Larkin in town perfectly sober, always neatly dressed. If he had come into Ned's store whenever she was working at the lending library, he always tipped his hat politely and addressed her with the greatest courtesy. Now she said, "Please, let me help. Tell me what to do."

The expression in Blaine's eyes changed from uncertainty to frank approval. "All right. Come in and together we'll make quick work of it."

While Blaine collected a number of bottles and disposed of them, Holly tidied the general disorder of the schoolmaster's small apartment. From the adjoining bedroom she heard the loud rhythmic sound of snoring as Larkin slept, oblivious of his rescuers.

As she picked up garments, carried used tumblers and half-filled mugs of old coffee into the kitchen, wiped table tops, and folded rumpled newspapers dropped on the floor, Holly also noticed the book-filled shelves in the tiny parlor. Pausing to read the titles, Holly realized Mr. Larkin was unlike her preconception of a drink-sodden derelict, a well-read man whose reading choice tended to the classics. There were books in Latin, philosophy and essays, Shakespeare plays. How had such a man of intelligence and taste ended up here teaching grammar school in a remote Oregon town?

On the table beside a well-worn leather reading chair was the scrolled silver-framed photograph of a pretty, stylishly dressed woman holding a beautiful baby. Holly had never even thought that Larkin might be married. That photograph seemed the most poignant evidence of all to Holly how much he must have lost through his addiction to drink.

Blaine's voice brought her back from her pitying thoughts. "Well, I think that's it. He'll sleep for hours and when he wakes up, he'll find nothing to drink to get him started again. He'll feel miserable. But he'll have time to get himself together by tomorrow morning. At least, I *hope* so. I'll ride out here early and check on him to be sure." Blaine's tawny hair had fallen forward onto his broad forehead from his exertion and he brushed it back with an impatient gesture. "You all set? Ready to go?"

"Yes," she replied, looking at him with new eyes. What compassion he had. His clear blue eyes were clouded now with concern; what strength of character in his face. How lucky Larkin was to have the doctor as a friend.

83

On the way back into town, Blaine said quietly, "I'm sorry our day together had to have this kind of ending."

"Please, don't apologize, Blaine. It wasn't your fault, and besides, I'm glad it was *us* who found him."

"I am, too. Only how long I can keep protecting him, I don't know. More for his own sake than for any other reason. It's a sickness, you know, contrary to what some self-righteous people would have you believe. It's not a moral weakness or a sin. One drink, and Larkin, for all the promises he makes to me and to himself, is off."

"I guess he could just not take that first drink?" murmured Holly.

"Of course, that sounds sensible to people to whom it isn't a problem. But so far, no one has come up with a way to really help someone like Larkin. At least not yet. There doesn't seem to be any cure or any medicine to take that will do the deed."

They went on a little farther, then Blaine turned to Holly and said softly, "You were a brick, Holly. Not many ladies would have handled the situation as well as you did. Thank you."

Holly felt a pleasurable warmth spread all through her; she could feel her face glow. Why, for heaven's sake? Hadn't she received dozens of compliments from gentlemen before? Flattering words about her dancing, her dimples, her hair, eyes, and complexion? Why did this unflowery comment from this practical doctor mean more to her than anything anyone had ever said to her?

Well, for one thing, she was rather gratified at how ably she had conducted herself in this really bizarre set of circumstances today. She had even surprised herself. And for another, she'd never been called "a brick" before! At this Holly almost burst out laughing.

Chapter 10

*H*olly had never known anyone to hold a grudge as long as Hetty! On Wednesday morning Hetty was still angry because Holly had returned late from her drive with Blaine and missed Sunday night supper. Bound by Blaine's request to keep the incident with Larkin secret, Holly could not explain. She knew that Hetty probably thought she was out "sparking" with the doctor instead of assisting him on his "errand of mercy." So, after her offer of household help was curtly turned down, to avoid another scene with Hetty, Holly left for the store earlier than usual to open the lending library.

A heated discussion was taking place around the potbellied stove where a group of "regulars" were gathered. Holly hung up her shawl and bonnet and slipped behind the counter of the Lending Library. She had discovered that Ned's store was the hub of the town. Here rumors, facts, whispers of scandal, tidbits, and tittle-tattle, along with reports of real events, were argued about, examined, and retold. Not a thing happened in Riverbend that did not eventually get thoroughly chewed over there long before it became a news item in the *Monitor*. Ned, as usual, remained a silent bystander, listening, but rarely offering an opinion or comment.

Today the voices were raised loudly and Holly could not help hearing every word. When she heard the name "Larkin" over and over, her ears pricked up.

"Well, it's the last straw, I guess," declared one of the men.

"We can't let it go on, that's for sure. Bad example for the young people." This next voice was indignant. "We've overlooked it long enough. But it's gone too far this time."

"Too many people know—"

"Too many people have *seen* him—"

"My Lorena said he fell asleep in class on Friday. Put his head right down on the desk and slept! Well, when her ma heard *that*—well, you know *my* wife, Tilly, is a 'Temperance'!"

Holly drew in her breath. Larkin! It was Larkin they were talking about. How had they heard about his latest binge? Her second thought sent a chill down her spine. Had someone seen him? Had someone, maybe, seen *her* and Doc with Larkin? *If so,* her next thought was, *Oh dear! Wait until Hetty hears about it.*

Another voice said emphatically, "You're right, we've got to do something about it."

"But school's just got started a few weeks. At this point in the school year, where're you going to find a teacher who hasn't already got a position?" This mild query came from Ned.

Concealed by the counter, Holly peered cautiously over the edge and saw that two of the men were Owen Roberts and Ed Morrison, two members of Riverbend Town Council. This elected body also served as the school board who did the hiring and firing of the Riverbend grammar school teacher.

Poor Blaine! He had tried so hard to protect Larkin. But the children had to be protected, too, didn't they? You couldn't blame the parents for being upset.

She had better go see Blaine, Holly thought, talk to him about how the word got out. Holly reached for her bonnet, tied it under her chin. The men around the stove were too involved in their conversation to notice her as she slipped by them, went out the door, and crossed the street to Blaine's office.

At her knock, he called, "Come in," and she entered his small waiting room. Through the open door to his inner office she could see him standing at his desk and packing his medicine bag. When he looked up and saw her, his face lit up.

"Why, Holly, good morning! How nice to see you. I hope this isn't a professional call?"

She shook her head, then looking left and right to be sure that they were alone, moved over to the door, and lowering her voice, said, "Blaine, have you heard about Mr. Larkin?"

The smile on his face faded, replaced by a worried frown. "Yes, he came by here last night. It seems that on Monday he was still pretty hungover and that evening came into town to the Nugget—as he explained it, 'to get a hair of the dog that bit him'—in other words, to get over the shakes." Blaine paused, his mouth grim, "Well, as luck would have it, the Town Council meeting was just breaking up as he came out of the saloon— he'd had more than one hair, it seems, and he ran right into them. He was nervous as well as a little gone in drink, and the encounter was not a mutually happy one, to say the least." Blaine shrugged. "Yesterday, he was notified they were demanding his resignation as schoolteacher, effective immediately."

"Then it's true," Holly said. "I heard them talking over at Ned's store."

"Yes. Poor fellow, he came by here, all remorseful, repentant, swearing off, and asked me if I'd speak for him to the council. But I had to tell him it was no good. They've given him his last chance, and he's out."

"Then, what will he do? And what about the school?"

Blaine shook his head again. "I put him on the morning stage. He was too ashamed to show his face in town, particularly to face the children. I sent him to a doctor friend of mine in California who may be able to help him get over his addiction. He's had some success with chronic alcoholics. I pray to God he'll get the help he needs."

Poor Larkin, Holly thought, remembering the books and the picture of the woman and child in his cluttered little living quarters in the schoolhouse. Her pity and concern must have shown in her face because Blaine stopped putting some small vials and bottles into his medical bag and gave her a long look. "Don't look so troubled, Holly," he said gently. I know this comes as a shock. But life is full of these kinds of tragedies. I'm sorry you had to—"

"Oh, no, Blaine, it's not that—it's just all so sad. . . ."

After a moment, Blaine said, "You look like you could use a

little diversion. Larkin asked me if I'd go out to his place, pack up his belongings, and send them to him in care of Dr. Logan. As a matter of fact, I'm riding out there right now before I make my other rounds. Would you like to ride with me?"

She nodded. It was true, the whole experience had affected her deeply. She looked up into Blaine's concerned eyes. "Yes, I think I would like to come with you, Blaine."

She was quiet as they rode out in the brilliant sunshine of the fall morning. The air was so clear, the sky so blue, the changing colors of the trees so beautiful, Holly felt that it was too bad for anyone, like Larkin, to be unhappy on a day like this.

The schoolyard was empty. In the absence of a teacher, school had been suspended temporarily. Maybe indefinitely, unless Riverbend could find a new one. Blaine unlocked the door and they stepped into the one large classroom. It smelled of chalk dust, charred wood from a stove that had been left to burn out, the mustiness of old books, unswept floors. The whole place had an air of neglect and indifferent care. *What a shame!* was Holly's first reaction. How hard it would be for children to try to learn in this kind of atmosphere. A schoolroom should be neat, clean, colorful.

"We can go through here," Blaine said, turning a key in the door behind the teacher's desk.

Holly followed him into Larkin's living quarters. The smells from the classroom were intensified by the sour odor of whiskey, unwashed clothes, and accumulated dirt. Holly looked around in dismay, unconsciously picking up her skirt. How could Larkin have made everything worse just since Sunday?

Blaine went ahead of her and opened the door into Larkin's bedroom. He was gone so long that Holly went to the door to see what he was doing. Blaine stood in the center of the room as if undecided where to begin. He held up his hand to halt her. "Don't come in here, Holly. I shouldn't've brought you into this! I'd forgotten how it can be when Larkin's been drinking steadily. Now, I don't want you to do anything—I'll see to it." He dragged out an old trunk from under the sagging mattress of the iron bed and told her, "Just wait there for me in the other room or go outside into the fresh air," he said as he began to toss things into the trunk.

Holly went back into the front room. When she had been here on Sunday she had been too nervous to notice much beyond the awful mess. This second time she took a closer look. This room was the same size as the schoolroom. There was an alcove with a table and chairs and, beyond that, a tiny kitchen area with a stove, a hutch, and a window. Larkin had as much space here at the back of the schoolroom as one would find in a cottage. Of course, it was in shambles now, but with a good cleaning, some paint and polish, it could be quite—cozy and charming. An idea began to stir in Holly's mind.

The more she thought about it, the more sense it made. Why not? Her heart began to race. *She* had as good an education as most women—perhaps better than some. She had finished the twelfth grade and then had two years at Blue Ridge Female Academy. Of course, to be truthful, Holly had not applied herself diligently or very seriously there. For one thing, the Academy had been too close to Penrose College for Young Men, and invitations to the parties, the fall and spring "Germans," and the social activities had occupied a great deal of her time.

Still, she *did* have a smattering of botany, geography, history and, certainly, as fond as she was of reading, she could teach spelling and reading! Arithmetic was another matter, however. But she was sure that if she brushed up on her multiplication tables she could manage reasonably well.

Of course, the main incentive for the idea growing in Holly's imagination was that with the job of teacher came living quarters. At such a possibility Holly's excitement soared. If she applied for the job of Riverbend grammar school teacher she could move out from under Hetty's inhospitable roof and be independent! Within those few minutes Holly decided that's just what she was going to do. Apply for the position of teacher at Riverbend grammar school!

Right then Blaine reappeared carrying out two boxes belonging to Larkin, then came back for the trunk, and took it out and lashed it to the back of his buggy.

"I wish we could take advantage of this lovely day and go on

89

a drive," he smiled regretfully as he helped Holly back into the buggy and picked up the reins. "But I've got to get this into town so it can be placed on the next stage, and I've patients to see."

Holly did not reply, only smiled vaguely. She had only half-heard the remark. Her mind was too busy plotting how she could go about the plan of acquiring the job of teacher and thus her freedom.

When Blaine let her out again at Ned's store, instead of returning to her task at the lending library, she crossed the street and hurried over to Vi's house. By the time Vi answered the doorbell, Holly was trembling with excitement. Vi had a customer being fitted in her sewing room, and suggested that Holly go into the kitchen and "make herself at home" until she could join her.

Vi's kitchen was like the rest of her little home, sparkling, spotless, serene, painted a sunny yellow and smelling slightly of herbs and spices. But Holly was too restless today to sit down on one of the pressback chairs and calmly await her hostess.

Of course, Holly had never thought of being a teacher before. Guiltily she recalled that she had always equated women teachers with plain, prim, proper spinsters who had no other choice but to teach! But as she'd often heard, "desperate times demand desperate choices," and Holly had become desperate enough living with Hetty to take any chance.

She knew that her educational qualifications lacked certification. But then her qualities compared to the failings of poor Larkin would be taken into consideration. What she did have she would use. Her ability to get along with children, her imagination, and storytelling talent could be put to good advantage. Surely there were textbooks she could read to help prepare lessons. The most important thing was to convince the Town Council that she was capable of doing the job. When she got it, then she could figure out how to go about teaching.

Vi's clear voice floated from the hall out to the kitchen. "Yes, Mrs. Abbott, your dress will be ready next week."

Abbott? thought Holly. *Wasn't her husband, Miles Abbott, on the Town Council?*

She heard the murmur of more conversation then the front

door clicked shut, and Vi came into the kitchen, her tape measure still hanging around her neck. "What a nice surprise, Holly. What brings you here today for a visit?"

"Oh, Vi, I know I shouldn't have just popped in like this during the week when you have ladies coming for fittings, but I just had to talk to you. Actually to ask your advice!"

"Well, if I am to be your oracle today, I believe we better have some tea, don't you?" Vi went to fill the kettle with water from the hand pump on the counter and placed it on the stove to boil.

"Oh, Vi, the most wonderful opportunity has come up. Well, I mean, due to certain sad circumstances, there may be a chance for me to move out of Hetty's, be on my own. I'm so thrilled at the possibility, but I'm also scared and—"

Vi held up her hand. "Slow down, Holly, I haven't the slightest idea what you're talking about."

Holly took a long breath then very deliberately told Vi about Larkin's leaving and the post of teacher being left vacant as well as the little apartment behind the schoolroom.

While listening attentively, Vi got down two china cups, arranged some thin wafer cookies on a plate, and set them on the table.

"So, what do you think?" Holly asked breathlessly.

"Have you ever taught before?"

"Well, no, but I'm sure I could. After all it's only grammar school. Certainly I could teach six-and seven-year-olds!"

"You'll have *all* ages, Holly. Or at least for part of the year. The older children attend during the winter. But in the spring the big boys are usually needed to help out on their families' farms, plowing and planting and so on. Strapping farm boys of twelve and fourteen can be a handful—"

"Oh, I've got dozens of young cousins that age, Vi. I don't think that would bother me," Holly said confidently. "My real worry is getting the job! I suppose I'll have to apply and go for an interview before the Town Council."

Vi didn't say anything right away. She poured their tea and offered Holly the plate of cookies, then she looked over at her friend seriously. "Have you prayed about this, Holly?"

Taken aback by Vi's question, Holly replied, "Well, no, not really. I haven't had time. I just got the idea."

"It's a pretty important step for you to take. Don't you think you should have God's guidance?"

"Yes, I suppose so. I just thought *you* could help me decide what to do," Holly said. Then she asked shyly, "Is that what *you* do, Vi? I mean, pray about it before anything else?"

"When it's something that's going to change my life as much as this would change yours, Holly, I think it's the wisest thing to do."

"But if I pray and do seem to get a 'go ahead'—will you help me, Vi? I mean, you do think it's a good idea, don't you?"

"Of course, I'll help you every way I can, Holly," Vi promised.

Holly breathed a sigh of relief. "Thank you." She stood up. "And I will do as you say, Vi."

As they walked to the door, Vi put her arm around Holly's shoulder. "I'm sure the children would love having you for a teacher—that is, if you decide to do it."

"After I *pray* about it, you mean?" Holly smiled.

"Of course, *after* you pray." Vi gave her a mock reproachful look.

At the front door, Holly asked, "Seriously, Vi, how should I pray about it to expect an answer?"

Vi hesitated a moment before replying. "Well, I don't recommend this practice as a general rule, but I must admit that when I've been under pressure to make a decision and have been at a loss for direction, I *have* done it. First, pray earnestly for guidance, then open the Bible at random and read the pages where it falls open. Search there for what God may be showing you in His Word. That's all I can tell you, Holly. I feel that somewhere in those two pages you're going to find your answer."

Something stubborn in Holly resisted this idea. It seemed too chancy. With all her heart she wanted this job. Mainly, of course, because it provided an avenue of escape from Hetty. Actually, when she thought about it, didn't it seem almost Providential? Great-Aunt Ancilla always said that it is sometimes in *circumstances* that God makes His will plain. Wasn't *this* just that sort of *circumstance*?

Back in the cramped bedroom at Hetty's house, Holly decided she might as well follow Vi's advice. After all, if Vi relied on this method of discovering God's guidance when unsure of what direction to take, why shouldn't she try it?

Holly got out the little Bible that Great-Aunt Ancilla had tucked into her trunk that day when she was packing to leave for the West. Holding it in both hands, she squeezed her eyes tight shut and prayed, "Dear Lord, show me what to do, and *please* make it plain!" then flipped open the Bible. When she opened her eyes again and looked down at the pages, she was surprised to see she had turned to the Book of Isaiah.

If Holly was familiar with any Scripture, it was mostly the New Testament, and this seemed very strange to her. But remembering Vi's instruction, she began reading from the top of the left-hand page, relying on the possibility that at some point a verse would "quicken" to her, as Great-Aunt Ancilla used to say.

The pages that lay open before her contained Chapters 49 and 50. Running her index finger down line by line, she came to this one: "This place is too small for me; give me a place where I may dwell," and almost laughed.

If that wasn't to the point, she didn't know what was! Did God have a sense of humor? Quickly hoping that He wouldn't think her irreverent, Holly read on. A kind of quiet settled over her as she did, and she realized that the Scriptures had effects other than just giving answers. Then her finger stopped on a verse, and as she read it over two or three times, she began to feel it *was* her direction to pursue the position of schoolteacher. Chapter 50, verses 7–8: "For the Lord will help me, Therefore I will not be disgraced—Therefore I have set my face like flint and I know I will not be ashamed. He is near who justifies me, who will contend with me?" If she was interpreting this as an answer to her own question, it seemed to Holly that she was to step boldly forward, with a "face set like flint," and God would help her.

She closed the Bible thoughtfully. This was all new to her. She had never before exercised faith in such a manner. But she admired Vi Dodd, and if Vi thought this was how to go about it, who was she to argue?

That evening at the supper table Holly took a deep breath and announced her intention. "Well, that's splendid, Holly," was Ned's immediate response. "I think that's a great idea, you'd make a fine teacher."

"Oh, Holly, will you teach me when I go to school?" Aurelia almost bounced off her chair in her excitement.

"I haven't got the job yet, honey. I'm just going to apply for it." Holly smiled across the table at her, then glanced at Hetty, whose fork had stopped halfway to her mouth; she had paled, her expression blank. For politeness' sake Holly asked, "What do you think, Hetty?"

Hetty put down her fork, got to her feet, and picked up her unfinished plate, took it over to the drainboard and said over her shoulder, "I never thought you were much for school when you were a pupil, so how come you think you can teach?"

Holly felt her face burn at this barbed comment. She knew that she had not been a prize student as Hetty had been. Still her marks were reasonably good, and she certainly was no dunce!

Suppressing her indignation at Hetty's attempt to embarrass her, Holly replied gaily, "Well, isn't there an old saying, that 'if you become a teacher, by your students you'll be taught'? I'm open to learning all I can even this late in my life."

"I think you'll do just fine, Holly," Ned said heartily, which was a brave thing to do in the wake of his wife's blatant disapproval.

Hetty said nothing more, but her opinion was obvious in the way she brought the dessert dish of blackberry cobbler and slammed it down on the table.

PART 2

I a small house and large garden have,
And a few friends, and many books, both true,
both wise and both delightful, too!

Abraham Cowley

Chapter 11

$\mathcal{T}$aking some liberty with the Scripture, Holly "set her face like flint" toward the coming meeting of the Town Council. Making many false starts and revisions of the text, Holly labored over her letter of application for the position of grammar school teacher until she was satisfied. Writing in her very best penmanship, she stated her qualifications and addressed it to the membership of the Riverbend Town Council acting in its capacity as school board. Within a few days Holly received a letter from Mayor Ed Morrison that her application was being studied and considered by each member. A decision would be announced at the next town meeting.

It was the longest week of her life. Finally on the morning before the meeting, Holly hurried along Main Street on her way over to consult with Vi on an appropriate outfit to wear. Preoccupied, she nearly collided with Adam Corcoran as she rounded the corner.

He took off his hat, made her an exaggerated bow, and greeted her, "Good day, Miss Lambeth. Rumor has it that you will be Riverbend's new schoolmarm in place of the lately departed but not lamented Larkin."

"Well, it certainly has not been decided, Mr. Corcoran, but I have applied for the position."

Regarding her with a skeptical smile, he said, "Perhaps I'm wrong, I often am, but my first impression of you was not of a schoolmarm. Probably that might be colored by the fact that I don't remember my own schooldays with much pleasure, due in large part, I'm sure, to a series of teachers who were neither pleasant nor charming nor even, I might add, erudite."

Although Holly knew he was teasing her, she was aware of a sense of irony in the situation herself but affected an air of indignant dignity and replied, "I find that very unfortunate, indeed, Mr. Corcoran. I myself have most happy memories of *my* school days *and* my teachers. And if I am awarded this important position, I certainly hope to emulate those paragons of wisdom and kindness." With satisfaction at matching Adam at his own game, Holly bestowed one of her most winsome smiles on him and moved past. "Now if you will excuse me, Mr. Corcoran, I have an errand to complete."

Holly might have been both flattered and disturbed had she seen the mixture of admiration and challenge in Adam Corcoran's glance following her.

At Vi's the two women put their heads together to decide just what Holly should wear the night she appeared before the Council. "You want to look well but not too fashionable," Vi told her. "That might put them off since most of them have wives who are busy, hard-working mothers with very few opportunities to dress up."

"Should I look drab, dowdy?" asked Holly worriedly, already thinking of the wardrobe of bright-colored stylish clothes she had brought with her.

"No, not that, but . . ." Vi hesitated. Looking at Holly, she could not help wondering how in the world this pretty, vivacious young woman could convince five middle-aged men she was capable of overseeing thirty or more children—no matter what she wore!

"Maybe, I can remodel something. I mean, take off the trimmings or flounces," Holly suggested, mentally reviewing her possibilities. Perhaps the blue traveling suit or her gray walking dress or even the cinnamon brown wool—she wrinkled her brow and asked Vi, "You think I should look more reliable and serious, don't you? Not flighty or—more Quakerish, right?"

"Well, not exactly, Holly," Vi laughed. "But I think you get the idea. You've got good taste and judgment. Just don't show up with too many feathers or flowers on your hat!"

Monday was the regular meeting night of Riverbend's Town Council. As usual the time and agenda was published in the *Monitor* with the added notice that the subject of hiring a new schoolteacher would be discussed after the previously announced items on the agenda.

Riverbend, so newly evolved from its raw mining camp beginnings, now had a citizenry eager to exhibit responsible civic interest and pride in its development. Therefore the Town Council meetings were usually well-attended. *This* Monday every seat was filled a half hour before the meeting would be called to order, extra chairs were even brought into place on the side aisles. It seemed that everyone in Riverbend had a personal reason to be present for this particular meeting.

It had already circulated around town that Ned Thornton's wife's cousin was applying for the teacher's job. Those who had met Holly through the lending library were pleased at the idea, confident that anyone who knew so much about books had to be a good teacher as well. Others who only knew her by sight had their own unexplored opinion that she was "too citified" and probably "stuck up." If she wasn't, why was it she never came along with her cousin Hetty to their Sewing Circle or Missionary Society? It didn't occur to those who held this attitude that Holly had never been invited. Others, mainly those with children in need of a teacher, were anxious to have the vacancy filled as soon as possible and had come to hear and see for themselves what the young lady from "back east" had to say for herself. Certainly no one who came to the meeting was disinterested in the outcome.

Holly herself had been in a frenzy of nerves all afternoon and at five went over to see Vi, who was going to accompany her to Town Hall, to get her final approval on her appearance. As she left for Vi's house, Holly paused in the kitchen and trying to keep her tone light, said, "Well, Hetty, I'm off to the lion's den, wish me luck!"

Hetty looked up from the bread she was kneading for the

next day's baking. Surveying every inch of her cousin, she replied coldly, "Hmmph, you'll need more than good luck."

Holly pretended to adjust the scalloped cuffs of her coffee-colored boucle-wool jacket and ignored Hetty's mean-spirited remark. What else could she expect from her cousin? Hetty had made no secret of how she felt about Holly's ability to get the job.

Keeping her voice even, she said good-bye and went out the door. As she walked briskly toward Vi's house, Holly thought she would never understand Hetty, not if she lived to be a hundred. *You'd think Hetty would hope I'd get the job and get out of her hair!*

But she had more important things now to be concerned about than Hetty's predictable attitude. She had to concentrate on making a good impression on the members of the Town Council, convince them that she was their best possible choice for teacher.

Holly knew that even if she embellished her educational qualifications it would not be enough. Her lack of references and experience were the first obstacles she had to hurdle. But then after the Larkin debacle, plus the fact that the school year session was already three weeks behind, put great pressure on the council to appoint someone soon. The time needed to advertise the position, receive and check applications, vote on the one to be selected, plus the expense of sending for someone were factors to be considered. Paying train or stagecoach fare for the person to get to Riverbend would seem prohibitive to the frugal council members and would strain the town coffers. All this might stand Holly in good stead, she told herself as she went up the porch steps of Vi's house.

Vi was dressed and ready to go when she let Holly inside.

"So, how do I look?" Holly asked her, spinning around slowly. "Like a potential, proper schoolmarm, I hope?"

Vi's critical eye reviewed Holly's outfit. The suit with its high collar over which a narrow rim of silk ruching peeked was subdued enough. Since Holly had taken Vi's suggestion to remove the small blue-feathered bird nested in green velvet leaves, leaving only the dark brown grosgrain ribbons, her bonnet was now acceptable. Vi nodded.

"Very nice indeed."

"Good! If you approve of my appearance, the Town Council will surely agree." Holly's eyes sparkled. "Come on, let's go."

On their way to the Town Hall, Vi tried not to let her own anxiety about the outcome of the meeting dim Holly's enthusiasm. "What a night!" Holly exclaimed. "Look!" she said pointing up to the stars glittering in the sky. "This is the kind of night that good things happen," she declared squeezing Vi's arm.

Inwardly Vi's heart sank. She was afraid that Holly's attractiveness might be the very thing that would do her the most damage. Even with her outfit carefully chosen for its conservative effect, Holly Lambeth was hardly anyone's idea of a schoolteacher.

There was a definite autumn crispness in the air and as they hurried up the steps leading into the brick building, Vi shivered. But it was more from nerves than cold.

Standing just outside the entrance was Adam Corcoran. "Why, Mr. Corcoran," Holly exclaimed, "What are you doing here? I shouldn't think you'd care who was hired for schoolteacher."

"Good evening, Miss Lambeth, Mrs. Dodd," he tipped his hat to both women. Then smiling at Holly said, "Of course, I'm interested in everything that happens in Riverbend. Especially who is appointed to the important position of teaching our young people. As I'm sure *you're* aware, a schoolteacher has great influence in a community. I wish you the best, even though I'm not quite sure why you are doing it."

He regarded her in that half-amused, half-skeptical way she had come to expect whenever they met. She felt sure that he knew about Larkin, probably knew about her helping Blaine the day they found Larkin inebriated along the side of the road. He may even have put two and two together and figured out why she was applying for the job. He had seen firsthand Hetty's illhumor, perhaps even read between the lines of her cautious answers to his often pointed questions about her situation at the Thorntons'.

Adam had not come to call on her as he had first asked permission to do. Holly was certain this was because of his wish to

101

avoid Hetty. But on the days she worked at the lending library he visited her frequently there. Of course, he made all sorts of excuses for doing so: returning books, looking for recent arrivals, then lingering to chat. In spite of his cynicism and sometimes barbed comments, Holly had come to know and like Adam. She even thought she could see through that veneer of superiority he affected. So now she replied in the same vein, "It is very encouraging to realize that the editor of the town paper is so interested." Then she added candidly, "I'm glad you're here. I need all the support I can get."

"Rest assured you *do* have my support, Miss Lambeth. Only I'm afraid I don't have the power to sway any votes on the Council. I'm here in the capacity of editor of the *Monitor*. I always cover the Town Council meetings."

"Nevertheless, it's nice to feel I have some friends in the audience."

"I'm sure you do, Miss Lambeth," he said and opened the door for them to enter the building.

Watching Holly as she walked inside, Adam thought, *What a plucky little creature she is!* He hadn't imagined that she had it in her to face a five-man board and a room full of strangers, some of them probably hostile, ready to criticize or condemn her for her Eastern looks and manners.

Adam sauntered to a place on the left-hand side in the front row where he could get a good look at the members, try to judge their reactions, see and hear everything he could. He was betting on Holly to win, but he was also hedging his bet. The men of the Town Council took their roles very seriously. No doubt they'd been coached, argued with, and given opinions about the last item on tonight's agenda from everyone and anyone who had cornered them, bent their ear, or buttonholed them in the general store.

The thought of the country store naturally brought Ned Thornton to Adam's mind, and he twisted around to look at the people still filing into the meeting room. He spotted Ned's rangy figure in the doorway, talking to someone, then making his way forward to find a seat. Well, at least Ned had come to lend familial support to Holly's application. Adam wondered

102

where Ned's "gracious, honey-tongued" wife was? Not even for appearance's sake would she come to wish her cousin well? The harridan!

Fiercely Adam hoped the vote would go Holly's way. She deserved better than putting up with Hetty's petty cruelties, her spiteful nonsense, just because Holly was personable and charming. Women, the gentler sex? Adam gave a scornful grunt and the man sitting beside him looked alarmed. Adam immediately pretended to stifle a cough just as Mayor Morrison pounded the gavel, bringing the town meeting to order.

When Holly entered the hall, two dozen or more heads turned in her direction. But to her, all the faces were so blurred that she did not recognize any of them. Fully aware that she was the focus of all eyes, she moved up the aisle. Vi pointed out two seats in the front row on the right, and Holly quickly sat down. She tried to control her breathing, which was rapid and shallow, and to look composed.

Behind her she could hear the buzz of voices. Without doubt she was the subject of much of the conversation and comments. Knowing that she was being discussed was torture. Closing her eyes briefly, she thought miserably, *What am I doing here? How in the world did I ever get into such a situation?* Tonight seemed far removed from any other experience in her entire life.

Glancing over at Vi, she wished fervently that she had her serenity and inner strength. Vi was the only really serene person she had ever met. Vi always seemed poised, collected. She always spoke quietly, purposefully, never said an idle word nor made an irrelevant remark nor made a useless gesture, which gave force to everything she said or did.

Holly's stomach knotted. Desperately she tried to pray and could think of nothing but "Help!" To calm herself, she applied the comforting thought that she used when she had to go to the dentist: *In an hour or so this will all be over!* As the five members took their places on the platform, she folded her hands in her lap and tried to look both intelligent and attentive.

When Mayor Morrison picked up the gavel and brought it down with a loud bang and the meeting began, some of the apprehension, the timidity that Holly had experienced earlier, began to vanish. A surge of determination replaced it. This was something she wanted, something she *needed,* something she intended to get. Unless she did—Holly firmly stopped that train of thought. She *had* to be appointed schoolteacher; for her to go on at Hetty's was out of the question.

Conscious that the hall was more crowded than usual because of the interest in the decision they were being called on to make about a new schoolteacher, Mayor Ed Morrison began going through the order of business more quickly than usual, initiating a quick consensus on several of the items and allowing for a limited amount of discussion on each. He was able to get a unanimous decision on most. All the members of the Council were acutely aware of the one subject everyone was waiting for, and each of them was conscious of the young woman seated in the front row, who was the most anxious of all.

Owen Roberts, a rough-hewn rancher in his fifties, had grown children and grandchildren. He'd seen plenty of schoolteachers come and go, some good, some bad, most pretty indifferent as far as that went. As a man who raised cattle, loved horses, he had taken the position on the Council reluctantly, and rarely came into town. Owen needed to have Holly pointed out to him one day when he was in the store where she was working at her lending library. Now as he squinted down at her he wondered—was she too pretty? Too young?

Miles Abbott, a surveyor, practical and close-fisted, figured the lady must have plenty of spunk to want to take on the mixed group of youngsters who would troop into her classroom at least six months of the year. Why not let her try if she wanted to? It would save money and time. It would cost the town both if they tried to fill the position otherwise.

Theodore Winsbrook had been trained as a lawyer back East but came to the West for his health in his youth, stayed to become a farmer, had observed Holly in the lending library, had privately looked over her selection of books, and had come to the conclusion she was "smart as a whip." He was willing to give her a chance. His own children, a boy and a girl, needed to have their minds stretched. And Larkin had been a disaster.

Matthew Healy, a short, rotund, ruddy-cheeked man, settled

back in his chair complacently. He already knew how he was going to vote. Before he left for the meeting tonight, he had been given orders by his wife, Geneva (who belonged to the Riverbend Literary Society and, of course, knew and liked Holly), to hire her.

Ed Morrison, the mayor, who would cast the deciding vote in case of a tie, had his doubts that anyone as dainty as Miss Lambeth looked could handle the big boys. He recalled enough of his own rambunctious boyhood, when school days were colored by plenty of sessions with the hickory stick, to feel uncertain about hiring a woman teacher. Those big fellows needed discipline, most often wielded by a strong man. Of course hiring a man, in Larkin's case, hadn't worked. She could probably do as well as Larkin had, dazed as he was with drink half the time.

"We will now consider the application of Miss Hollis Lambeth for the position of schoolteacher of Riverbend Grammar," Ed announced. "Will Miss Lambeth please take her place at the podium and present her credentials for this job."

Afterward, Holly could not remember a word she had said. She had rehearsed dozens of times in front of the mirror and also for Vi. She had planned to give a brief background of her school attendance history, enumerate the subjects she had studied, and finish with a little speech about the value of education and her love of children. When her mind went blank, she decided she must be finished, and she resumed her seat amid a nice spatter of applause. She hoped she had covered everything she wanted to say, but she wasn't sure. Vi reached over and squeezed her hand.

"How did I do?" Holly whispered anxiously.

"Fine, just fine," Vi reassured her. The waiting had been agony.

Mayor Morrison stood up and told the assembly that the council would retire to a private session to discuss their decision, and the five men filed out. There was an immediate breaking-forth of voices that was almost deafening.

Rigid with tension, Holly watched the five men come back onto the platform. Mayor Morrison moved to the edge of the stage and held up both hands for quiet and the hum of noise ceased.

"The Town Council of Riverbend has voted to award the position of grammar school teacher to Miss Hollis Lambeth." He turned to the other members, and asked "So say we all?"

Five resounding "ayes" were raised, and an enthusiastic clapping of hands followed. Vi hugged Holly, and afterward Holly went up to the council members and shook each hand and thanked them individually.

Her sense of relief was almost greater than her elation. It was only later that she realized that this was the first time in her life she had ever gained something important—not because she was pretty, pleasant, popular, or because she was a Lambeth! This time she had got it on her own—and maybe even in spite of those very things.

Chapter 12

*M*oving day for Holly came on the loveliest autumn day she had yet seen in Oregon. The morning was bright as a new gold piece, the sky a cloudless blue, a brisk breeze rustled leaves of trees along the road out to the schoolhouse. The minute Holly awoke that morning, a feeling of joy soared through her. Today she would actually be leaving Hetty's house and going to her own place. This definitive step of independence gave her intense satisfaction. Surely this *was* "the day the Lord hath made," and she fully intended to "be glad and rejoice in it."

Ned had offered to take her with her belongings over to the schoolhouse, and Vi, along with Geneva and Matt Healy, had promised to meet her there to help her. Even Blaine told her that he would try to come by if no patient needed him.

In spite of her own good spirits, Holly dreaded the actual time of departure when she would have to say good-bye to Aurelia and Teddy. She had come to dearly love her little cousins in spite of the tension with Hetty. And what was she to say to Hetty before she left?

The night before, after the children were sound asleep, Holly had quietly packed all her things and had Ned place them in the wagon. Pretending to be still asleep, she waited until the children woke up and went out for their breakfast before getting up and dressing. She then delayed going out to the kitchen until she heard Ned go out to hitch up the wagon. One look at her woebegone face, however, and Holly knew that Aurelia realized this was the day she was leaving.

"Do you *really* and *truly* have to go, Holly?" the little girl asked plaintively.

Teddy's spoon of oatmeal stopped halfway to his mouth, and his large blue eyes widened.

"Go? Go where?"

"Today Holly's moving to the schoolhouse," Aurelia informed him.

Teddy's lower lip began to tremble, his eyes grew bright with tears. He dropped his spoon, spattering his porridge. "No!" he said, thumping his little fist on the table. "No! I don't want her to go."

Quickly Holly tried to avert a scene or, worse still, a Teddy-tantrum.

"But, Teddy, you can come visit me, you and Aurelia; we'll have a tea party and . . ."

Aurelia, always sensitive to a possible storm, added, "And next year I'll be a pupil, and Teddy can come some days with me to school, right, Holly?"

Knowing that next year was problematic, to say the least, that *she* might be a long way off by next fall when Aurelia would be six and ready for first grade, Holly attempted to divert an onset of tears. "Teddy, you can come anytime and visit the school, look at picture books, and play with the children," she said appeasingly. Then glancing at Hetty, she added tactfully, "that is, anytime your mama says you may."

Hetty maintained a stoic silence.

"Can I, Mama?" asked Teddy. "I want to go. Now."

"You can't go now," Hetty said sharply. "Sit up there and finish your porridge." Teddy opened his oatmeal-rimmed mouth and a wail began to emerge.

Hetty turned a furious face to Holly. "Now, see what you've done?"

Holly knew there was no use arguing or trying to explain. She hurried over to Teddy, kissed his round little face contorted with unhappiness, and said over the howls, "Teddy, please don't cry! Do what your mama says, and I promise you a nice surprise! I'll send it back with your papa," With that, after giving Aurelia a quick hug, Holly made her exit.

From the kitchen window Hetty watched them, the anger still like a hard fist in her chest. She saw Ned put his hand under Holly's elbow and assist her into the wagon. Hetty's lip curled scornfully even as her heart wrenched. Ned probably admired Holly, and that admiration would make him offer comfort and support to her. Men had always admired and helped Holly even when she didn't deserve it. *Especially* when she didn't deserve it, Hetty thought resentfully.

Things usually happened just the way Holly wanted them to; she always had the last word. Men had always flocked around her, wanting to do her bidding, *asking* to do whatever she pleased. Why? What made Holly so—so attractive to men? Even in Willow Springs, there had been far prettier girls, yet Holly had been the most popular. She did not even flirt—well, at least, not as blatantly as some of the other girls did, Hetty had to admit. Still, Hetty could never figure out just what it was that Holly did that men so liked, to make them circle her like moths around a flame. She did not even seem to have to lift a finger—

But she'd lost Jim Mercer, hadn't she? *That had brought her crashing down all right*, Hetty thought with some satisfaction. She remembered how she used to envy Holly when Jim came home from West Point in his dashing cadet uniform, with the red-lined gray cape and the jaunty cap. She recalled how indifferent Holly had seemed to his adoration, how casually she had accepted his worshipful eyes, his eagerness to do her bidding.

Well, Ned was twice the man Jim Mercer had been. And *she* was the one who had caught *him!* Suddenly Hetty was convinced, recalling Ned's remonstrative look when Holly announced so hopefully that she was going to try for the schoolteacher's job. All that week, in spite of his gentle prodding, *she* had remained aloof, unhelpful. Even last night he had gently asked if she wasn't even going to wish Holly well as she started her new endeavor. But why should she? Stubbornly Hetty justified her actions. It was all right for Ned to say. But what did *he* know? Ned couldn't possibly know what Holly was really like or what it was like for Hetty, all the years of being in Holly's shadow, being compared to her, and envying her while watching everyone else—even family—under her spell.

Hetty's hand shook slightly as she drew the curtain back just enough so she could peer around it. Ned and Holly were both seated in the wagon now. Ned was bending solicitously toward Holly. Listening? Or was he sympathizing? Hetty saw Holly's pert profile turned to him, her hair, upswept from the slender neck, gleamed like rich mahogany in the autumn sunlight, the blue bonnet tipped coquettishly forward, the small plum-colored plume fluttering in the brisk wind. Hetty felt the sour taste of jealousy rise up within her.

The wagon started out, and at the same time Hetty became aware of the scorching smell of something burning. Her biscuits! She whirled around, snatched up a pot holder, grabbed the oven door open, and pulled out the blackened baking sheet. She ran with it to the back door where she banged it down on the porch railing. Somehow she had also burned her fingers, and as she dropped the pan and shook her hand, scalding tears sprang into her eyes and coursed down her cheeks. It seemed the last straw.

Hetty leaned her head against the porch post and sobbed.

Outside, Holly climbed into the wagon where Ned waited patiently. She felt bad that there had been no mutually pleasant last words with Hetty. But there certainly had been no opening there. Unconsciously, Holly sighed. Ned raised his eyebrows. "Storm brewing in there?" he inquired, jerking his head toward the house.

"'Fraid so," Holly sighed.

"The kids adore you, Holly," he said as he lifted the reins, clicked his tongue for the horse to start forward. They rode a little way before Ned said sadly, "I'm sure sorry about Hetty—" He halted as though not sure that whatever he said might not seem disloyal to his wife. But then he went on, "You know Hetty hated Willow Springs, and I guess, in a way, you're being here reminded her of all the things she hated most about it."

"It's all right, Ned, I understand. I'm just sorry she can't let bygones be bygones. I realize now that back home I was pretty thoughtless sometimes."

Ned didn't offer any more, and they went the rest of the distance with only a few words exchanged. When they got to the schoolhouse, Ned unloaded Holly's trunk and boxes and carried them into the little apartment behind the classroom. "I wish I could stay and help, Holly, but I've got to go open the store. Saturday's one of my busiest days," Ned said as he stood awkwardly in the doorway.

"Oh, of course, Ned. I understand. And thank you for all this." Holly gestured to her assorted boxes and bags and her trunk. "You've done so much for me already. You go ahead. There are others coming to help."

"I wish you all the luck in the world, Holly, and if things don't work out—you can always come—" he broke off, turning beet red. Holly knew that what he had been about to say was something he really couldn't offer with any assurance.

"Thanks, Ned, I appreciate that. But it's going to work out, don't worry." She smiled confidently, adding mentally, *It's* got *to work out!*

Holly was only alone a short time when the Healys arrived.

"We're here to get you settled right," Geneva declared as, armed with scrub buckets, brushes, brooms and big cakes of yellow soap, she mounted the steps and set to work. "You, Matt, start on the windows outside," she ordered her hefty, muscular husband who winked at Holly as he saluted his wife and went to comply with her instructions.

Annie Olsen and Elly Rogers, both members of the Literary Society, came soon after, and then Vi. Holly was so grateful. All these women knew exactly what to do to turn the dusty, dirty place into clean, sanitary, and shining living quarters. Less experienced in housework skills, she was glad to follow their expert directions.

At noon they stopped for a hearty lunch. Besides cleaning equipment, Geneva had brought a hamper of delicious food: ham, deviled eggs, potato salad. Annie had brought a jug of sweet apple cider freshly pressed from their orchard's fruit, and

Elly provided home-baked bread and a custard pie. Vi's contribution was one of her delicate lemon sponge cakes.

"What a feast!" exclaimed Holly. "You're all so wonderful! How can I ever thank you."

"You're thanking us aplenty by teaching our children," Geneva said.

"Maybe you won't be so grateful after a couple of days with our two rascals!" laughed Matt.

"Matt's right, Holly, that's the truth. And I know *my* Billy and Tom can be as mischievous as a barrel of monkeys, I can tell you," Annie shook her head.

"Don't be afraid to use the proverbial hickory stick, Holly," counseled Elly who had five children, all under the age of twelve.

"I just hope I can do the job!" declared Holly.

"You'll do just fine," Vi told her, and they exchanged a look. Holly was reminded of Vi's advice, "Pray hard and let God do the rest." She meant to take it.

After they ate, they all went back to work. Early in the afternoon, to Holly's astonishment Adam Corcoran appeared.

"What in the world!" she gasped as she saw him dismount and approach the schoolhouse, holding a bouquet of autumn flowers. She met him at the door and surveyed him with mock severity. He was immaculately groomed as always.

"Oh, no, Adam!" she shook her head, "you'll never do! This is hard, dusty work, and you're not dressed for it."

He looked momentarily abashed; then, pointing to Vi, with her head tied up in a scarf and wearing a coverall apron, he asked, "Why can't I have one of those?"

Holly giggled, "I guess we can find an extra one for you if you really want to help."

"Why else would I have come?" he demanded. With that he handed her the flowers, took off his gray broadcloth jacket, and rolled up the sleeves of his white shirt.

At four o'clock Geneva said that she and Matt would have to leave. She had left her brood with a neighbor, and, this being Saturday night, there were baths to be given in preparation for the Sabbath and church the next day. Holly thanked them profusely, and they departed. Elly and Annie, who had come together, gave their particular job a final "lick and promise"; then they left, too. Vi was next to leave. Promising to come to visit soon, she got into her small buggy and rode off.

Adam was the last to leave and seemed almost reluctant to go. He pulled an immaculate linen handkerchief out of his pocket and wiped his forehead. "Whew, you were right. I never saw so many cobwebs, so many spiders. What did old Larkin do with them, I wonder, raise them for scientific experiments?"

"You're not quitting?" Holly, hands on her hips, demanded as if shocked.

"Isn't everything done? The place looks like it underwent a complete transformation. But if there's anything else, it'll have to wait until I just have a little rest before tackling it," he told her, adding, "The spirit indeed is willing, but the flesh is weak."

Holly blinked her eyes, "Why, Adam Corcoran, quoting Scripture?"

"Every educated man knows plenty of appropriate quotations, as many from the Bible as Shakespeare."

"But you know who quotes Scripture for his own purposes, don't you?" she teased.

"I am also aware of that," he answered, nodding his head sagely. "And I only quote it rarely when the occasion calls for it."

Holly found his coat for him and gave it to him.

"I was joking. Everything is done. I can't thank you enough for lending a hand. I didn't expect it."

"Life is full of surprises, isn't it?"

"And thank you, too, for the flowers," she said as they walked out onto the schoolhouse porch.

"You're more than welcome. And I really *do* wish you . . . well, everything you need to succeed . . ." here his voice changed into his supercilious tone, ". . . at this enterprise you've so rashly undertaken."

He went down the steps and untethered his horse from the hitching post. For a moment he stood by his horse's head, adjusting the bridle then tightening the stirrup buckle. Then he turned and looked up at Holly standing on the porch steps above him and asked doubtfully, "Sure you won't be lonely here?"

"Lonely?" she repeated his question, and paused before answering slowly. "I'm really not sure. I've never lived completely alone before. But to be quite honest, I hadn't given a thought to being lonely. I just wanted to be free."

His smile was slightly sardonic, but his eyes were understanding, and he did not comment.

After Ad had ridden off, Holly went back inside her new domain. Smiling, she looked around. She had never worked so hard physically in her life before; she had never felt so tired, but she knew she had never felt so happy.

The entire place smelled of scouring powder, ammonia, and vinegar, and of furniture polish and wax. Holly drew a long breath. The clean astringent odor seemed as sweet as any perfume. She circled the room, trailing her fingers along the tops of the polished double-desks, stopping to straighten a picture, then she paused to gaze out the clear windows onto the schoolyard and the surrounding hills.

She'd read somewhere that it takes a person at least three weeks or twenty-one days to get accustomed to a new place, a new set of circumstances. In time, she knew, all this would become as familiar to her as her room at home in Willow Springs.

She had come to Oregon with no other purpose than to escape the swirl of gossip around her, of "hiding out" comfortably until she felt she could slip quietly back into town, no longer the target of wagging tongues. She remembered her feeling of dismay when she arrived—"end of the line"—how bitterly she had regretted coming. Now, instead of regret, she was filled with hope. It wasn't just by chance she was here. She was more and more convinced there was a plan, some kind of Divine plan to all this.

Holly smiled. She seemed to be thinking in clichés: end of the line, closing one door, opening another, turning over a new leaf, or starting a new chapter. This experience would be a blank page. Nothing had been written on it yet. Its contents would be up to her. Until now, Holly had spent a lot of time looking back.

But, no more. Now was a new beginning—Holly felt a tingle of real excitement—she spun around, pirouetting several times— and she was going to enjoy it, make the most of it.

Several loud knocks on the schoolhouse door jolted her out of her unaccustomed reverie, and Holly heard a man's voice shouting, "Anybody here? Where's the new schoolmarm?"

Holly stood still, startled, listening.

"Miss Lambeth! Hello, are you here?"

It was a voice she recognized, vibrant, pleasantly pitched. For some reason Holly's heart skittered!

The voice came again, "It's me, Blaine Stevens!"

Blaine Stevens! That's what had been missing today, she thought. Blaine! She ran through the hallway joining the small apartment in back to the schoolroom, feeling unreasonably happy to see his tall figure standing in the doorway. He was holding a huge orange pumpkin.

"I guess I missed the housewarming party?" he asked abjectly.

Holly tried to look severe. "You missed the *work* party."

Blaine looked sheepish. "Sorry."

Holly laughed and put her hands on her hips and eyed the pumpkin, saying, "So! You think bringing *that's* going to make up for it?"

"I guess you could put it like that," he drawled.

"You know what they say about Greeks bearing gifts, don't you?" she demanded.

"Well, not being a Greek—I'm not sure—but it doesn't sound good."

"If I were a Trojan, maybe not—," she dimpled, "but under the circumstances . . ."

Blaine shook his head. "What those poor, unsuspecting children are in for! A teacher who knows the classics."

"Only by hearsay!" Holly smiled, then with her head on one side, she examined the size of the pumpkin and asked warily, "I hope you're not expecting me to bake a couple of pies with this?"

"Not at all. I thought I'd show off my surgical skill and carve you a jack o'lantern—thought it would be a nice touch for your first day of school."

"Why, Blaine, what a delightful idea. Shall we go into the kitchen?"

"No, let's sit outside on the porch and I'll do it there. It's such a nice afternoon, and from the looks of this place you've spent enough time inside today. It'll do you good to get some fresh air and sunshine!"

Holly put a finger under her chin as if in obedience. "Yes, Doctor. Thinking of my health, I see. So, what do you need?"

"Just some old *Monitors*, if you've got them. I come equipped with scalpel," he joked and walked out onto the front porch while she hurried into the kitchen and gathered up a stack of newspapers in a box by the stove.

Watching Blaine's hands as he first outlined triangular eyes, nose, and a wide, grinning mouth with the point of his knife, Holly thought how strong and capable they were, blunt-tipped, flexible. She was fascinated by how quickly and smoothly he cut into the flesh of the pumpkin, neatly scooped out the meat and seeds, then finished off the comical face, leaving two jagged teeth on the top and bottom of the smile.

"There! How's that?" he asked leaning back and surveying his handiwork.

"A work of art!" declared Holly. "You're a genius!"

"Ah, madam, you exaggerate!" he murmured with mock humility.

"Only slightly. It is certainly one of the handsomest jack o'lanterns it has been my privilege to meet—the children will love it!" she assured him. "Now, I'll just gather up this mess and reward you with a piece of lemon sponge cake."

"That sounds great—if it's no trouble."

"None," said Holly starting to fold up the remains of the pumpkin.

"Wait! Don't throw away the seeds," cautioned Blaine. "Rinse them thoroughly, put them on a baking sheet with a little butter and into the oven for about fifteen minutes and—"

"Then what?"

"Eat them! They're delicious and *very* good for you besides. Very healthy!"

Holly teased, "Always the doctor!"

"'Fraid so." Blaine looked abashed. "I guess it goes with the territory—, as they say."

"Never mind. I should be glad you're concerned about my health! All this good medical advice for free," she said laughingly over her shoulder as she started inside.

"Don't be so sure of that," Blaine retorted.

"Sure of what?"

"That it's free. I may present you with a bill."

"Oh, so what is your usual fee?"

"Well, it's not *usual,* not what I *usually* charge my patients," Blaine said as he followed her into the kitchen.

"So? What is it?"

"Would you like to go on a picnic with me next Sunday afternoon?"

Holly was glad that her back was turned to him so that he couldn't see how his question had brought the warmth rushing into her cheeks, starting her heart thumping.

She tried to keep her voice steady as she replied casually. "Why, yes, that sounds like fun—that is, if this good weather lasts."

After Blaine had gone, Holly lighted a candle and placed it inside the grinning jack o'lantern and stood looking at it for a long time. Was she becoming too interested in Blaine? Everything about him appealed to her: his strength, his confidence, his manner, and underneath all that, his quiet sense of humor. She realized that when she was with him, things seemed to fall into place as if it were all as it should be. Strange?

For awhile that evening she puttered around, setting out her personal things to make the little parlor more hers. She set out the double-framed pictures of her parents, the watercolor of their home that her Aunt Sylvie, the "artistic" sister in her mother's family, had painted, and then she placed her photo album containing all the special pictures on the small chest of drawers.

The flowers Ad brought, the white and gold chrysanthemums, were already filling the room with their spicy scent, and the pillow that Vi had needlepointed for her went on the rocker. Holly looked around with infinite satisfaction and drew a long breath of contentment. She couldn't remember feeling so happy for a long time.

That night before getting into bed, Holly stood at the window, watching a harvest moon move slowly across the sky. After she blew out the lamp, the moon shining in the window made square patches on her bedspread.

After this eventful day, sleep didn't come easily. She missed the feel of Aurelia's warm little body curled beside her and realized the one thing she would miss from moving out of Hetty's house were the children. Finally she closed her eyes and whispered the childhood prayer that Great-Aunt Ancilla had taught her, "I will lay me down in peace and sleep, for Thou, Lord, only, makest me dwell in safety."

PART 3

If ever I am a teacher,
it will be to learn more than to teach.

Madame Deluzy

Chapter 13

The first morning that Holly was to take charge of the Riverbend grammar school so many butterflies were fluttering in her stomach that she could hardly manage to swallow a half cup of coffee. And not very good coffee at that. She had been so distracted making it that it tasted more like bitter hot sand than anything else.

Dressed in what she hoped was a "schoolmarm" outfit, over her plainest blue merino dress with a simple white collar, she put on the patterned calico pinafore Vi had made her to protect her dress from chalk dust and ink and "whatever the children may have on their hands when they tug at you." She swept her hair up and back into a prim knot and looked in the mirror to assure herself that at least she looked the part, then Holly went out into the schoolroom for a final check before school started.

Everything in the schoolroom looked perfect. The worn, scratched pupils' desks had been cleaned and varnished, the scarred floor was waxed, blackboards washed. The teacher's pointer hung neatly by the wall map of the world, chalk was in the boxes, the slates were on each desk, pencils and erasers on top of the polished teacher's desk at the front of the room. The finished result was all due to the help so generously given her, Holly recalled with gratitude. For the short time she had been in Riverbend she had made some really good friends.

In spite of Hetty. That last awful scene with her cousin flashed into her mind and Holly gave a little shiver. She quickly banished the memory. She refused to think about it now. Or to think about it any more, for that matter. She wanted to forget it. She had enough on her mind without thinking about Hetty.

Morning sunshine poured through the sparkling windows and, peeking out, Holly saw a few of her students were coming into the schoolyard. She consulted her fob watch pinned to her apron bib for at least the dozenth time. It wasn't yet eight o'clock, the time she was supposed to go out on the porch and ring the bell announcing the opening of school.

Suddenly Holly felt the grip of doubt. Perhaps she had underestimated the pitfalls of what she had undertaken. In less than an hour twenty-five children would be thronging through that door. And *she* was expected to teach them! In the euphoria of privacy and freedom she had experienced over the weekend, obtained with the schoolteacher's position, the responsibilities of it, only dimly perceived, had floated somewhere on the periphery of her mind as "next week." Now *next week* was *now!* The first day of school was *here!* Her first day of teaching was about to begin.

All at once came a terrifying vision of this room filled with children of varying ages, noisy, squirming, staring at her curiously while she was supposed to not only keep everything in order but teach them something as well. Oh, why had she ever thought she could do this? What on earth was she doing here?

Then suddenly, out of Holly's past came a memory of something her father had told her when she was a little girl and refused to go by a neighbor's house because they had a big black barking dog, "Holly, a dog senses when someone is afraid of it, and that's when a dog will bite!"

Why that came back to her now, Holly couldn't imagine. However, it did the trick of steadying her. "If I look as scared as I feel, the children will see it, and it will all be over for me," she told herself, the ridiculous image of the children pushing through the doorway jumping on her with bared teeth almost made her laugh out loud.

Her feeling of panic subsided. Holly walked over to the teacher's desk and picked up the handle of the heavy teacher's bell, walked out onto the schoolhouse porch, and, pumping back her arm, began to swing it. The loud clanging ring reverberated into the clear morning air. Riverbend Grammar School was now back in session.

At the end of the day Holly's head was throbbing. As the last little "scholar" trailed out of the classroom, she sank into the teacher's chair with a sense of infinite relief and total exhaustion. *How did people manage to teach year after year?* she wondered wearily, thinking of the grammar school teachers she knew in Willow Springs who after forty years were still teaching—like old Miss Wilkins who had taught Holly's own mother!

She had moved through the day in a whirl. The projects she had planned for the children to do that she thought would take twenty minutes were either completed or ruined in five! The variety of ages and diversity in ability of her pupils was confusing. The tasks that she thought would be simple proved difficult. The ones she thought would occupy them long enough to give her a breather were completed in record time. She would go to help one group with something, repeat instructions, and get them started, when another group would need help.

And always at the back of the room were the big boys! She had been warned about them. It seems once a boy got to the age and strength he was of real use on the farm, he only attended school haphazardly and regularly failed to appear during spring planting and fall harvesting. These fellows, ranging in age from twelve to fourteen, were a continual source of interruption. They carried on a constant conversation between themselves, talked through her directions, and asked for repetitions just, Holly suspected, to divert her from her explanations and irritate her. She would have to find some system to get them under control. But right now she was too worn out to think how.

She was so tired that she went to bed early that night, then overslept the next morning. She had to rush, with only time to grab a quick mug of coffee and a few bites of bread and jam, to be ready when the first little pupils arrived. They were the Healy twins, scrubbed and shiny-faced, eager to begin their day of learning.

At the end of her second day of teaching, Holly concluded it was far worse than the first had been. *Why did I ever think I could do this job? Was having the little apartment in back really worth all this?* she demanded of herself as she sat slumped at her table sipping tea that afternoon.

If it hadn't been for Vi's unexpected arrival with a meat pie and a pan of cornbread wrapped in a padded cloth to keep warm, she might have been tempted to write a letter of resignation to the Council right then.

"Oh, Vi, why did I ever take this on! I'm not up to it! I don't think I can ever get the hang of it. A teacher I'm not!" she moaned as they sat at the kitchen table together.

"Nonsense, you're going to do fine. It's always hard starting any new venture," Vi assured her.

"I don't know," Holly said, gloomily shaking her head.

But the next day things went a little better. Some of the children were really eager to learn, quick to follow directions, and touchingly sweet. Holly decided to separate the big boys, give them physical tasks to do, like bringing in water from the well and filling the drinking bucket in the classroom each morning, splitting kindling, and chopping wood to keep the woodbox for the stove filled even though the days weren't cold enough yet to have a fire going.

She found a box of *McGuffey Readers* that Larkin had evidently ordered and never unpacked, and these were a great help. For the children who knew how to read, she could assign them a lesson while she taught the younger ones their ABCs. By Friday, although her nerves were frazzled and she was physically spent, Holly felt she had gained a little more confidence that she would survive the year ahead.

It would only be until spring, she encouraged herself. The school year in Riverbend only went until the first of May; then Holly would make plans to go home to Willow Springs.

Chapter 14

*T*he second week of school had gone incredibly well, Holly thought, as she stood at the schoolhouse door on Friday afternoon, watching the last group of children leave the play yard and start their meandering way home. None were in any hurry, probably because they knew the chores that awaited them there.

Little Joel McKay and his sister, Cissy, were the last to leave. Cissy turned at the gate to wave one more time to Holly before hurrying to catch up with her brother. These two had already made inroads into Holly's affection. Skinny and under-sized for their ages, with threadbare clothes and bare feet. She worried about them now especially when early fall frost covered the grass.

Holly was just about to close the door when she saw a familiar small buggy and horse coming down the road toward the schoolhouse. Her heart gave an unexpected little leap as the buggy turned into the schoolyard. *Blaine!* she thought happily.

He reined up in front of the porch, leaned out, and greeted her. "Well, Miss Schoolmarm, how's it going?"

She placed a hand on her breast and heaved a dramatic sigh. "Better than I had any right to expect!" she admitted with a laugh.

He reached into a basket beside him on the floor of the buggy then held out his hand, "An apple for the teacher?" he grinned, opening his palm revealing a round bright red apple.

"Why, thank you, Blaine!" Holly took it and dropped a curtsy.

"Thank the Fosters; they gave me a whole bushel in payment for taking care of their last baby," Blaine laughed.

"Ummm, delicious!" Holly said as her white teeth bit into the rosy skin and took a bite of the sweet, tart fruit.

"Know someone who can bake a superior pie? I can't possibly eat all of these myself."

Holly thought a moment, then warned laughingly, "Well, don't look at *me*, Blaine, I never was able to get the crust right. But I was thinking you could leave some of the apples here to share with the children. Some of them seem to forget to bring lunch sometimes or else come without it, and it would be nice to have something on hand for them to eat."

"Good idea!" agreed Blaine. "I'll bring the basket inside for you." He got out of the buggy and led his horse over to the edge of the yard where there was some scraggly long grass for him to nibble on; then he lifted out the split-oak basket of apples and carried them into the schoolroom.

Holly held the door open for him and he set them down behind the teacher's desk.

"I'd say it's more likely some of them come without lunch because there isn't enough in the larder at home to spare," Blaine told her frowning. "A few of the families around here have quite a struggle to make a go of it. A lot of folks came out here from the East without much farming experience, just wanted to get a new start, maybe; when offered land to homestead they grabbed on to it. Turned out to be a lot harder than they had any idea it would be—"

"The proverbial Promised Land?" Holly commented.

"Something like that." Blaine shook his head. "Only for some of them it hasn't worked out all that well."

Then turning to Holly, his serious expression was replaced by an engaging smile. "Since this is Friday and the youngsters get a holiday from school on weekends, so how about the teacher? What would you say to going on that picnic we talked about, tomorrow?"

"Oh, yes, I'd love that."

"While this weather holds—it might be really nice farther up on the river—I might even do a little fishing. That is if you wouldn't object?"

"Object? I like to fish myself; my Grandfather used to take me fishing with him. And I've caught a few nice trout myself a time or two!" Holly gave her head a little toss.

"Were you a tomboy, Miss Lambeth?"

"You *might* say that, Doctor." She lowered her voice conspiratorially. "Would you believe that my mother quite gave up on me several times! She would say to my grandfather, 'Papa, how do you expect me to bring Hollis up a lady if you keep encouraging her this way?'"

"Well, I'd say she managed to do that just fine," Blaine commented as he gazed at Holly appreciatively, adding with a mischievous grin, "But then I've never seen you with a fishing pole, have I?"

"You'll have your chance tomorrow."

As they walked back to the door she asked, "What about the picnic food? What shall I bring?"

"Yourself. I'll provide most of it." He held up his hand when she started to protest. "Really, most of my patients pay me in wonderful ways—you'll see." He went down the steps. At the bottom he turned and looked up at her. "So, then, I'll come by—say ten o'clock tomorrow morning?"

"Yes, fine."

Blaine started walking to where he had left the buggy, and Holly's eyes followed him. *If* she planned to stay in Riverbend, Holly could not think of a nicer "beau" than Blaine—good-looking if not handsome, intelligent, gentle, and with a fine sense of humor—but then, she amended quickly, she wasn't planning to stay. There was certainly no point getting any ideas about the doctor.

True to his word, Blaine arrived promptly at ten next morning, and Holly was ready and waiting in a blue calico dress with a pattern of tiny flowers, her hair out of its coil and gathered with a blue ribbon at the nape of her neck.

"I feel like a kid playing hooky from school!" he told her as

127

he helped her into his small gig, picked up the reins and they started off.

"But that's impossible! You're *with* the 'schoolmarm'!" Holly laughed gaily.

"That's right! I almost forgot or else you don't *seem* like a schoolteacher to me!" he looked at Holly, thinking how lovely she looked with the sun's sending dancing gold lights through her hair, the rose color of her softly curved cheeks. "You see, Miss Lambeth, I never had such a pretty teacher as *you* when I went to school."

"Why, thank you for the compliment, sir," Holly replied. "It's hard for me to believe, too. I never thought I'd end up a schoolteacher."

"What do you mean 'end up'?"

Holly hesitated. Surely she didn't know Blaine well enough to reveal her sorry story, to tell him that by this time she had expected to be an Army officer's bride, not teaching school in a frontier town. No, she couldn't confess her humiliating experience of being jilted. Instead, she answered, "I just never *planned* to teach school. It just never occurred to me that I would. But I'm discovering as they say that 'life is full of surprises,' right?"

Blaine gave her a searching glance as if he knew she was holding something back, but he didn't ask anything more. Instead, he spoke of himself. "I always wanted to be a doctor. My uncle was a doctor and as a little boy I used to go with him in his buggy when he made his calls. The whole idea of being skilled enough to help people when they were hurt or ill seemed a great way to spend my life."

"From what I hear, Riverbend is very lucky to have you."

Blaine shrugged, "I'm just glad I can be of use." Then he changed the subject. "I'm going to pull off the road here, we'll have to leave the buggy and walk down to the river bank. I started to get another horse from the livery stable and a sidesaddle for you to bring out, but I didn't know whether or not you rode. Do you?"

"Yes."

"Next time, we'll do that. Then we can ride right to our picnic spot."

Holly felt a little spurt of pleasure that Blaine had said "next time."

Blaine unhitched the horse and led him over to a shady spot to graze, tying him loosely to a small aspen. Then he got the wicker hamper and his fishing gear from the back of the buggy and said, "Come on, it's not far."

It could not have been a more beautiful day for a picnic. Holly had never seen deep forests like these in Oregon. She loved the feel of the pine needles under her feet like a soft brown carpet on the path through the woods to the river. The sun was warm on their backs as they came to a clearing overlooking the clear, rock-rimmed river. They both stood for a moment, savoring the quiet, the only sound being the rush of the water below, the gentle swish of wind high above in the trees.

Blaine set down the picnic basket, and Holly spread out the blanket for them to sit on. It was so lovely and peaceful that neither of them spoke for a few minutes.

"Are you hungry? Or do you want to try your luck at fishing first?" Blaine asked after awhile.

She considered her choices, then said, "Eat? I am rather hungry."

"Good! So am I." Blaine opened the hamper and began putting out the food.

"My goodness, such a lot!" Holly exclaimed.

"I have a lot of grateful patients!" he laughed as he continued bringing out a loaf of home-baked bread, sliced ham, a chocolate cake, and peach pie.

Holly opened her own much smaller basket and brought out her contribution. "And *I* have a lot of *grateful students!* Or at least their mothers are!" she announced putting down a daintily arranged plate of deviled eggs and a square of gingerbread. Blaine looked surprised, and Holly explained, "Danny Glenn's mother sends me a dozen eggs every week, and Geneva Healy always bakes something extra for me on her baking day."

"If I were the suspicious type I'd say some of your pupils are angling for good grades," he commented as he sampled one of the eggs.

"And it pays, doesn't it?"

"Hmmm." Blaine rolled his eyes as he popped the rest of the

129

egg into his mouth, then licked his fingers. "I'd give them all A's for sure."

They made sandwiches of the ham and thickly buttered bread, drank the lemonade, and finished with cake.

"What a feast!" declared Blaine, leaning back against a large rock, his arms folded beneath his head. "It's a real treat for me, I can tell you. I usually get my meals at the Hometown Cafe, and believe me, I don't know *whose* hometown they're advertising with that name, because the food leaves a great deal to be desired."

"Well, maybe we should go on picnics more often!" Holly quipped then blushed. Immediately she wished she hadn't said that. It was the sort of thing the "old Holly" would say, coy and flirtatious. Wasn't she done with that sort of foolishness? She hoped Blaine wouldn't take it wrong. She looked over at him. His eyes were closed. He seemed to be entirely relaxed, maybe even dozing.

Holly got up and walked over to the edge of the river and looked down at the clear, sun-dappled water. How peaceful, how beautiful it was. She felt a kind of awe at the splendor of this country. The surprising thought came to her of how lucky she was to be here. She couldn't remember ever having been so touched by the majesty of natural beauty before. Maybe she really was changing, becoming a different kind of person. Someone who was aware of beauty, able to appreciate nature, capable of reflection.

"Ready to try your luck fishing?" Blaine's voice behind her made Holly turn. He was on his feet, roused from his short nap and getting out his fishing rod.

"I think I'll just tag along down the stream with you," she said.

She followed Blaine as he moved from one rock to the other, casting and spinning. She saw the flashes of gold and brown of the plentiful trout in the crystal water. Blaine landed several but released them, explaining offhandedly that he didn't cook enough to take them home, and besides it was just the fun of testing his skill that he enjoyed most.

All too soon, the shadows began to lengthen, the towering trees soon hid the lowering sun and the wind off the river turned chilly. "Guess we better get started back," Blaine said reluctantly.

They repacked the hamper, folded the blanket and walked slowly to where they had left horse and buggy earlier. Holly debated whether or not to invite Blaine back to the schoolhouse for a pick-up supper from the remains of the picnic, make a pot of hot tea. Would it be proper for a spinster schoolmarm to entertain the town's bachelor doctor alone?

Vi had warned Holly that a small-town schoolteacher had to be careful about her reputation, so, regretfully, she decided against such an invitation. But with someone like Blaine it seemed such a silly rule to be kept.

In the buggy on the way toward town, Blaine said, "I hated to leave. I haven't enjoyed a day so much in . . . well, I don't know how long."

"It was lovely, Blaine; I'm glad you suggested it." Holly smiled at him.

As they jogged along, they carried on a bantering conversation, while Holly enjoyed the scenery of meadows fenced with rails where placid cattle grazed and where orchards were now heavy with autumn fruit: golden pears and russet apples. Suddenly the peaceful scene was shattered. Coming down the road toward them was a horse in a frenzied gallop with its rider waving one arm frantically and shouting. Blaine pulled on his reins. "Whoa!" He leaned forward as the breathless rider slid his mount to a stop alongside.

"Thank God, Doc! I found you! You gotta come quick! It's my boy Chad! Fell off the hayrack, split his head near clear open—he's bleedin' somethin' awful—please, come, right away!"

"Sure thing, Jesse," Blaine clicked his reins, and as the man whirled his horse around and started galloping ahead, Blaine urged his jogging horse forward. "Come on, fella, let's get going!" They started off at a fast clip.

"That was Jesse Renner. His farm is not far from here. A widower with three boys all under twelve who do a man's work along with their father."

"Oh, you mean Ev and Henry? They come to school. But I don't think I know Chad," Holly replied.

"He's probably been helping his father by not attending school since their mother died last spring."

"Ev and Henry don't come regularly either. But I didn't know why."

"A motherless home has a lot of problems," Blaine said grimly. "I'm sorry, Holly, you'll have to come along. There's no time to take you back into town."

"Of course not, Blaine. I understand."

They were going so fast that the fragile little buggy swayed perilously from side to side as they bumped down the rutted country road. Holly had to grip the side handles of the seat to avoid being tossed from the jolting vehicle. Swerving, almost on one wheel, Blaine turned into the gates of the Renner farm. Near the barn, lying on the ground, she saw the prone figure of a boy; two other boys, looking pale and frightened, stood over him. The father, who had made it back only a few minutes before, handed the reins of his horse to one of his sons, with a terse order, "Take him in and rub him down," then knelt beside the inert body of the boy.

"He's still a-breathin' Doc, but I dunno." The man's voice broke as Blaine jumped out of his buggy and ran to where the man was kneeling beside his son.

Over his shoulder, he called back to Holly, "Get my medicine bag, it's under the seat."

Mechanically, Holly ducked her head and saw the black medicine bag, dragged it forward, grabbed it. Gathering up her skirt, she got out of the buggy and hurried over to Blaine. Looking down at the child, she saw blood all over his face, matted into a shock of sandy hair. Instinctively she shrank back, fighting down the instant nausea at the sight, the scared pounding of her heart, and the flinching of every nerve. She set down the medicine bag beside Blaine and stepped back, quelling the urge to run away.

Blaine made a quick examination of the boy, running his hands over his limbs, arms, taking his pulse; then, placing practiced fingers on the base of the boy's throat, he bent his head close to scrutinize the still bleeding gash on the boy's forehead. "He'll be all right, Jesse, but we've got to close up that wound.

He's lost a lot of blood and will go into shock if we don't act fast." He turned aside and snapped open his bag, brought out a square of cotton gauze, and applied it. It immediately turned crimson and Holly felt herself gag.

Blaine spoke again. "We'll take him into the house. Jesse, get on the other side and easy now, gently. Careful—," he instructed the father. To Holly he said, "Bring my bag, please."

Like an automaton Holly followed them. They entered the house into the kitchen. It was dim, dingy, smelled of old grease, dirt, and the odor of cabbage and fried meat hung in the air. A widower, Blaine had said. Certainly no woman lived in this fetid atmosphere.

Blaine issued orders like an army drillmaster, and Holly scurried to obey. "Clear that table. Scour the top, see if you can find a clean towel—"

She found a large cake of lye soap in a cracked dish on the counter, and there was some water in the kettle on the stove. It was almost impossible to get a lather up, but she did her best; then, as rapidly as she could, she washed off the surface with a wadded dishrag.

There wasn't a tablecloth in sight. Blaine and Jesse were still holding the boy, waiting. Realizing that every minute counted, Holly made an impulsive, instantaneous decision. Blaine and Jesse both had their backs to her, still holding Chad. Quickly Holly moved into the corner and lifted her skirt to one side and unbuttoned the waistband of one of her petticoats. Holding it so it wouldn't drop on the floor, she stepped out of it carefully, then whipped it over onto the kitchen table. Then the two men eased the boy on the top.

Outside, the autumn evening was rapidly darkening. The kitchen was full of shadows.

"Light a lamp," Blaine said to Jesse. "I need to see what I'm doing. I'll have to suture that cut; it will take stitches—" Blaine was almost talking to himself.

The boy began to moan. Blaine put his hands on the boy's shoulders soothingly. Holly could hear Jesse fumbling as he lighted an oil lamp with shaky hands.

"Jesse, hold the lamp right here so I can see," Blaine said calmly.

The father stepped up to the table. Then Blaine spoke directly to Holly. "Chad will have to be held absolutely still so that we don't start the bleeding all over while I sew up his head. Think you can hold his head for me?"

Holly's face whitened and her eyes darkened with fear. She knew she had no time to hesitate. She was needed in a way she had never been before in her entire life. The only thing that deeply troubled her was whether she was up to this task that had been thrust upon her. She swallowed over a throat dry with fear and nodded.

"All right, just step here and put your hands on either side of his head, hold it steady," Blaine ordered. He gave her one long look, then he seemed to forget her and concentrate totally on his patient.

Holly clamped her teeth together, so they wouldn't chatter and she wouldn't scream. Eyes riveted, she watched as Blaine removed the blood-soaked cloth, wiped the child's forehead gently, then began his skillful surgery. His hand never shook as he expertly, quickly moved the needle back and forth closing the gaping gash.

It wasn't until she heard Blaine speaking to Jesse that Holly snapped back to consciousness and knew the ordeal was over. She heard Blaine say, "Let's wrap him in a blanket, get him into bed, heat some bricks, and place them at his feet; see that he doesn't get a chill. He'll be fine. I'll look in on him in the morning, but I don't think you have to worry, Jesse. He may have a mild concussion from the fall, but the wound on his forehead will heal, and he'll just have a slight scar, that's all."

Left alone in the dark kitchen, Holly stripped off the blood-spattered petticoat from the table, rolled it into a tight ball, and stuck it under her arm. Shuddering, she walked over to the door, opened it, and stepped out onto the porch and took a long, shaky breath.

Every muscle in her body ached with released tension. She began to tremble and felt suddenly cold. How had she ever been able to do what she had just done? The Holly *she* knew was one

134

who grew faint at the merest drop of blood on a pricked finger and turned away from a plucked chicken or a dead mouse!

Within a few minutes, she felt a firm hand on her arm and Blaine's voice saying solicitously, "You all right?"

She nodded.

"Come on, then, I'll take you home."

They drove back to the schoolhouse in silence. When Blaine took her up to the door, he asked softly, "Will you ever go on another picnic with *me?*"

Her laugh sounded slightly hysterical. "Of course."

"You were splendid, Holly. Thank you."

"You're welcome," she said faintly.

There was much left unspoken, but there seemed no adequate words to be said. This was the second time they had shared something for which there seemed no words.

"Good night, Holly. Bless you."

"Good night, Blaine."

One morning about two weeks later Holly was awakened out of a sound sleep by an unusual sound outside. Reaching for her wrapper, she got out of bed and padded barefoot to the window and looked out. To her surprise she saw Jesse Renner and Chad unloading a cart of firewood and stacking it beside the schoolhouse.

She realized it was their way of saying thanks for her part in helping Blaine when Chad was injured. She rapped on the window, and they both looked up; and she smiled and waved her appreciation. Jesse shook his head as if to say "No need!" and went on working.

Somehow the incident made her feel a special bond with Blaine. This was the kind of payment for "services rendered" he usually received. They had shared something important, and now she understood something else about him: the warmth of people's gratitude. It made her feel a new closeness to Riverbend's doctor.

Chapter 15

*R*iverbend, Oregon, October 1882

"Dearest Mama," Holly wrote,

I have now been a full-fledged teacher for over a month! From your letter, which I received today, I am aware of the full extent of your and Papa's surprise at the news. It is so like Papa to say, as you quote him: "Well, well, maybe all the hefty fees I paid out to Blue Ridge Female Academy are being put to some practical use after all." I can just see his eyes twinkle while he says that. But in all seriousness I seem to have taken to teaching like the proverbial duck to water.

Of course, I would not be entirely truthful if I didn't relate some of the mishaps that have occurred, although in retrospect some of them have been quite comical. For example, I have certainly been put to the test as people tell me all new teachers are. Particularly by some of the older boys. Because they only attend school sporadically, when they are not needed on the farms, they do not have the desire to learn as do most of the other children. The three who are most troublesome have played some tricks. I will not go into full detail but just mention a few—such as putting old rags in the classroom stove so that one chilly morning when I decided to light a cozy fire, it smoked terribly creating such a cloud of fumes that I had to evacuate the building and conduct the rest of the school day outdoors. Thankfully, the weather here is still warm in the middle of the day so we all rather enjoyed the change of location! Another time a small garter snake was found in the bottom of the drinking water bucket, much to the horror of two screaming little girls.

But I think my stern reprimand and threat of worse has straightened these youngsters out sufficiently—at least temporarily. Nothing untoward has happened recently. They are woefully behind in their studies, so I have separated them from their usual places in the back of the classroom and set them to practicing their letters and doing sums.

The children who come to school are all ages, so I have to be quite versatile in planning each day's schedule. On the whole, I find them all anxious to learn and attentive. I try not to have favorites, but two of the children are especially appealing—a little boy named Joel and his younger sister, whom he calls Cissy. He is about eight, I think; she about six. Both have angelic expressions on not-always-too-clean faces, curly golden hair, large brown eyes. Sadly enough, they are the poorest-dressed children at school. There is an air of neglect about them, although it is touching to see how Joel, such a manly little fellow, is so protective of his sister.

Holly stopped writing for a minute as she thought about Joel and Cissy. How to explain children like these to her comfortable, well-fed family? How could they possibly understand? Try as she might, Holly could not remember having seen any *really* poor people in Willow Springs. Had she actually been *that* sheltered or too-self-centered to notice if there were?

These two children had become a matter of concern to Holly. Both came to school barefooted even now when the weather was getting cooler. Holly had worried what they would do when winter really set in. She soon found out. One particularly chilly, damp morning Cissy was wearing shoes, much too big for her little feet, but no stockings.

They both looked small and underweight for their ages, and Holly wondered if they got enough to eat. Most of the other children came with full lunch buckets, but one day Holly had seen Joel sitting with Cissy at recess, sharing what appeared to be a meager one. It looked as though it might only be a piece of crumbly cornbread. Another time she had seen Joel picking up one of the Healy boys' discarded thick ham sandwich and giving it to Cissy, who devoured it hungrily. After that, Holly felt she must do something.

She remembered one of her favorite folk tales from her childhood: "Stone Soup"—the story of a beggar who came into a poor village and cleverly got everyone to contribute something to what was only a stone in a pot of boiling water until a rich concoction of meat, potatoes, carrots, lentils, and beans was soon bubbling over the fire with enough to feed everyone. So Holly told it to the children one afternoon and suggested that the next day they make some stone soup and each child could bring something to put in it. The idea delighted them, and the following morning Holly, who had purchased a nice soup bone with plenty of meat on it at the butcher shop, placed it in a pot on the schoolroom stove. It was sending up a delicious smell as the children filed into the class. Each child had brought something to add; Joel and Cissy had brought wild onions. By lunchtime, Holly ladled out a delicious bowl of soup for everyone, and she felt *this* day Joel and his little sister had gone home with full stomachs. The children were so enthusiastic about stone soup that it became a weekly treat.

When Holly confided in Geneva that she felt some of the children did not have adequate lunches, Geneva suggested putting potatoes in the warm ashes of the stove at the end of each day and letting them roast overnight. That way any of the children who wanted one could have one the next day with no one being pointed out as not having enough to eat.

Holly realized she was learning something every day: how to deal with problems, meet challenges, use good judgment in ways she had never before been called upon to do. She had been used to living in a world where all her wants had been met, where there was always someone to take care of things, see that food was provided, that her clothes were not only warm and comfortable but fashionable as well. All that was changing for her; she was seeing things with new eyes; a different kind of world was coming into focus for her. This new awareness in her feelings seemed to be centered on Joel and Cissy, not only because of their physical needs but they also seemed hungry for care and affection. What was their home life like? Holly wondered.

One rainy morning she found them both wet and shivering on the schoolhouse porch long before time for school. Holly brought them inside, back to her own warm little kitchen, dished them each a bowl of oatmeal and hot tea with plenty of sugar. While she dried Cissy's hair and rubbed her cold little feet in her own hands, she noticed the bruise on Joel's forehead and his swollen eyes. What kind of parents did these children have?

When she asked Geneva what she knew about the family, Geneva just shook her head. "Not much. No one does. The McKays always keep to themselves. They don't attend church. I do know he came out here originally to mine, and when that didn't work out he tried farming. But I don't think he was ever much of a farmer; he's sold off his land piece by piece, cut most of the timber too. The few times I saw her, she looked a poor, beaten thing. When I tried to be friendly and talk to her, she just scurried away. Not much I can tell you, Holly."

For not being able to tell her much Geneva had given Holly a lot of information about the McKays. However, it was nothing that made her feel very good about the children. Holly frowned and said, "Joel is so bright. He's one of the smartest children in school. Eager to learn, wants to recite—," she halted midsentence as Geneva regarded her curiously. Holly could guess what her friend was thinking—what her own good sense told her, that it was unwise getting emotionally involved with her students. Especially since she'd be leaving in the spring. Holly knew she was already growing almost too attached to the little boy and his sister.

But it was true. Joel was always the first to raise his hand, first to volunteer for any little job she wanted done around the schoolroom. They were always the first children to arrive at school and the last ones to leave in the afternoon. It was as though *this* was a place where they felt warm, happy, and safe. Safe? *That* thought that came unbidden into her mind troubled Holly most.

139

Holly decided not to write any more about Joel and Cissy in her letter home. It would only distress her soft-hearted mother to hear the things that bothered *her* so much. Dipping her pen in the inkwell, Holly went back to writing an "edited" version of her life in Riverbend.

As to my "social life," Mama, about which you inquired, I cannot say my calendar is crowded! I find I need much time to prepare my daily lessons and have only the weekends for "fun and frivolity," of which there is not a great deal in Riverbend! I keep the lending library going one Saturday a month so I get to see some of my acquaintances, and the Literary Society meets once a month. I've told you about Viola Dodd and Geneva Healy, both have become dear friends.

Her pen halted a second, then she wrote, "I don't see as much of Hetty or the children as I would like, but she has a busy life and, as you can see, my own is quite full." Here Holly's pen stopped moving across the page. She had never been able to tell her mother about the situation between her and Hetty or that it had been the spur that moved her to apply for the teacher's job. It would grieve both her own mother and Aunt Dolly to know that their daughters did not get along, that, in fact, there had been a clear break in their relationship.

Holly tapped her teeth with the end of her pen thoughtfully for a moment. "Well, it isn't *my* fault!" she said to herself before starting to write again.

I have also attended performances of two plays put on by a traveling acting group who were in Riverbend for two nights. Both were well-attended and received enthusiastic applause from the audiences. One presentation was of Shakespeare's *As You Like It*. So you see we are not completely without cultural amenities here. I was escorted to this performance by Adam Corcoran, the editor of the town newspaper, a gentleman of refined taste and intellectual background.

Holly halted the flow of her pen; *that* description did not *exactly* describe Ad. Actually, she knew that his sophistication and his satirical bent in conversation would make her mother uncomfortable, and she might not consider him a suitable escort for her daughter. However, Holly found Adam intensely attractive and interesting and enjoyed hearing his comments, listening to his views, and sometimes arguing with him. He took delight in prodding her to defend her opinions and that was stimulating to Holly, who spent most of her time with minds under the age of twelve.

The other, a modern melodrama, was *The Fate of Jenny Osborne,* and to this one I went with Dr. Stevens, our town physician. He was, however, called out in the middle of the performance by a seriously ill patient and had to leave. He made arrangements for me to be escorted safely home by our mutual friend Mr. Corcoran.

In her letter Holly did not mention the other times she had spent with Blaine. Her mother would have been shocked to know about her helping Larkin and that she had assisted him in an emergency surgery! How could she put into words her relationship with Blaine? She and Blaine had established a special bond that was more than friendship but a little less than love. At least there was nothing the least bit romantic between them—

Quickly Holly dipped her pen into the inkwell, unable and unwilling to explore her own feelings about Blaine. She went on to finish the letter, saying,

I will take this into town to the post office now so that it will go out with the mail on the morning stage. I don't want you to worry about me if it is a long time between my letters. From what I have described of my life now you will understand. Do not imagine for one minute that you are not all often in my thoughts and always in my love. Your affectionate daughter.

Just before Holly sighed it with a flourish, she scribbled a postscript along the margin.

Please thank Great-Aunt Ancilla for all the tracts!

Afterward, when Holly thought about it, she told herself that perhaps she should have been more alert to the restless atmosphere in the classroom that afternoon. But when the children had filed back in from lunch hour, she was preoccupied with finding written work for the fourth- and fifth-graders to do while she drilled the third-graders on their times tables. She had received a letter of intent from the District that the County School Supervisor was making his annual rounds of the grammar schools of the area and would be in Riverbend within the next few weeks. Holly was anxious that her students would make a good showing.

Still, if she had been a more experienced teacher, she might have sensed an unusual undercurrent in the classroom. It wasn't until she had to interrupt her drills three times to quiet the other children and settle a squabble between the Healy twins, that she had noticed that the three older boys, Sam Durkin and Ben Hostler and Wes Spurgeon, were missing.

She stood up and looked around. She hoped that all three of them hadn't gone to the "necessary" behind the schoolhouse at the same time. If they had, that meant they were probably jostling and roughhousing outside instead of coming straight back into the classroom. She frowned; now that she came to think about it, she didn't remember having seen them since before lunch. She usually put them to doing more sums than she knew they could finish before the day's end when they got back from recess. This usually settled them down quickly after their vigorous outdoor playtime.

But no, they weren't in the classroom. Walking to the back of the room, she looked at their desks and saw no open workbooks. Where had those rascals got to? Holly heard snickering behind her, and she turned around to see all heads swiveled in her direction, all eyes upon her. Aha! Everyone knew something that *she* didn't. She marched to the front of the class and, folding her arms, glanced around. Sly glances were exchanged one to another, a few hands were suddenly clapped to mouth, cov-

142

ering guilty smiles, and a few suppressed giggles could be heard. Something was definitely afoot.

Holly employed her sternest schoolmarm voice. "If anyone is keeping the whereabouts of Sam and Ben and Wes a secret from me, he or she will be punished as severely as they will be when I find out."

Dead silence. Holly scanned the room, searching out her most vulnerable prey. Who would break first? She maintained her severest expression and began to pace up and down, then walk slowly along the aisles between the desks. The silence grew heavier. Finally reaching the front of the classroom again, Holly casually took down her pointer and tapped it on the teacher's desk. At this, one or two tentative hands were raised. She spotted Suzanne Rogers.

"Well, I see that one of my pupils is honorable enough to speak up." She gave the rest of the class a scathing look, then said, "Suzanne, do you know where the big boys went after lunch?"

"Yes, ma'm, I-uh, I *think* so," the little girl stammered.

"I do! I do!" Tommy Mason waved his hand wildly.

"So do *I!*" shouted Fred Kohl, not to be outdone, and jumped up. "I heard them talking at lunch."

"Well, then?" Holly waited.

Full of himself, Fred squared his fat little shoulders and announced, "They said they wuz goin' to a saloon and get them a beer!"

A shock wave of gasps and titters echoed throughout the room. Holly blinked and tried to maintain a straight face. "You're sure, Fred, that they really said that's where they were going? They weren't just showing off? Teasing you younger boys?"

Fred shook his head from side to side vigorously. "No ma'am, I sure as anything heard them say that. And so did Billy, didn't you, Billy." Shy Bill Sanders nodded solemnly.

"So did I hear 'em, Miss Lambeth," piped up Bucky Jensen.

Holly took a deep breath, trying not to lose her composure. This was a serious matter. This was insurrection at its worst. If the Town Council learned that three of her students had taken off, heading for one of the town's drinking and gambling establishments during the school day, they would be convinced that she had lost control. They would dismiss her without a doubt. Holly knew a couple of them had had grave reservations that a young female teacher could not handle the big boys who worked on farms alongside the men who didn't think much of "school larnin" anyhow.

Holly knew this was a crisis. She had to take action. But what? She was fully aware that she was the focal point of every child in the class room. They were all watching her to see what she would do.

"All right, children. Settle down," she said automatically although nobody was making any noise. It just gave her something to say while she tried to put her thoughts in order. "Back to your lessons."

She must do something right away. Bring back those truants, make them an example. Inwardly, she quailed. Ben was big, brawny, and although Wes was thin he was wiry and strong, and Sam towered over her. How in the world could she order those huge farm boys back to school, make them come?

Well, she had to try. A half-hour before the regular time for school to close, Holly rapped for attention and said, "Children, we are going to dismiss early today. Tell your mothers there was an emergency that teacher had to attend to. That will be all then; bring your readers up to the front and clean your slates," she told them in a voice that she tried to keep from sounding wavering.

As usual, some of the children dawdled. She noticed Joel eyeing her curiously, taking time helping his sister on with her jacket and edging slowly to the classroom door. She knew they were trying to figure out what she was going to do. Very deliberately she put on her bonnet and took her shawl down from the hook beside the door. "Hurry up, Joel. Time to go. I have to leave, lock up. I have an errand to do downtown."

Reluctantly he took his sister's hand and went out the door. Holly quickly closed the schoolhouse and shooed the children lingering in the play yard out, urging them homeward; then she set out for town. She knew that some of the children who lived

144

in town quickened their lagging steps to follow her. She almost had to laugh, thinking she probably looked like the Pied Piper of Hamlin with a line of children behind her.

A saloon, eh? If that was true, which saloon? When Holly reached Main Street, it had its usual middle-of-the-day deserted appearance. She halted for a minute, squinting at the signs proclaiming the business that had enticed the boys to try out the wares inside. The Nugget, Last Chance, the Doggone Best.

Her heart bounced like a sledgehammer gone wild as she started down the street. She would just have to check each one, she guessed, and pray that the Lord was with her. She was about do something that she never in her imagination had dreamed she would do! But gritting her teeth and with only one last-minute panicked hesitation, Holly pushed through the slatted, swinging doors of the Doggone Best and took a few steps inside.

The first thing that hit her was the stale air. The combined strong odor of cigar, sour whiskey, sweat, and sawdust wrinkled her nose in distaste. The interior was so dense with smoke, so murky and dim that it took Holly a full minute to adjust her eyes enough so that she could see. As soon as she could, what she saw was a blur of startled faces—the weathered faces of old miners standing at the long bar, the open mouths and widened eyes of the cardplayers huddled at the tables, the dropped jaws of the cowboys holding brimming beer mugs half-raised, and the painted masks of the "girls" hanging around at the pool table.

The stunned, bald bartender, in a striped shirt was the first one to find his voice. He leaned forward, his elbow on the bar top. "Can I do something for you, lady?"

Holly's gaze was still circling the room, searching for the boys as he spoke. A second later she spotted three pairs of scared-looking eyes gazing back at her. They stumbled up from the table where they were sitting with some rough-looking characters and started backing up against the wall.

In a clear, strong voice Holly spoke. "Sam Durkin, Ben Hostler, Wes Spurgeon, get over here at once. Get yourself out of this place and home. Tell your folks I'll be there to talk to them later."

She had managed to put more authority and command in her tone than she would ever have thought possible. Her words snapped in the air like firecrackers going off on the Fourth of July. To her own amazement she saw the three shame-faced truants, shoulders hunched, slouch forward and slink past her and through the doors.

Then Holly, hands on her hips, swirled around and swept the room with a long, slow, disgusted look. Turning back to the bartender, she riveted on his now-reddening face. She tried to make eye contact, but he averted his head. Still, Holly had her moment.

"All you men should be ashamed of yourselves. You had to *know* those boys were underage. They should have been ushered out the minute they came through those doors, not encouraged and plied with drink." Her tone was scorching. "I don't know how many of you have children, but if you do, how would you feel if someone served them an alcoholic drink that could start them on the road to ruin." She took another long breath and, pointing her finger at the bartender, said, "There's a law in this country about selling strong drink to minors. If I report this to the sheriff, this place could be closed."

Holly wasn't at all sure that this was the case, but it sounded threatening and rang true enough.

By now she was trembling. Doing this had taken all her energy. Her knees felt so weak that she wasn't sure she could manage to walk out the door. Somehow she did, and once she stepped outside and was able to draw her breath again, the three culprits were nowhere in sight. There were, however, a few of her students gathered at a little distance from the entrance of the saloon as well as a few interested adults who evidently had been told what was going on. As Holly started down the steps and back toward the schoolhouse, there was a light smattering of hands clapping. She didn't look back but walked on.

Chapter 16

$\mathscr{T}$he next Sunday morning at the door of the church, Owen Roberts, the head usher, greeted Holly and, handing her a bulletin, whispered, "That was a splendid thing you did, Miss Lambeth. Everyone is mighty impressed." Remembering that Mr. Roberts had been one of the members of the Town Council who had been most reluctant to appoint her to the position of schoolteacher, she appreciated his comment all the more.

Holly found a seat at the end of one of the rear pews. The Macready family, already seated in it, moved over with nods and smiles to make room for her. The Willis family in the pew in front of her all turned and smiled.

Holly recalled with what trepidation she had attended church the first Sunday after she had assumed the job of schoolteacher and moved to the school house. She knew that the town's schoolmarm was expected to attend church. When she had first arrived in Riverbend, she was forced to accompany Hetty and Ned and sit with them. Already aware of Hetty's feelings about her, Holly had felt very uncomfortable. Locked in her own misery, surrounded by strangers, filled with resentment and a critical attitude toward her cousin, Holly knew that her heart had not been right for worship.

She had spent the entire hour feeling sorry for herself and thinking of the neat white clapboard-and-stone steepled church

147

at home. By contrast, in Willow Springs, church had been a pleasant weekly event with the enjoyable hymn-singing and an inspirational sermon followed by fellowship after the service that was almost a social occasion. That month of miserable Sundays was now past, Holly realized with a sense of relief and gratitude.

Of course, the story of the incident at the Doggone Best had made its rounds, probably embellished each time it was retold. Its effect had been apparent almost immediately as the very next day children had brought presents from grateful parents to a teacher who knew how to take charge. Gifts of home-baked bread, canned peaches, sweet potatoes, and plantings had all been shyly offered by her students. Why, her cache was beginning to rival Blaine's, she thought with some amusement. Well, it was nice to be appreciated and complimented and feel accepted. Now when she came to church, she was greeted with shy smiles from students, approving nods from their parents. She felt welcomed and enveloped by their friendship.

But just as she was basking in this new security, she saw Hetty and Ned enter. Hetty marched first down the aisle, looking neither to the right nor left; Ned was behind, holding Aurelia and Teddy by the hands. As Aurelia passed her pew, she twisted her head around and smilingly waved with a wiggling of all five fingers. Holly smiled and raised her hand in a demure wave back. How she loved those children. And how sad it was that she and Hetty had so much animosity between them.

The congregation rose for the opening hymn. As she stood, Holly noticed that some of the elders were preparing a table for the Lord's Supper and realized that it was Communion Sunday. The Reverend Mobley took his place in the pulpit and announced, "We will now take up the tithes and offerings. Before we do, let me remind you of the biblical admonition in Matthew 5:23 to meditate on: 'Therefore when you bring your gift to the altar and there remember that your brother has something against you, leave your gift there before the altar and go your way. First be reconciled to your brother, then come and offer your gift.'"

Conviction tingled through Holly at these words. She

glanced over at the back of Hetty's head, but the stiff black bonnet never quivered. Hetty remained staring straight ahead. What *did* Hetty have against her? Holly wondered. What had she ever done to her to make Hetty so resentful? Oh dear, sighed Holly, what was there to do about it? What *could* she do about it?

The day's sermon didn't help. Reverend Mobley took his text from Mark 11:25 and read, "And whenever you stand praying, if you have anything against anyone, forgive him, that your Father in heaven may also forgive you." Convicted, Holly listened carefully to what the minister said. As he ended with— "Forgiveness is the key to the Christian life, let us always be aware of all that the Lord has forgiven us and not be in judgment of anyone else," Holly bowed her head and, with as much sincerity as she could muster, forgave Hetty.

When the Communion tray was passed and she partook of the elements, she promised that she would make an attempt to speak and be as pleasant as possible to Hetty after the service.

It became a promise impossible to keep. Before she could leave, one of her pupils' mothers tapped her on the shoulder and engaged her in a long conversation about her Billy's progress. By the time Holly was able to get away and hurry out to the church steps, she saw Ned's wagon pull out of the churchyard. So Holly missed the hoped-for opportunity.

For the rest of the afternoon Holly was very thoughtful. In Willow Springs she had never seemed to need time alone to think, reflect, and pray. But today she felt newly troubled about the rift between herself and her cousin. She knew that both their mothers would be grieved if they knew how deep and wide was the chasm separating their two daughters. Should she go to Hetty? Try to somehow bridge the gap? What could she say that would help?

She needed someone to talk to about it, someone whose advice she could ask, someone she could trust. Naturally, Vi came to mind. Holly bundled up again, for the day had clouded over, and walked to her friend's house. Vi was always comforting to confide in, sensible yet sensitive, practical yet inspiring.

"Come in, come in!" Vi welcomed her. "What a pleasant surprise!"

"I'm not sure you'll think it's so pleasant when you hear what I've come to complain about."

"Well, what are friends for anyway but to lend a listening ear or a shoulder to weep on, if that's called for?" Vi took Holly's coat and waited while Holly unpinned her hat and veil. "You'll have some tea, won't you?"

"That sounds lovely. It's getting colder outside." Holly rubbed her hands as she followed Vi out to her neat little kitchen.

After the tea brewed, Vi put her pink and white pot, two cups, and a plate of caramel cookies on a tray and carried it into the parlor. Vi's parlor, with its starched lace curtains, dark-blue velvet love seat and curved "lady" chairs, was as feminine and fashionable as she was.

"Now, what's the trouble?" she asked as she handed a cup of the fragrant steaming tea to Holly.

Trying to divide the fault as equally as she could, Holly poured out the still unresolved situation between herself and Hetty, confiding the conviction that she now felt she had to do something about it.

"She won't even let Aurelia and Teddy come to see me. I do miss them and . . ." Holly lifted her chin defensively, "I think they miss me, too. Ned says they do."

Vi's eyes were sympathetic. "I understand. So what do you plan to do to heal things between you?"

"Well, today at church what the minister said really hit home. Do you remember the Scripture passage he used?"

"About forgiveness?"

"I intended to make a point of going up to Hetty after the service and as the quotation says 'be reconciled,' but I didn't have a chance."

"Maybe you're going to have to make the opportunity yourself," Vi gently suggested.

Holly made a face. "Oh, I really dread doing that, Vi. You don't know how Hetty can be—"

"No, but I know everyone can be difficult at times. Some of the ladies I sew for can be *very* difficult, *indeed*."

Holly was thoughtful for a moment then finally said, "Other

150

than going to see Hetty, is there something else you think I should do?"

"Praying is the most important thing, Holly. Since you don't feel ready yet, ask the Lord to prepare your heart to go to see Hetty."

"I *have* prayed, Vi, but so far it hasn't done any good. Maybe I'm praying the wrong way."

"I'm not sure there *is* a really wrong way to pray, Holly. I do think when there is something between us and someone else, we need to ask God to do the necessary healing. He knows both hearts. If you're sincere in your desire to make things right between you and your cousin, ask him to prepare *her* heart to receive whatever you say to her. Your part is praying; God will do His."

"Oh, Vi, how did you get so much wisdom?"

Vi laughed. "Through lots of trials and tribulations, Holly, and *lots* of praying!"

As the afternoon was getting late, Holly said she must be going. She gave Vi an impulsive hug before she left and thanked her for her tea and her advice.

That evening Holly got out her Bible and decided to try Vi's method, the same one she had successfully followed when she started the lending library. It wasn't foolproof, as Vi had warned her, but Holly didn't really know what else to do about herself and Hetty. This time the Bible fell open at Proverbs, Chapter 27. Holly squeezed her eyes tight shut and ran her finger down the page, then stopped. Opening her eyes, she glanced at the verse on which her finger had landed, verse 19: "As in water face reveals face, so a man's heart reveals the man." That didn't seem to make much sense or at least didn't satisfy her with the direction she was searching for. Disappointed, Holly closed the book and blew out her lamp and got into bed.

Lying there in the dark, it came into her mind that Hetty had been in church that morning just as she had! Had the minister's words touched *her* heart? It seemed to her that there was fault on both sides, but Holly didn't know how to end the impasse. She sighed, turned her pillow over, and bunched it under her head.

But she couldn't sleep. Although her experiment to get guidance had not seemed to work, the words "be reconciled with your brother" kept repeating themselves in her head. In biblical times a cousin was considered a "brother." Hetty was, after all, her "brother," and she should try to make peace with her.

That was her last thought before going to sleep. In the morning the verse still remained foremost in her mind. By the end of the week Holly knew she must take the first step toward reconciliation, as hard as that was going to be for her to do.

So, on Saturday morning she resolutely walked over to Hetty's house. She took with her a new picture book, from the latest box sent by her mother, for Aurelia and Teddy. The children's presence would break the ice if her cousin met her with the same degree of chill she usually did. Whatever her reception, Holly was determined to get to the bottom of the problem and achieve some kind of truce with Hetty.

To her dismay, Ned had taken the children to the store with him, and Hetty was in the midst of a vigorous end-of-week housecleaning. She met Holly at the door, enveloped in a "coverall" apron, a dust scarf tied around her head, and a stormy expression on her face.

At first Holly did not think Hetty would even ask her in, for she stood there arms crossed, glaring for a full minute before grudgingly opening the door for her. Finally, Hetty stepped back, and Holly walked inside.

Already intimidated by the hostility in Hetty's eyes, Holly realized she was trembling. Holly prayed for courage.

"I brought a lovely new book I'm sure Aurelia and Teddy will enjoy," she began. "Mama sent it, and she sends her love, too, Hetty."

Hetty did not respond immediately, then reluctantly offered, "Would you like some coffee; there's some left from breakfast."

Hardly a gracious gesture, Holly thought, feeling her temper rise. Forcing a tight smile, she said, "Yes, that would be nice." She was determined not to leave before she had a chance to straighten out whatever grudge Hetty was holding against her.

She took a seat at the kitchen table and groped desperately for something noncontroversial to start the conversation.

152

Nothing came. She began to feel tense as Hetty silently got out two cups and then shook the blue-enameled coffeepot before filling them.

Holly saw that Hetty was going to do nothing to make this easy, so in total frustration she just blurted out, "Hetty, why do you dislike me?"

Hetty put the coffeepot back on the stove with a bang. She stood with her back toward Holly for what seemed a long time. When she whirled around, her eyes were flashing. "Dislike you? I don't *dislike* you. Sometimes I even feel sorry for you," she sneered. "You're so pitiful! For the first time in your life you found out that you couldn't have everything you want, so you run away, come out here and then try to take over here just like you did back home. You think you can sweet-talk your way just like you did in Willow Springs, have everyone eating out of your hand. I don't blame Jim Mercer one little bit. In fact, I applaud him. You treated him like dirt, like you did any fellow that was fool enough to show he was interested." She gave a harsh little laugh. "Oh, I've seen you plying your little tricks, using people—my husband included—just like always. Maybe you think you're foolin' folks here, but they'll catch on pretty quick. They'll see through you. Just the way I do."

Shocked, Holly stared at her cousin. "I don't know what you mean, Hetty. When did I ever hurt you?"

Red blotches were coming out on Hetty's face now, her hands were clenched into fists at her side, her lip curled as she continued, "You hurt me plenty. Lots of times. Dozens of times. You ignored me, treated me like I didn't matter—"

"If I did—and I don't remember doing it, I never guessed—"

"How could you?" Hetty demanded furiously. "You were always too busy playing the belle of the ball to notice anyone else!"

"If I did, I'm truly sorry," Holly said contritely.

"Sorry? What good does it do to be sorry *now?*"

"Well, that was *then*, Hetty, this is *now*. If I was a thoughtless, self-centered girl who didn't know she was doing it—we're both women now, can't we possibly put all that aside, be friends?"

Hetty shook her head. "It's too late, Holly. I don't need your

153

friendship. I don't need *you*. I've made a place for myself here. I've got a husband and children, my own friends, and I don't need you anymore."

Holly felt sick and shaken by the bitterness in Hetty. Gone was any pretense of relationship, cousinliness, now even the possibility of friendship. Holly got to her feet, not knowing what more she could say. Then before her horrified gaze, Hetty's features began to break up; she turned away and put her face in her hands and began to sob, the harsh, painful sound of someone who had not cried since childhood.

Helplessly, Holly stood there, knowing if she reached out in comfort she would be rejected. Then Hetty's muffled voice said, "Please go—"

"Hetty, I—"

"I said *go!*"

Unsteadily, Holly made her way to the door, then she turned and looked once more, struggling for something to say. All that came was a broken, "Believe me, I *am* sorry."

But Hetty did not move, turn, nor reply, and Holly left.

Once outside she realized she had been so upset that she had forgotten to leave the book for the children.

She walked through town in a daze, the things Hetty had said ringing in her ears. Had she really been that indifferent, that selfish, that unsympathetic? Vaguely she remembered Mama's urging her to see that Hetty had a good time at one of the impromptu gatherings of young people that seemed to happen so often at their house. She couldn't honestly remember making any concerted effort on Hetty's behalf. With belated realization, Holly knew she had found it flattering and enormous fun to be the center of attention herself and gave little thought to any of the other girls who might be longing for some of the spotlight she had always taken for granted.

How hard that must have been for someone like Hetty, painfully shy, awkward, tall and skinny, and insecure. Holly was genuinely sorry that she had been the cause of some of Hetty's unhappiness, but she couldn't take the blame for all of it. Holly recalled how she had once overheard Aunt Dolly, Hetty's mother, complaining to Holly's mother that Hetty was "impossible, glum, moody, uncooperative—"

Mounting the schoolhouse steps and letting herself into her own apartment, Holly said aloud, "Well, at least I *tried*, didn't I!" She made herself some tea and feeling rather sorry that her sincere efforts for reconciliation had been so rebuffed, she went over some of Hetty's accusations, trying to justify herself.

Unkind? Indifferent? Unfeeling? Maybe she *had* been. She thought of the Scripture she had found at random: "As in water face reveals face, so a man's heart reveals the man."

She had gone to see Hetty to try to make right the difficulty between them. In her heart Holly had believed it was all Hetty's fault. But instead of getting the expected apology from Hetty, she had heard a lot of unpleasant things about herself.

Maybe *her* heart wasn't right. Maybe *she* needed to think about all the things Hetty had said. Whatever Hetty had perceived her to be she *was* different now. She remembered her feelings upon her arrival in Riverbend when the stagecoach driver had shouted—"End of the line!"

In a way, it had been the "end of the line"—at least of one part of her life. That frivolous life she had led with all the careless abandon of a butterfly, the life that had ignored people like Hetty. Things had happened to change her. She had closed that chapter of her life, and she had opened a new one. New things were being written in it. Why couldn't Hetty see that?

Maybe, in time, she would, Holly sighed but with little hope. Hetty had told her to leave. Would she ever feel comfortable returning to Hetty's house after today? When would she get to see Aurelia and Teddy? Sadly, Holly drew the beautiful new edition of *Alice in Wonderland* out of her basket. Idly she turned the pages, looking at its colorful illustrations, pausing to read some of its amusing verses. She had loved *Alice* when she was a child and had wanted so much to share it with Aurelia and Teddy. She stopped at one of Alice's encounters with the White Queen and read, "Consider what a great girl you are. Consider what a long way you've come today. Consider what o'clock it is. Consider anything, only don't cry!"

She too had come a long way from Willow Springs. She had

managed and coped, accomplished and overcome a great many things she would never have thought she could before. She had even often "imagined six impossible things before breakfast!"

God bless Lewis Carroll, Holly thought, closing the book and feeling much better.

If, in spite of all her attempts, Hetty refused to be friends, hadn't she gone the extra mile? Holly shrugged, What else could she do?

Just then she heard the sound of horses hooves, buggy wheels outside. Blaine! Holly felt her heart lift immediately. She jumped up, took a quick glance in her mirror, patted her hair, straightened the brooch on her collar, and hurried to open the schoolhouse door.

Her eager smile faded when she saw that it was *Ad!* He had just thrown the reins over the hitching post and was putting the block on the ground when he looked up and saw her standing at the door.

"Good afternoon, Miss Lambeth," he greeted her making a sweeping bow. "It was such a pleasant day, I rented this and took the liberty of coming out to see if you were free and to suggest we take a nice ride through the countryside? You look like you could use a little outing—or did I mistake the expression on your face for something else? Disappointment?" his smile was slightly sardonic. "Were you expecting someone else?"

Quickly Holly assured him. "No, of course not! And I'd enjoy some fresh air and sunshine! Wait until I get my bonnet and shawl," she told him and ran back inside.

So what did it matter if she had hoped it was Blaine? Holly scolded herself. Ad was always amusing and took her mind off her troubles. And she was foolish to spend time thinking about Blaine Stevens who was a man totally dedicated to his career and far too busy to spend a Saturday afternoon frivolously.

PART 4

Heap on the wood! The wind is chill!
But let it whistle as it will,
We'll keep our Christmas merry still.

Sir Walter Scott

Chapter 17

One Friday early in December as school was dismissed, there was a little more than the usual scramble for the door. As was her practice, Holly followed her students out onto the porch to see them off, to make sure that the older boys didn't start a scuffle or fight. But the excitement that erupted as the children poured through the door, down the steps, and out to the play yard were for a different reason. "It's snowing!" came glad shouts. Holly looked up into the pewter-colored sky. When she saw large snowflakes drifting lazily down, she, too, experienced the same childlike thrill at the sight of the first snow of winter.

Holly had always loved snow, perhaps because her birthday was in December, and at home it had always been celebrated festively. In her happiest memories of childhood, it always seemed to be snowing. Maybe because her parents always gave her a wonderful party. There had been one birthday she remembered with particular joy. She must have been about eleven, and her father had rented a sleigh and all her friends had been invited for a sleigh ride. She could still feel the cold air that made it almost hurt to breathe, the bite of the wind in her face that made her eyes sting, and the merry sound of the sleigh bells ringing as the sleigh skimmed over the icy roads and fields. . . .

Holly wondered if anyone in Riverbend owned a sleigh or if there ever were sleighing parties or carol sings? She put some wood into the stove and got the fire going again, glad she had the whole weekend to herself with no lessons to prepare for the next day.

The following morning when she woke up, the room held a peculiar brightness. Had she overslept? Then she realized that it was Saturday, and there was no school today. She could look forward to a day all her own, a welcome break in the routine of the week. When she finally got up, she saw to her delighted surprise that the ground was covered with a light powdering of snow, and it was still snowing.

It was still snowing when, after her leisurely breakfast, she decided to indulge herself and spend the day reading. It was a perfect day to reread one of her favorites, Charles Dickens' *A Christmas Carol*. Before settling down with it, she looked out the window again. The snow was coming down thicker and faster now. Maybe she'd even get snowed in! She had plenty of wood and food and lots of reading material, so she smiled to herself as she pulled her rocker close to the stove and opened to page one. "Marley was dead, dead as a doornail. . . ."

The next thing she knew, the room was gray, and it was getting hard for her to see. She got up to light her lamp and, at the window, saw that it was still snowing, and in the quickly falling darkness the pine trees at the edge of the road were new shapes of white pyramids. It looked like a Christmas scene, Holly thought. Christmas! An unexpected wave of homesickness surged through her. She'd be spending this Christmas thousands of miles from home. . . .

At Christmas the Lambeth home was very Dickensian. As they had said of Scrooge at the end of the book, her family "really knew how to keep Christmas!" There was a gaily trimmed six-foot cedar in the front hallway by the staircase, its banister and post entwined with evergreen boughs and red ribbons, the mantelpiece in the parlor decorated with red candles and poinsettias, and in the dining room, on the sideboard, was a big cut-glass bowl of eggnog to be offered to the many guests who came calling during the holidays, to be served along with slices of Mama's heritage fruitcake.

There had been parties every night of the week between

Christmas and New Year's and the annual Christmas pageant and program at the church—

A Christmas program! That's what this school needed—a project in which everyone could have a part! One that they could put on for the parents to come and see the children perform. Why, they could have carol singing, and after the Nativity play she could have a party right here in the schoolhouse—

What an inspiration, just the thing to bring parents and children together. Of course, it would mean a lot of work, but it would have such rewards that it would be worth it.

In the weeks that followed, Holly would have to remind herself often of her first enthusiasm. There were days when nothing went right and everything went wrong. The children were inattentive, couldn't remember their lines or the lyrics of the simplest, oldest carols, some of which, to Holly's astonishment, they had never heard before. The old piano badly needed tuning, but she struggled along with it to keep the various-ranged voices on key or at least partially so.

She divided the Christmas story into what she judged were basic scenes with minimal lines for each of the speaking parts to memorize. Even so, such phrases as "Lo, I see yonder Star" and "Be not afraid" proved almost impossible for some to learn or remember. There were moments when Holly was close to desperation that it would not all come together, and many times when she was ready to give the whole thing up.

But the excitement of the children, their eagerness to participate, their anticipation of wearing costumes, and the idea of performing before an audience was contagious. And when Holly was at the point of losing heart, something or somebody rescued her from the brink of despair.

Holly sent notes home with the children, announcing that there would be a Christmas program and a party afterward on the evening of the last school day before the ten-day holiday period.

After that, the days seemed to fly by. Every day Holly used the incentive of play practice and carol singing to get through the regular lessons with dispatch and inspire more effort on the part of the children. She was encouraged by the willingness of

161

most of them to cooperate. Although there was much discussion about the role each one was to play, there seemed to be less squabbling, shoving, pushing, and general naughtiness with the prospect of the Christmas program always ahead.

"I'd like to think it's the Christmas story itself having an effect," Holly sighed half-humorously to Vi one afternoon when she went over to consult with her about costume descriptions to send home to the children's parents.

"Don't underestimate the power of the Word," Vi replied as she went through her scrap bag, getting out materials Holly could use to put together shepherd's robes and strips of sizing to stiffen angel wings.

"While you're here, come see what I've done," Vi suggested, her eyes shining, and she beckoned Holly down the hall and opened a door at the end. "I've redone Avesta's room for a surprise when she comes home for the holidays!" Vi said excitedly watching for Holly's reaction.

"Oh, Vi, it's any girl's dream!" declared Holly stepping into the room and gazing around. There was a white iron bedstead with gracefully scrolled enameled loops and gilded curls covered by a white matelasse woven spread, and a white painted bureau and washstand on which stood a china pitcher and bowl covered with painted pansies. The windows were curtained in gauzy white organdy tied with lavender ribbons. "Oh, she'll love it, Vi," Holly exclaimed.

"I hope so," Vi beamed. "Avesta likes things pretty, feminine, and she loves this color." Vi touched the lace pillows threaded with lavender satin ribbon.

Holly hoped Avesta appreciated her mother and knew she was the center of Vi's life. Now that she was so far away and on her own, Holly had begun to realize how much her own mother had done for her when she lived at home, all the little things that went unnoticed and unacknowledged. Holly left Vi's and headed for Ned's store.

She was anxious to find out if the small Christmas gifts for the children had arrived yet. She had ordered them from one of Ned's catalogues: spinning tops in all colors for the boys, hair slides and ribbons for the girls. She was going to wrap them with each child's name and then tie them to the branches of the Christmas tree in the classroom.

One new experience that Holly was particularly enjoying was managing her own money. At home she had gone to her father whenever she wanted money. Although the Riverbend teacher's salary was small, it gave Holly a feeling of independence to know she had earned it and could spend it any way she liked. She loved using a small part of it to plan the Christmas party.

Before, when Holly ran the lending library, she had discovered that the little world of Riverbend revolved around the General Store. There was always a group of men discussing the weather, the crops, the current topics. Even the women shopping for groceries or dry goods often gave their opinion, made a comment, or expressed their views.

This Saturday when Holly entered there seemed more hubbub than usual in the voices of those gathered around the potbellied stove in the center. The jangle of the bell over the door seemed to go unheard, and she moved immediately over to the counter where Ned was ringing up a purchase. As she waited for Ned to finish with his customer, she overheard the men, inasmuch as none of them were making any attempt to lower their voices. In fact, it seemed they were raised, indignant, and argumentative.

When Ned was free, he smiled and greeted her. "Good morning, Holly, what can I do for you?"

He came over to where she stood, and she leaned toward him, nodding her head to the group at the stove and asking in a low tone, "What's all that about?"

Ned lifted an eyebrow, slipped a folded copy of the *Riverbend Monitor* in front of her, tapped his forefinger to the bold-faced column headed "Editorial."

"Oh, dear, what's Ad been up to now?" she sighed, her eyes racing down the rows of print.

WHO STILL BELIEVES THE RAILROAD IS COMING THROUGH RIVERBEND?

Only the people who will benefit continue to perpetuate this

163

myth; namely Miller's Brickyard, Tidwell's Lumber Mill, Bankers, Realtors, possibly the politicians if they can convince their constituents that their clout will make the planners and the Eastern owners of the railroad companies change their minds—which of course won't happen! These decisions are usually made in Washington, D.C., and that's where the "Big Boys" play.

All the usually "reliable sources" we've checked have told me the railroad is NOT coming to Riverbend; the town of Medford will get the proposed branch line from San Francisco to Portland, NOT Riverbend.

"Uh-oh!" Holly said softly as she raised her head and met Ned's eyes. "Ad's in big trouble now." Ned nodded solemnly and gave a shake of his head.

The store was filling up with people getting their weekend supplies so Ned and Holly had no more time to discuss their friend's latest published opinion. Ned checked the shelves of the post office, found Holly's package, and she left.

The day was windy and overcast, and Holly's thoughts were as storm-tossed as the clouds overhead as she walked home. Why did Ad always stir up something, "trouble the waters"? Maybe it was his "exile mentality," the thing that he claimed was *their* bond, that neither one of them really belonged in Riverbend, that their stay was temporary and they had no stake in what happened, that they were both "birds of passage."

But Ad was wrong about her, Holly thought, as she turned into the school yard. Something definitely had happened to her. She wasn't sure just what. She could feel it. Everything was drawing her in, deeper, closer—almost as if she was becoming part of everything—the hills, the river, the town, the people— like the Healys, the members of the Literary Society, the friends she had made, Vi, the Bodine sisters, Mr. Clegg, and Rupert Benson—and the children, especially the children—Aurelia and Teddy, of course, and Joel and Cissy, *and—Blaine Stevens*.

Holly let herself into the schoolhouse door. No matter if she left in June, she *did* care about this community, about the people.

Since Vi had volunteered to make the more elaborate costumes needed for the Three Kings, having, as she did, a great many odds and ends of trimmings for the robes of these potentates from the Far East, Holly was left with the more mundane task of fashioning costumes for the lowly shepherds. She was busily sorting among piles of flour sacks that had been washed then dyed, mounds of old curtains, and pieces of quilting on the Saturday before the program was scheduled when Ad dropped by the schoolhouse.

"Oh, it's you," she said offhandedly when she opened the door.

"Well, that's not much of a welcome," he pretended offense.

"I'm sorry. I'm just feeling rather cross. I'm not a great hand at sewing, and I have a half-dozen shepherds to garb properly for the Christmas play," she explained, settling down again.

Ad sauntered around the kitchen, stopping at the table where some of the material and balls of varicolored yarn were stacked. He picked up a piece of material at random. "What are these for?" he asked curiously.

Holly looked up briefly, then back at the stiff cloth through which she was trying to push her needle. With one finger free, she made a circle around her head. "It's for one of those towel kind of things they wore on their heads, and we'll braid the yarn for what goes around it to hold it in place."

"Oh, you mean a 'kufiyya' and an 'iqal,'" nodded Ad.

Holly blinked a couple of times, demanding in astonishment. "How do you know that sort of thing?"

"Oh, editors have all sorts of sources of information," Ad shrugged. "Or bored bachelors do crossword puzzles to wile away lonely evenings, read dictionaries, peruse encyclopedias."

Holly threw him a quizzical look. "Maybe that's time better spent than writing inflammatory editorials."

"So, you heard about that, huh?"

"Who in Riverbend hasn't?"

Ad scowled. "People don't like to hear the truth."

"Well, you sure started a firestorm with this one. You should hear what they're saying at Ned's store."

Ad did not reply. He walked idly around the room, then stopped at the chest where Holly's photo album was placed.

Busy with her work, Holly did not notice at once that he was looking through it. After a few minutes she realized he had stopped turning the pages and was studying one in particular. She glanced over, and he turned his head to meet her gaze. His tone was indifferent, but his eyes held hers intently as he asked, "Who's the dashing soldier boy?"

For a second, Holly was tempted to retort, "None of your business." But then she thought, *Why not?* and with a slight shrug replied, "Lieutenant Jim Mercer. We were engaged."

"To be married?"

"No! For the next dance!" she said flippantly, then, "*Of course,* to be married."

"What happened? Did you change your mind?"

Holly hesitated then blurted out, "No. He did."

"When was this?"

"About two months before I came to Riverbend."

Ad closed the album abruptly. "Then why do you still keep his pictures?"

Again Holly shrugged, "I'm really not sure."

"He must be some kind of fool," Ad said quietly.

"Oh, no, he's very bright, very smart. He graduated way at the top of his class from West Point," she said continuing to take stitches.

"Then why—?"

Holly put down her sewing with an exasperated sigh and said, "Adam Corcoran, did anyone ever tell you that you ask too many questions?"

"It's the reporter in me; it's in the blood."

"Well, if you want to know the truth, he married someone else."

As soon as the words were out of her mouth, Holly was surprised that it didn't hurt. The old feelings of humiliation and shame seemed somehow to have disappeared. In fact, she felt an unexpected sensation of freedom as if she had shaken off an old burden.

"I'd get rid of the pictures if I were you," Ad said casually. He sauntered over to the door. There he turned back and looked at Holly for a long minute. "You're a very special lady, Miss Holly

Lambeth." At that he made an obeisance, said, "Shalom," turned on his heel, and walked out of the room, then she heard the schoolhouse door shut.

The last day before the holidays was the date of the Christmas program. That week was fraught with mishaps and anxiety. Holly had always heard dress rehearsals were usually disasters, and that a bad one guaranteed a wonderful opening performance. Considering how terrible theirs was, she fervently prayed that the old adage was true. The children stumbled over lines that had been word-perfect in practice; some tripped over the unaccustomed shepherd's robes; angel wings fell off; the Kings' crowns toppled; and the beard refused to stay glued to the Innkeeper's chin.

When Adam had come by to get the details of the program so he could do a preview article and announcement for the paper, Holly told him about the party she was having after the performance. "I want to have a tree and all the trimmings. I'm sure some of the children have never had a *real* Christmas," she confided. "I've sent away through one of Ned's catalogs for paper cornucopias, colored crepe paper. I'm going to have the children make their own decorations, cut and paste rings to drape on the boughs, and we'll pop corn and string cranberries too."

"You really love doing all this, don't you?" Ad asked her with an appraising look.

"Yes, I do," Holly replied almost defensively. "I always assumed that everyone had the same kind of childhood I had, but I'm finding out that people coming to settle out here had so many other things—*survival* things—to do, that some of the fun things, the things that give flavor and lightness to life—got lost." She paused for a minute, then said, "I guess they were considered less important, and maybe they are—but, no, not really. I *do* think they're important. And it's so much fun for me to see how happy these things make the children."

At last the night of the program arrived. The schoolroom had been turned into a theater. Matt Healy had donated chairs from the Town Hall and brought them over in his wagon the afternoon of the performance. As he helped Holly set them in rows, he said, "Riverbend children have never had something like this, Miss Lambeth. Everybody's mighty excited about it. I think the parents don't know what to expect, but they're proud that their kids are being treated special."

"I'm glad. I hope everything goes well!" Holly said. She couldn't remember ever feeling more nervous.

Geneva had offered to help backstage, where a flimsy curtain had been strung across one end of the schoolroom. As the parents began to assemble, Holly greeted them at the door, trying not to let the sounds of loud whispers and shuffling behind the stage distract her too much.

Holly was even pleased to see people who didn't have children in school arrive to support this first dramatic effort on the part of the school. When she saw Ned come with Aurelia and Teddy, Holly thought that perhaps in the spirit of the season, her cousin had put aside her animosity and come. But Ned mumbled that Hetty had a sick headache and wasn't up to coming. Holly sympathized even though she knew it was only an excuse.

Her rueful feelings were fleeting, however, because her attention was needed elsewhere. With everything in readiness, she had to begin the program. As she stepped forward to make her opening announcement, she saw, with happy surprise, Blaine step into the back of the room. She was glad she had chosen a very becoming red taffeta dress frilled with Irish lace to wear for the occasion.

To her amazement and everyone else's delight, the production came off without any hitches—at least none that were visible to the audience. Of course, there were actors whose minds went blank at the novelty of wearing a toga or the sight of his or her parents' faces in the crowd; loud promptings from Holly were seemingly unheard by the rapt viewers. The audience, at Holly's invitation, joined in the final singing of "Hark, the Herald Angels Sing" with reverent gusto, and then rose to give the players a standing ovation.

When the grinning cast had taken three curtain calls, Holly held up her hand to quiet the applause and spoke, "I want everyone to please stay for refreshments and for each child to take a gift off the tree."

The party started in full force and the little schoolhouse rang with voices, laughter, and merriment as people mingled, greeted one another, helped themselves to the variety of food provided by the parents; and the actors and actresses, still resplendent in their makeshift costumes, enjoyed being the center of attention. There were cries of excitement as the children found their presents from Holly tied to the tree; the boys began top-spinning contests immediately, while the girls helped each other with the hair slides and ribbons.

Ad complimented Holly and remarked dramatically, "I shall give this a four-star review in my newspaper. Theatrical agents and managers from all over will be beating a path to the door, wanting to sign up all these youthful thespians."

"Oh, Ad!" Holly dismissed his teasing. "But do be sure you check with me so that you get all the children's names and spell them right before you print it in the paper. I know every parent will want to save the clipping when they see it."

Just then Blaine came up and joined them. "Great show, Holly. Everyone did splendidly. You have a real gift for working with children."

"Why thank you, Blaine." Pleased and flattered by his comment, Holly was annoyed to feel herself blushing and even more annoyed to see that Ad noticed it.

After the evening was over one particular incident stood out in Holly's mind. During the party she had felt a tug on her sleeve and turned to see Joel standing beside her holding the hand of a pale, hollow-faced woman. Cissy, looking anxious, stood beside her. "Miss Lambeth, this is our Ma," Joel said.

"Oh, I'm so pleased to meet you, Mrs. McKay," Holly exclaimed. She extended her hand to the shabbily dressed woman and felt a thin, work-roughened hand in her grasp. "Your children are so bright, a real pleasure to teach."

The woman seemed ill-at-ease and hardly looked up as she stammered something in reply.

Holly wanted to talk to her more, try to draw her out, see what she could find out from the mother, but one of the other parents, who was leaving, tapped her on the arm, and Holly had to give them her attention. By the time they had left, so had the McKays.

Later, as she tidied up the remnants of the party, Holly found among the presents that some of the children had given her, a booklet Joel had made for her of carefully pressed leaves. With it was a small card, soiled by much redoing, laboriously printed lopsided letters, "Luv from Cissy." Both gifts brought tears to Holly's eyes. Most of the presents from the other children were the handiwork of their mothers—crocheted pot holders, jars of candied peaches, boxes of homemade fudge—Holly knew *these* were the ones that she would cherish most.

With school closed for two weeks for the holidays, Holly enjoyed the first free time she had had for months. Knowing the slowness of the mails, Holly had sent her Christmas gifts to her friends and family in Willow Springs right after Thanksgiving. But some things she had ordered by catalog had only just arrived. Even though she knew they would get there late, she wrapped them and planned to mail them anyway. She was on her way into the post office, located at Ned's store when she met Vi coming down the steps.

One look at her friend's face and Holly knew immediately that something was wrong. Usually so poised, Vi seemed distracted and distressed. Holly had to catch her arm and speak to her or else Vi might have gone right past her. "Oh, sorry, Holly, I didn't see you—"

"What's the matter, Vi? Has something happened?"

Vi's eyes brightened with unshed tears. She quickly tried to blink them away.

"Oh, it's nothing really! I just got a letter from Avesta, and she's not coming—"

"Not coming?" gasped Holly, knowing what a keen disappointment this must be to Vi. "After all you've done to get ready for her? Why not?"

Vi whisked out a handkerchief and dabbed her eyes before the traitorous tears could overflow. She tried to smile, but her lips quivered at the attempt. "She's had a lovely invitation to

170

spend the holidays with one of her classmates. The girl's family lives in California, and they've asked Avesta to come with them to San Diego to stay at the Del Coronado. It's a beautiful place, a luxurious resort. They have all sorts of things planned for the girls—it's a wonderful opportunity for Avesta to meet the right people." Vi's voice cracked a little, and Holly pressed her friend's hand.

"I'm sorry, Vi, I know how much you were looking forward to Avesta's coming," was all she could think to say to comfort her.

"But, I'm really happy for her, Holly. Really! I mean that's why I sent her away to boarding school. I wanted her to have nice friends, girls from good families who would open doors for her—" She smiled bravely. "There wouldn't be much for her to do here during the holidays, anyway. What girl of sixteen wants to sit home with her mother and sew, for goodness' sake, when she could be horseback riding and dancing and going to parties and balls?"

Holly nodded sympathetically. She felt a sharp twinge, remembering her own former life of parties and festivities—she, too, would probably have chosen the same option as Avesta had at that age.

"It's all right, Holly. I'll be fine. I think I'll have a party on Christmas anyway. You'll come, of course, won't you? Unless you have other plans."

"Yes, of course. I mean, no, I have no plans," Holly agreed, sure that no invitation from Hetty was forthcoming. "I'd love to come, Vi."

Chapter 18

*W*hen she first heard about the town's annual Christmas Dance, Holly wasn't sure she wanted to go. But she discovered there was no way of getting out of going. The town schoolteacher was expected to be there along with everyone else in Riverbend. Once she had resigned herself that her attendance was, in fact, a "command performance" due to her position, she found she was looking forward to it. She began to think that it might be fun. It had been such a long time since she had had a chance to get dressed up and step out.

As she thought about what to wear, she remembered with some chagrin that it was only at her mother's insistence that she had brought a suitable party dress with her. Now, as she got it out from her trunk, Holly recalled the day she had watched indifferently as her mother carefully packed it in layers of tissue paper. Then, feeling utterly rejected by Jim, she had felt she would never want to go to another party or dance as long as she lived. She was going to Oregon to "lick her wounds," not to dress up or go to parties! How long ago that seemed. Her life had changed so much since she had left Willow Springs, brokenhearted. Strangely enough, days went by when she hadn't even thought of Jim.

Holly shook out the dress, spreading the skirt across her bed and trying to see it through the eyes of the other ladies who would be in attendance. She knew that as the schoolmarm she would have to pass a gauntlet of criticism as to the appropriateness of what she wore. Examining it critically, she decided that it was much too frothy, too ruffled, too much décolletage for Riverbend. She would have to do something about the neckline for sure—

Maybe she should consult Vi, ask her expert opinion, Holly decided and bundling the dress up in a box, she walked over to Vi's.

Vi ushered her into her fitting room and had Holly put on the dress.

"It's such beautiful material, I'd hate to do anything drastic to change it," she murmured. "But, truthfully, it is a little dressier than most of the Riverbend ladies would wear to the Christmas party—"

"Well, I certainly don't want to wear anything inappropriate."

"No, of course not. Let me think what we can do," Vi circled Holly, "Uh-huh. Well, now, just let's see." Narrowing her eyes Vi surveyed the dress critically. With another "Uh-huh," she held out the material and, nodding, began snipping here and there, making a few tucks with pins taken from the red tomato pincushion strapped on her wrist. Her "magic" needle did the rest.

"How's that?" she asked Holly turning her toward the full-length mirror. Holly saw that Vi had filled in the scoop neckline with some judiciously placed netting, removed some of the roses and rearranged them, and taken off two rows of ruffles. "There now, you'll look pretty as a picture, but you won't cause any 'green-eyed' remarks about looking too citified. A schoolmarm has to be as 'without reproach' as Caesar's wife—or in *Riverbend*," she added dryly, "—as the minister's wife."

"Thanks, Vi!" Holly gathered up her things and started to leave, then asked, "You're coming, too, aren't you?"

"Oh, yes, I will for awhile. The Bodine sisters asked me to go with them, so we'll be there."

"Good! Then, you'll see me in all my finery. Thank you so much, Vi." Impulsively Holly gave her a hug. "You're a wonderful friend. I don't know what I'd do without you."

"Good-bye, Calpurnia," Vi laughed, and Holly went out the door.

As she walked down the street toward the schoolhouse, the

door of the *Monitor* opened and Ad stuck his head out and greeted her. "Afternoon, Holly. Just wanted to make sure you were going to the dance tomorrow night?"

"Yes, I am, are you?"

"Wouldn't miss it," he grinned. "Polishing up my dancin' shoes."

She regarded him skeptically. "I thought you didn't mix socially."

"Well, I've got to cover it for the paper since I don't have a society editor," he said straightfaced but with twinkling eyes.

Holly shook her head, smiling.

"Be sure and save me a dance," Ad called, as with a wave of her hand she walked on.

The morning of the dance, Holly washed her hair in the newly collected rain water, then sat in front of the stove, drying and brushing it until it crackled and shone with russet lights. Early in the evening she bathed, lavished herself with her rose cologne, put on two petticoats, one cotton and one taffeta that rustled and swished with each movement; then she slipped into the remodeled gown.

Holly did not realize how her new life had enhanced her looks. The rigorous routine of keeping up the little apartment and schoolhouse, chopping wood, carrying pails of water from the well, the exercise of playing games like "Run, Sheep, Run" and "Drop the Handkerchief" with the children outside in the schoolyard, her long walks in the woods and back and forth to town, all had contributed to not only a feeling of well-being, but a radiantly glowing complexion and a slenderly rounded figure.

Even with its altering, the dress was very becoming. For an added effect, Holly tucked some of the silk roses removed from the skirt into her hair.

The dance was not scheduled to start until nine o'clock. Party or no party, farm chores had to be done, cows milked, livestock brought in and fed. Town folks had to close their stores and places of business. Men working in the woods, the local "lumberjacks," had to get into town, pick up their paychecks, patronize the barber shop and hotel baths before going over to the

Town Hall. People living in outlying areas or coming from other districts had to drive their wagons long distances. But no one would miss this annual event, the high spot of the year for most people, a chance to get together for some fellowship and fun no matter how far they had to come or what the weather was like.

The weather was clear but with a definite bite in the air, Holly discovered after sticking her head out the door, trying to decide whether to wear her fur tippet and carry her muff or just her hooded cape. She decided on the cape. The fur ensemble might appear too fancy, as if she were showing off. Her acceptance in Riverbend had been too hard-won to gamble on losing the ladies' goodwill.

It was after eight-thirty when the pounding on the door announced the arrival of Matt and Geneva Healy, who were to take her to the Town Hall.

"Well, if you don't look like a picture, all duded up," was Matt's hearty comment when she opened the door.

"Thanks, Matt—I *think!*" Holly laughed. "I'll be with you in a minute."

"I'll wait for you in the wagon."

Holly flung her cape around her shoulders, wound the delicate knitted "fascinator" over her hair, gathered up her gloves and small velvet evening bag, and hurried outside. The sky was a satiny dark, pin-pointed with a few brilliant stars. Matt assisted her into the wagon alongside Geneva who exclaimed, "My, oh, my, Holly, you smell good enough to sprinkle on my best linens!"

"Oh, Geneva, I love the way you put things! I hope it's not too much!"

"Not a bit, darlin', just lovely like a spring garden." Geneva reassured her. "And like Matt said, you look so sweet; you're not going to have a chance to set down all night, you'll have so many dance partners."

A chorus of greetings came from the back of the wagon where all the little Healys were bundled down, scarfed and mittened. In Riverbend children were welcome at every event; besides, there was usually no one to leave them with at home.

After returning their greetings, Holly turned to Geneva and asked, "Tell me what to expect at this party."

"Well, first we just sorta socialize, you know, just mix and mingle with folks, some of the ones that come from Mills Flat we don't see but once or twice a year; then the music kind of gets agoin', and the dancing begins—"

"And then we eat, and that's the best part!" Matt chuckled.

"Now, Matthew, you know you like to square dance as much or more'n anybody," Geneva chided. "Well, around eleven or so, when folks are gettin' a little hot and tired, we set out the food—I brought my fried chicken and my marble cake—all the ladies try to bring their very finest recipe—"

"Oh, dear, should I have brought something?" Holly worried.

"Oh, no, honey, nobody'll expect *you* to bring anything!" exclaimed Geneva.

"Single gals are there to set their caps for the bachelors in the bunch!" Matt put in.

"Now, you hush, Matt, you're goin' to have Holly all nerves 'fore we get there. Listen here, Holly, there's going to be so much those tables are going to be groanin'. Not only desserts but hot dishes and pies, and I don't know what all."

"I'm sure countin' on Annie Olsen's bringing her stack cake and Hazel Burrows her 'Impossible' pie—" Matt smacked his lips in anticipation.

Ignoring him, Geneva patted Holly's hand again. "Believe me, Holly, you're going to be a special guest at this party. You're just there to enjoy yourself. You've worked hard all this time with all our young'ns, and everybody's so grateful you took over and done so well. Why, everyone's still talking about the Christmas program. We never had one like it before. All the parents are so pleased that their youngsters had a part and did them proud."

As Matt pulled the wagon up into the row of buggies and wagons lined up at the fence in front of Town Hall, lights were shining out of the oblong windows. They could hear the sound of voices, laughter, and the squeak of band instruments being tuned. Holly felt her spirits lift happily.

"Give me a hand with this basket, Matt," Geneva directed,

and Matt helped her down, then offered an arm apiece to both and escorted them toward the hall, with the Healy youngsters trailing along behind.

Outside, ranged along the steps, were a number of young men. All heads turned in their direction as they approached. A wave of sound, muted whistling, and mumbled comments reached Holly's burning ears as she felt at least a dozen pairs of eyes upon her. Geneva squeezed her arm and whispered, "Don't pay them no mind, Holly; they don't have polished manners, but they're all nice fellows. That's just their way of admiring a lady."

Inside it was bright, noisy, and warm. All along the sides of the big room were plank tables resting on sawhorses covered with white paper and festooned with crinkly yards of twisted red and white paper ribbon. Women were busily scurrying about putting all sorts of platters, bowls, and covered dishes out on each one.

"I'll just take my things over there and see if I can help out," Geneva said and went bustling off, the youngest Healy child holding onto her skirt while the others ran to be with friends they had spotted. Matt had stopped at the door to talk to some men, and Holly found herself left standing alone.

Then, directly across the room she saw Hetty in conversation with another woman. Hetty must have seen her come in with the Healys, but when Holly tried to catch her eye, her hand raised in a little wave of greeting, Hetty turned her head. Deliberately! Holly was sure.

Holly felt the old rage rise up in her. Where was her cousin's holiday spirit? Couldn't she at least make an effort at Christmas? Holly knew that her mother and Aunt Dolly would be sick at heart if they knew the situation between their daughters. Well, she certainly wasn't going to walk over and barge in where she obviously was being ignored.

Embarrassed to be snubbed so blatantly, Holly pretended to admire the festive appearance of the room. The decorating committee had done a fine job. Boughs of cedar tied with shiny red ribbons were draped all around, wreaths bright with holly, and glistening gilt bows hung over the doorways and in the windows. The little band on the raised platform at one end of the room was tuning up, sawing at their fiddles, plucking the strings, and twisting the tuning pegs, as the piano player tried to help them by striking one key.

Still smarting from Hetty's snub, Holly looked around for a friendly face and saw the mother of one of her pupils nearby. After exchanging greetings, she asked where she should put her wrap and was directed to an annex that had been utilized as a cloakroom for the ladies. Besides a coat rack, makeshift cots lined the walls so that sleeping babies and worn-out tots could be put to sleep if the hour got late and the party was still in full swing. In one corner were piled quilts, blankets, and pillows belonging to those who had come from so far away that they would stay overnight rather than face a cold ride home in the chilly dawn.

On the far side of the room a mirror hung over a long shelf. Loath to return immediately to the main room and perhaps experience again the humiliation of having her cousin ignore her publicly, Holly spent longer than necessary fussing with her hair and checking the tiny buttons on her gloves. For the first time in her life Holly understood what used to puzzle her back in Willow Springs—why some of the less popular girls had virtually hid out in dressing rooms at dances and parties, afraid to venture back to the ballroom where their dance cards might be left blank and they would be relegated to being "wallflowers."

When she could delay no longer without being conspicuous, Holly swallowed her pride and reentered the main room now filled with people. To her relief just then, she saw Adam walk in the door. Dressed in a fine dark suit, a frilled white shirt, and a flowing black tie, he could have been on his way to some fancy San Francisco social event. She was grateful when she saw him heading toward her.

He greeted her with a lavish compliment. "Good evening, Miss Lambeth, if you aren't looking as dazzling as a star on top of the Christmas tree! And may I have the first dance and sign your card for a few other dances before those rascals lining up over there fill it all up?"

"Of course, you may, but I don't think this will be a card dance."

"No, I don't suppose so. It's just first come, first served, I understand. I just wanted to make you feel at home where, I imagine, you barely get inside the door of any ballroom before your dance card is filled."

"Oh, Ad, don't tease!"

"Homesick?"

"Not exactly. But Christmas is a kind of sentimental time, don't you think? Thoughts of home and family and that sort of thing."

"But you have family right here. Aren't you spending the holidays with your cousin?"

Holly lowered her eyes, biting her lip, wondering how to tell the truth without making Hetty a pariah for not inviting her. "Oh, the music seems to be starting!" she exclaimed, skillfully diverting the conversation and the necessity of answering Ad's question.

There was immediate comprehension in his eyes. Ad held out his hand to her and as he spun her out onto the dance floor, he said, "Well, don't fret about it. I believe Vi is having a party for all of us who are a long way from home, and I'm *sure* you're invited there."

"Aren't you going, too? I know Vi mentioned that she was inviting you."

"Yes, she was gracious enough to do so; however, I don't plan to be here over the holidays. I'm going out of town."

"On a rail? After that editorial I wouldn't be surprised!" Holly teased, her eyes sparkled wickedly.

"No, folks have been surprisingly tolerant—or maybe it's just the Christmas spirit. So far no one has volunteered to provide tar and feathers. But just between me and thee, I may look around, test the waters, so to speak, for another position while I'm gone."

"In case the town fathers are secretly searching for a new editor?"

"Not that either. I think I may just be ready to end my exile."

"We'll miss you," Holly said, realizing that it was the truth.

179

"Perhaps absence will make the heart grow fonder."

"On the other hand: Out of sight, out of mind!" she laughed.

Ad pretended a scowl. "There's no verbal sparring with a schoolmarm."

Although they had some trouble measuring their steps to the band's first halting attempts at a waltz, Adam was a superb dancer with a strong lead and was able to make the set enjoyable in spite of the struggling band. Gradually the musicians seemed to get their instruments into harmony, and the next set, consisting of a lively polka then a popular schottische, was better. That was the last of the round dances because after that, Bill Hanum got on stage and began calling, "Gentlemen, choose your partners; we're going to do some high-steppin' square dancing."

At this there was applause, and before Adam could offer his arm to Holly, Matt Healy had come up and claimed her for his partner.

People lined up, men on one side, women on the other; then the command "Circle round" was shouted, and everyone joined hands and started moving. It was great fun, exhilarating and energetic. "Do-si-do, round you go, find yourself a pretty gal and swing her to the right." Sounds of clapping hands and shuffling feet were mingled with shouts and much laughter. Holly had to listen to get things straight because there were some new calls here in Riverbend she had never heard before. She found herself being swung right off her feet by some hearty man at times and giggling as she made mistakes and was pulled into line by others as she tried to keep up with the dance.

Finally the music reached a high crescendo and, with a loud twang of a fiddle, stopped at last; everyone was flushed, breathless and nearly exhausted.

"Just so you *old folks* can take it easy for awhile 'fore the next Virginia reel, we're goin' to have a Paul Jones," Bill Hanum announced, and the band began playing a soft, gentle melody. The idea of this dance was that when the caller blew his whistle and the band stopped playing, whoever you were facing became your partner. Whether by accident or design, Holly was never sure, but she found herself in front of Blaine.

180

Surprised, she said, "Why, Blaine, I didn't know you were coming!"

"I wasn't sure myself. I just got here, as a matter of fact. I had to make a call out on the old Mine Road. But now I hope everyone in Riverbend is alive and well, and from the looks of things, they are all right here!" he laughed.

There wasn't time for any more talk then because the circle began to move again, the music flowed and then stopped again. Holly had a succession of partners until the end of the piece. When intermission was called, Blaine magically appeared at her side again. People were thronging toward the tables, where cups of refreshment were being ladled out of huge punch bowls.

"May I see you home, Holly?" Blaine asked as they left the circle.

Pleased that he had asked, Holly wasn't sure if it would be considered proper since she had come with the Healys. As she hesitated, a look of disappointment crossed Blaine's readable face. "You've promised someone else?"

"Oh, no, it's not that; it's just that I came with Geneva and Matt and—well, actually, it's really out of their way to go around by the schoolhouse since their farm is out in the other direction—"

"You don't need an excuse to say yes, Holly," he teased. "I'm sure that Geneva and Matt won't mind; in fact, they'd probably approve."

A little embarrassed that it was so transparent she *had* been doing exactly that, Holly unfurled her little fan and fluttered it, murmuring, "My, it is very warm in here, isn't it?"

Still looking amused, Blaine said, "I'll go get us some punch; you wait here." With his hand under her arm, he guided her to one of the chairs along the wall and headed toward the punch bowl.

With the press of people and all the exertion of the lively dancing, the room did seem very hot. Holly fanned briskly to cool off while she looked around. As she did, she saw Ad's towering figure pushing through the crowd, carrying two cups of punch.

"Here you are!" he said triumphantly as he handed one to

her. "I wasn't sure I was going to make it through that mob," he sighed as he sat down in the empty chair beside her.

"Thank you, Ad, that was very kind of you, but Blaine just went to get me some," Holly said, a little apologetically.

Ad frowned. "Well, you can drink two cups, can't you? It's hot enough in here."

Holly took a sip, knowing that Adam was miffed.

"Well, I better ask you for the next dance *now*, I guess," he grumbled.

"I *think* I heard somebody say it's going to be a Paul Jones."

Ad made a sound of disgust. "I'm not sure I approve of this kind of dance rather than card dances," he growled. "Well, the first one after the Paul Jones then?"

Before she could reply, they saw Blaine approaching. Ad stood up, leaving the chair next to hers empty for him. While the two men exchanged greetings, Holly gulped down the rest of the cranberry punch, then she quickly slid her first empty cup out of sight under her chair and accepted the one that Blaine handed her. Ad left them, and a few minutes later the Paul Jones was announced.

During the dance Holly had several partners because every time the music stopped she was standing in front of a different man. This way Holly had a chance to chat with some of the fathers of her students, and she enjoyed hearing them say that their children were enjoying school.

When the Paul Jones ended, the band played a fanfare and the caller shouted, "Gentlemen, claim your ladies for the last dance."

Ad was at her side instantly and, making a great show of checking a nonexistent dance card and giving an elaborate bow, said, "I believe this one is mine."

"Well, I . . ." began Holly, looking uncertainly at Blaine who had also come up.

Blaine motioned toward the Healys and said, "I'll give you the pleasure, Ad, since I'm taking Holly home. I'll just go tell Matt and Geneva. I'll meet you at the door, Holly."

Ad said nothing, just bowed and held out his hand to lead Holly onto the dance floor, but his expression was ironic as he remarked, "I thought the proper etiquette was for your partner for the last dance of the evening to escort you home. Evidently I was wrong."

Holly tried to soothe his evident irritation. "Weren't you the one who informed me that Riverbend affairs followed no prescribed pattern?"

He made a grimace. "Hoisted on my own petard."

"*Or* 'snared by the words of your *own* mouth'," she retorted, reminding him of his contention that he knew Scripture.

"I'm just a little surprised that our serious, dedicated young doctor has time to attend dances and see young ladies home!" He glanced over her head around the room, asking in an aggrieved tone, "Why couldn't one of those overfed men or chubby children suddenly get an attack of food poisoning? Or one of the ladies faint and need the ministrations of our town physician? I'd counted on seeing you to your doorstep myself."

"I'm sorry, Adam. Thank you, anyway," Holly said, feeling a little rush of satisfaction. *How* flattering having two such attractive men vying for her favors. It was like old times in Willow Springs!

Almost at once she felt the prick of conscience. Wasn't she over all that sort of foolishness? Had she only thought she was? *What a silly shallow person I am after all!* Yet she still couldn't help the little bubble of excitement inside as the music ended and Ad reluctantly released her to Blaine.

"Ready?" Blaine asked.

"I'll just get my wrap," she told him.

"I'll wait for you at the door."

Holly hurried to get her cape, but when she came out, Blaine had disappeared. In another minute or so he reappeared and apologized, saying that one of the women had asked him to take a look at her child who seemed feverish. As Blaine took Holly's arm to assist her down the steps now coated with an icy glaze, he said, "Sorry about that."

"I hope it wasn't anything serious."

"No, probably too much cake, pie, and punch. He'll be fine in the morning. A doctor's never 'off duty' even at a party."

"It's all right. I understand," Holly said.

"Do you? Most women—I mean, most people don't." He helped her into his buggy then went around and took the blanket off his horse. He folded it over his arm and, as he patted the horse's neck, Holly heard Blaine speak to him. "What a good old fella. Long time out here in the cold. Well, we'll be getting warmed up, trotting out Lincoln Road to take the schoolmarm home." Holly smiled in the darkness, touched by Blaine's unselfconscious concern for his horse, his gentleness.

He got back into the buggy, picked up the reins, flicked them a couple of times, and they started off through the night. At least a hundred thousand more stars seemed to stud the sky since earlier, and the horse's hooves on the frost-skimmed road made a crunch sound in the stillness.

"Nice party. At least the end of it," Blaine remarked. "I hadn't planned to get there so late, but just as I was leaving my rooms Seth Hilliard rode in to say all three of the children had real bad coughs and the baby was having trouble breathing, so I went out there to take a look at them." Blaine shook his head. "Never can understand why folks wait so long to call a doctor. I could have given them something days ago and none of them would be this bad—" He broke off. "Sorry, shouldn't bore you with shop talk."

"You're not, and Denny Hilliard is in school. How is he— and the others? Are they going to be all right?"

"Yes, the older ones, certainly. I'm a little worried about the baby. I'll take another ride out there tomorrow and see," Blaine said, then changed the subject abruptly. "—You warm enough?"

"Yes, it is very cold, though. Think it will snow again?"

"Possibly." Blaine turned to glance over at her. "That's right—this will be your first Oregon winter, won't it? I almost forgot. You seem to have become a part of the community, fit in so easily, like you'd always been here."

"Why, thank you, Blaine. That's nice of you to say so."

"Well, of course, your coming has made a difference."

"Really?"

"Sure you have. The parents really liked the Christmas program; I've heard nothing but good about it."

"That's nice to know. I hoped they would. It means a great deal to have the parents think I'm doing a good job with the children and all."

"And of course, you've also brightened up the place, prettied the scenery too, as they say around here," he laughed.

Pleased, Holly smiled in the darkness. Blaine didn't toss compliments around lightly. Not like Ad, whose charm was second nature; flowery phrases came easily to him.

Even though her toes were freezing in her thin dancing slippers, the ride to the schoolhouse seemed to Holly to come to an end too soon.

"Whoa!" Blaine reined to a stop at the side of the school building, then jumped out of the buggy, came around, and held out both hands to help Holly down. He accompanied her up the steps and unlocked the door for her.

As he handed her back her key, their fingers touched. For a minute, Holly could not breathe. All at once everything became dazzlingly focused: the snow-scented wind, the brilliance of the stars overhead.

Both of them stood very still, their frosted breath mingling in the darkness. Holly swayed slightly toward Blaine, felt his hands tighten on her elbows as he steadied her. Holly felt that Blaine was about to kiss her, and instinctively she started to close her eyes—

Then, suddenly, through the clear night air came the sound of horses, the jangle of harness bells, voices ringing out Christmas songs, and around the bend of the road came a wagon load of merry-makers from the Town Hall, the swinging lanterns sending arcs of light onto the snow and throwing the two figures on the schoolhouse porch into full view.

"Howdy, folks!" the voices called heartily as the wagon lumbered by. "Merry Christmas, Miss Lambeth, Merry Christmas, Doc!" The laughing faces were illuminated, and Holly recognized most of them— all people she knew, parents and pupils alike, folks she had met through the lending library.

After the merry group had passed by, their songs still echoing, an awkwardness descended on them for a full minute. Then Blaine said with a chuckle, "Small towns! God bless 'em." He

185

started down the steps, saying, "Well, Holly, I guess I better say good night."

Conscious of keen disappointment, Holly managed to keep her voice light, "Good night, Blaine; thanks for seeing me home."

Once inside, Holly watched as Blaine got into the buggy and turned it around. After awhile, with a last look out, she sighed and walked back into her bedroom. Slowly, one by one, she began discarding gloves, slippers, cloak, and fan. The Christmas dance was over, the sound of the toe-tapping music faded away. Suddenly she was left with an awful sense of emptiness.

Tonight she had felt so happy being with Blaine as if they were on the brink of something—falling in love? What? Was she beginning to think of Blaine romantically?

Oh, what a perfect fool you are, Hollis Lambeth! What did it matter whether Blaine kissed you or not? Blaine was undoubtedly handsome, warm, sincere, understanding, but—after all, in the spring, when school was over, she was going home—home to Willow Springs. Wasn't she?

Chapter 19

A few days before Christmas, when Holly was in the store, Ned had issued an embarrassed invitation for her to come to Christmas dinner at their house. Aware of the probable discussion with Hetty that must have preceded it, Holly tried to make her refusal as easy as possible for him. "Oh, Ned, thank you, but I've accepted an invitation to Vi Dodd's. It turns out that he's going to be alone for Christmas after all, and so she's having a few friends to share the holiday with her. I do have some gifts for the children and for you and Hetty, too. So I'll stop by on Christmas Eve before the service at church if that will be all right?"

Ned's face flushed as he shifted the glass candy jars on the countertop nervously and said, "That's mighty nice of you, Holly; I'll tell Hetty, and the children will be so happy to see you."

Holly could see that he wanted to say more, obviously struggling with his own need to be honest with her and his loyalty to his stubborn wife. Holly felt sorry for him, but she felt sorrier for her cousin. Why was Hetty making life so difficult for everyone? Her husband and children especially? What possible pleasure could she be getting out of this feud?

Holly dreaded the prospect of the encounter with Hetty. It was enough to spoil Christmas Eve for her. But since she had promised Ned and did not want to disappoint the children, there was nothing to do but go. It had been fun, picking out their presents, poring over one of Ned's catalogs, selecting just the right gift, anticipating their happiness at what she had chosen. Afraid that anything of a personal nature she might give Hetty would not be acceptable just because it had come from her, Holly decided to give Ned and Hetty a joint present, something for the house. She hated thinking that way about her cousin, but in her heart she knew it was probably true. After much deliberation, she had chosen a cranberry glass bowl suitable for flowers or fruit or to be used as a decorative centerpiece. She wrapped all the presents in paper she decorated with holly leaves and berries and tied with scarlet ribbon.

She delayed going until late afternoon when, she knew, the children would be up from their naps. She did not want to be alone with Hetty. On the walk over, Holly kept thinking, *What a shame it is that things aren't normal between us.* It would have been so much fun to be included in all the traditional Christmas plans, trimming the tree, the holiday baking, filling the children's stockings. That's certainly the way things *should* have been for two cousins, both so far away from home.

Hetty's greeting was about as frozen as the ground over which Holly had trudged to get there. But the affectionate welcome Holly received from Aurelia and Teddy, who flung himself into her arms, made up for the iciness of their mother. "Will you have some tea or coffee?" Hetty asked stiffly after a few minutes. Holly would have loved to stay longer, talk and play with her small cousins, but the atmosphere was too stifling. Hetty's attitude made relaxing and enjoying impossible. Making the excuse that she had other stops to make and some last-minute shopping to complete, Holly moved to the door. Before she reached it, Hetty thrust a small, wrapped package toward her. "Here," she said shortly. "Fruitcake, made from Grandma Granville's recipe."

Holly managed a "thank you" even as she thought, *What an impersonal gift from one cousin to the other* and, at the same time, of the half-dozen same such fruitcakes sent by some of her pupils' mothers, lined up on her own kitchen table!

Back outside in the crisp December air, Holly felt incredibly let down. As she had known it would, her visit to her cousin had depressed her. A sudden wave of homesickness and nostalgia for other Christmases struck her, and she fought an overwhelming urge to cry. Holly hurried along toward town, her head bent against the wind.

"Whoa there!" a familiar voice rang out, and Holly came to an abrupt halt. She had almost collided with Blaine coming from the other direction. "And where are you off to in such a hurry?" he asked, grinning. His face was ruddy, and his blue eyes merry as he held out both hands to steady her from her sudden stop.

"Well—eventually to the Christmas service, but it's a little early yet."

"Believe it or not, I had the same thing in mind. Would it fit your plans if I offered you a little holiday hospitality before attending church? One thing I'm good at is making coffee, and you should see my waiting room. It's absolutely filled. Not with patients but *payments*. Most of which look and smell suspiciously like fruitcake."

"Sounds like *my* kitchen!" Holly laughed, feeling her heart already lifting. "And Hetty just gave me another one!"

"Well, come along," Blaine said heartily, offering his arm. Linking arms, they walked the short distance to the doctor's office. While Blaine moved briskly about stirring up the fire in the stove and brewing coffee, Holly examined the framed certificates on the wall. Ad was right. Blaine's qualifications were impressive.

"I'm surprised you're not spending Christmas with the Thorntons," Blaine remarked casually as he handed her a mug of steaming coffee. "It seems such a family time."

Holly accepted the coffee and took a sip before answering. Why not be honest? Surely Blaine would understand.

"The truth is, Blaine—, Hetty and I are not on the best terms. Please don't ask why. I really don't know, myself. I've tried to figure it out, but—" She shrugged.

"Hetty doesn't seem to be a very happy person," was his only comment. Then he deftly changed the subject, for which Holly was grateful.

"You will be at Vi's tomorrow, then?"

"Yes, it was lovely of her to invite me."

"And other homeless folks as well," Blaine smiled. "Vi always takes pity on us."

"A very fitting way to celebrate Christmas, don't you think?"

They chatted easily together for a half hour or so then left to walk down the street to the church to the simple but meaningful Christmas Eve service. Afterward, Blaine took Holly back to the schoolhouse in his buggy and escorted her to the door. "I'll see you tomorrow at Vi's? I have to make a few house calls first, but I'll be there." He started down the steps then turned back, grinning. "You know something? It's been years since I've looked forward to Christmas the way I'm looking forward to tomorrow." With that, he ran the rest of the way down the porch steps, whistling "Jingle Bells."

And so am I, thought Holly, smiling to herself.

Christmas Day at Vi's was lovely. As Holly had expected, Vi served a meal that was both a pleasure to the palate and to the eye. The table was spread with an embroidered cutwork linen cloth, silver candlesticks, and ivory china. She had fashioned a centerpiece of red-berried pyracantha and white geraniums in a milk-glass bowl. Turkey roasted to perfection, mounds of snowy potatoes, glazed carrots, pearl onions in cream sauce, and fresh cranberry relish was followed by a frothy lemon sorbet, and later by mince pie and coffee.

Holly, whose own culinary skills had not evolved much further than necessity required, thoroughly enjoyed being in a real home, eating delicious food, and being with pleasant adult company for a change. After dinner they had all had a fine time playing "Quotations" and "Charades." Although Holly knew Vi had been sadly disappointed about Avesta's not coming, she covered it well and could not have been a more gracious hostess.

Blaine helped Holly on with her cape and handed her her muff as they both thanked Vi and said good night. "It was a lovely party, wasn't it?" Holly commented as they walked along the darkened, quiet streets of town. "It reminded me a little of Christmases at home. Our family always held open house on Christmas Day with friends and relatives flowing in and out, my father presiding proudly over the eggnog punchbowl—" She broke off, hoping she didn't sound homesick. "Do you have Christmas memories, Blaine?"

"Yes, of course, I suppose everyone does. The lucky ones do, anyway, those of us who had good parents, happy homes."

"Yes. I'm surprised I haven't missed things as much as I thought I might," she said thoughtfully. "Do you miss yours?"

"Not so much anymore. Of course, I've been away from my childhood home for a good many years. First, away at college, then in Scotland and Germany for two years for further study— then I came out West," he replied, then looked at her. He smiled and said, "And I must say that Riverbend has its compensations—especially recently."

When they reached the schoolhouse, it was only early evening. Holly hated to see the lovely day end. She especially wanted this time with Blaine to last a little longer. Remembering Vi's caution about how careful the schoolteacher must be about her reputation, Holly hesitated to invite Blaine into her little parlor. As she debated about its propriety, Blaine made the decision for her. "Would it be improper for me to suggest that you might offer me something warm before I brave the chill again on my walk back to town?"

She knew —, he must have been reading her mind.

"Not improper at all but very probably inhospitable!" she declared with a toss of her head. "I might even offer you a slice of fruitcake!" she teased.

She took off her bonnet, hung it up, and Blaine assisted her with her cape. They walked into the parlor.

"Certainly *I've* found things I used to think were so very important don't really matter a fig to me now," she said. "Why don't you sit down here, and I'll bring us some tea?"

In the few minutes it took Holly to heat the water in the kettle, arrange a tray with teacups, and pour the water into the teapot, Blaine had picked up her photo album and was turning its pages. He looked up as she entered with the tray and said, "Hope you don't mind? It was lying here open, so I thought it was all right to look."

"Oh, sure. A little bit of Willow Springs I brought with me.

191

Have you ever seen so many aunts, uncles, and cousins?" she asked gaily as she proceeded to pour out the fragrant jasmine tea.

"I'm curious about all the empty spaces. Have you banished or disowned some of your relatives. Don't tell me *your* family has black sheep?"

"Doesn't everyone's?" She dimpled, eyes mischievous. "Or are all the Stevens clan impeccable pillars of society?"

"I don't know about that; never have been one to go into genealogy." He paused for a minute as he accepted the cup she handed him; then he regarded her thoughtfully and said, "You haven't answered my question."

Holly recalled Ad's same inquiry, and also that afterward, acting on his advice, she had removed all Jim's pictures from the album. How freeing it had been! She had taken them all out the very same evening Ad had been here, and since then she had rarely given Jim a thought.

Now, looking into Blaine's frankly interested eyes, she found it almost easy to say, "They were pictures of someone who's no longer in my life. It seemed a good idea to take them out. You see, we were engaged, and he broke the engagement. It pains me to confess that I have only myself to blame. For quite a while I spent time in futile regrets. It's over now, and it seems a long time ago and actually sort of unreal to me now."

"Did you love him very much?"

Holly thought a minute before answering. "I'm not sure I even knew what love is. As painful as it is, I must confess that I was to blame for what happened to us. I hurt him deeply—but it's all in the past now. Taking the pictures out was just a step in realizing that and going on with my life."

Telling Blaine was much easier than it had been telling Ad— Ad performed the surgery, the sharp cutting advice; Blaine's sympathy, understanding, brought healing. Then Holly said, "I was very young, and it seems a long time ago. So much has happened; I've changed so much." She took a sip of tea then quoted softly, "'When I was a child I thought as a child, I spoke as a child—now, I've put away childish things.'"

"Good for you. Out here you grow up fast, or you don't survive," he said quietly.

192

As Holly met his eyes, she felt disconcerted for a moment. She saw something in Blaine's eyes that she had seen in them earlier in the evening at Vi's. She had been asked to play the piano, and Blaine had come over and leaned on it while she played. He was looking at her now as he had then. His eyes regarding her with a mixture of admiration and incredible tenderness. Or was it something more? Before she could answer her own question, he went on, "It would do for all of us to put the past behind us—painful or otherwise. As a doctor, I've learned that life is precious—too precious for wasteful lingering over mistakes we've made or having vain regrets." He smiled, then drained his cup, set it upon its saucer, replaced it on the tray, and said, "And that's enough unsolicited philosophy from a country doctor. Now, I must be off." He stood up and started toward the door. "Thank you for a most delightful ending to a particularly happy Christmas Day."

Holly rose and went with him into the hallway and handed him his coat. Around his neck he wrapped the red-and-purple striped muffler the Misses Bodine had given him for a Christmas gift, and he plunged his hands into his pockets for his gloves. Then a slow grin broke across his face as he said, "Well, well, what do you know? I wonder how this got in here?" and instead of his gloves, he brought out a small sprig of mistletoe.

Still smiling, Blaine dangled it above her head.

Tilting her chin up and leaning down, he kissed her. Her response was instantaneous. Slipping her arms around his neck, she returned his kiss. She felt his arms tighten, and he kissed her again. She closed her eyes, savoring its sweetness. This was the kiss she had hoped for after the holiday dance, but it was much more tender, more intense than she could have imagined. With a little sigh, she looked at him. When she saw Blaine's expression, a tingle of alarm went through her. She recognized something in his eyes that frightened her a little. They were searching for some—what? Encouragement? Confirmation? Commitment?

She recognized something familiar in the way her heart was beating, too! Was she—*could* it be?—she was falling in love? Or was this the old Holly's response to the thrill of being the object of a man's admiration? Especially a man like Blaine Stevens? She stepped back out of his arms, feeling confused. Before she could say anything, Blaine said, "Merry Christmas, Holly, and good night." Then he was gone into the dark, chilly night. She remained standing in the doorway, still feeling the warmth of his lips on hers.

The week between Christmas and New Year's flew by. There was fresh snow, and Holly was invited out to the Healys' farm to go sledding on the hill behind the house; then she stayed for one of Geneva's bounteous suppers.

One day Ned brought Aurelia and Teddy to the store, where Holly came to meet them and take them out to her little school-house home to spend the day. Aurelia wanted to play school in the classroom, and Holly let her draw on the blackboard to her heart's content while Teddy sat on the floor, looking at picture books and playing with the bean bags the school children used at recess.

Holly served them a "pick and choose" lunch made up of all the gifts of cakes, pies, fruit jams and preserves, nut loaves, and candy she had been given by her pupils. The children had a glorious time and didn't want to leave when Ned came for them after he closed the store.

"Why don't you live with us anymore, Holly?" Teddy asked plaintively as she helped him into his warm jacket.

"It's not fun any more at home without *you*, Holly," Aurelia added wistfully.

Holly's eyes met Ned's over the children's heads and then looked away quickly. She said, "But, I have to live at the school because I'm the teacher, Teddy. And, Aurelia, you and Teddy can come and visit during a real school day sometime if your mama says you may."

That seemed to cheer them up a little. But as Ned led them down the steps and out to the wagon, they kept turning back and waving to Holly, who stood at the door.

Returning to her apartment, it suddenly felt empty. She had loved having the children here. Why was Hetty so stubborn? Why couldn't they all be pleasant and happy and *family*, for goodness' sake! Holly sighed with frustration. It ought not to be like this. She thought of the fabricated letters she wrote to her mother to pass on to Aunt Dolly. Did anyone read between the lines? Probably, if anyone did, it was Great-Aunt Ancilla. If not, why then in the latest batch of tracts from her were ones with such Scriptural admonitions as: "Ephesians 4:31: Let all bitterness and wrath and anger and clamor and evil speaking be put away from you with all malice," and "Proverbs 15:1: A soft answer turneth away wrath, but grievous words stir up anger"?

New Year's Day dawned crisp and clear and blue. There were still patches of snow on the ground, but the sun was shining brilliantly. To Holly's surprise, she received an unexpected New Year's caller: Adam Corcoran, looking dapper, as usual, in ruffled white shirt, string bow tie, dark blue coat, and a biscuit-beige waistcoat.

"Why, good morning and Happy New Year, Adam!" Holly greeted him at the door.

He leaned against the door frame, looking at her; then from behind his back he brought a package tied in bright paper and ribbon and handed it to her. "Happy Birthday."

"What on earth makes you think it's my birthday?"

"Everyone has a birthday every year, right? Since I don't know the exact date of yours, New Year's Day is as good a day to start a new year as any, don't you agree? So let's just say, it's a little gift to give you a good start on your year." He held it out to her.

"Why, Ad, that was very sweet of you—"

"Not sweet at all. I enjoyed doing it very much. I never do anything I don't enjoy," he said. "Well, hardly ever—as I recall one moving day doing a lot of things I didn't particularly enjoy."

"Yes, I know, and you were quite marvelous, and I appreciated every grubby unpleasant chore you did. Come on in, sit down, and I'll make us some tea." Holly carried the gift box over to the table and set it down. She placed the kettle on the stove.

"Aren't you going to open it?" he asked.

"Of course. Just delaying my pleasure."

"What a martyr you are," he remarked, seating himself on one of the straight chairs and stretching out his long legs with his shiny boots out in front of him.

Holly poured the boiling water into the teapot. While it steeped, she put the honey jar in the center of the table and cut two slices of the stack cake Rebecca Clay had brought her the day before on a plate.

"What do you suppose the year 1883 will bring us?" Ad mused.

"Is that a rhetorical question, or do you expect an answer?"

"I hope it means the end of my exile," Ad said, stirring honey thoughtfully into his cup.

"Has it really been that bad for you here?"

He lifted an eyebrow and gazed at Holly across the table for a second, then said slowly, "I'd say it's been better since sometime—about the end of August. . . ."

Ignoring his implication, Holly said seriously, "You've done a great deal with the paper. Everybody reads it; there's always lots of talk about your editorials!"

Ad shrugged. "Maybe start a little brush fire now and then. But that soon dies down. Besides, there's not much the locals can get too excited about. This Town Council's made up of the proverbial 'salt of the earth,' all upstanding, honest types. My meat is usually corrupt politicians. Not that *that* did me much good!" he remarked ironically. "Going after one particularly bad one landed me here! That should have taught me something, right? What do they say, teacher, if you don't learn by your mistakes, you're doomed to repeat 'em? Maybe I'm a slow learner." Ad made a dismissing gesture. "But that's enough about me. Open your present."

Affecting a simpering smile Holly pretended coyness. "Oh, Mr. Corcoran, you *shouldn't* have!"

"I know I shouldn't have but open it anyway!" ordered Ad.

Laughing, Holly untied the ribbons, pushed away the paper revealing a small, square box. Lifting the lid, she brought out a tiny rosewood clock. "Oh, Ad, thank you."

"It not only tells the time, it shows the date," he pointed out the small dial on the face.

196

"How clever! I never saw one like this or one so pretty. Thank you very much."

"Well at least now you can keep track of your prison sentence," he said gesturing to the schoolroom.

"I don't think of it *exactly* like that," she protested.

"Maybe not, but it takes one to know one, as they say, and I believe you're counting your time in Riverbend as much as I am."

"No, Ad, I'm not. You're wrong."

"If I am, I stand corrected. Has something happened to change your attitude about this town?"

Holly hesitated. Would Ad understand if she tried to tell him? Truthfully, she knew *much* had happened. It wasn't just one thing; there were many turns of events that had changed her thinking about Riverbend. Some she knew, some she only guessed, some she didn't want to admit. At least not to Ad.

But he was looking at her so curiously, she had to say something. "Well, for one thing I found I love teaching! That's a big surprise and probably accounts more than anything else for my change of attitude. And the children. They're wonderful."

Ad yawned elaborately, tapping his hand over his mouth, "Ho-hum, now I have heard everything!"

Holly pretended indignation. "But it's true!"

He frowned and gave her a long, scrutinizing look, then said, "Yes, I believe it really is. Who would have thought it?"

He finished his tea, put his cup down, and got up to leave. "Well, I guess I better be on my way; I have an important editorial to write—predictions for the New Year I think will be my subject."

"Do try to be optimistic, Ad," Holly begged as she walked with him to the door.

With his hand on the doorknob, he lingered as if he were about to say something else. Instinctively Holly braced herself for what might be some last cynical comment on Riverbend, its banality, its provincialism, its lack of excitement. She had no idea his mind was on something else altogether. She was unaware that the pale afternoon sun streaming in through the narrow windows created a golden aura behind her head.

Unexpectedly, Ad reached out and softly touched her hair;

197

his finger trailed down her cheek. Holly sensed that perhaps she should step back, but she didn't.

"You know, your eyes are extraordinary," he murmured. "I thought at first they were hazel, then I thought they were blue, but in this light—they're almost green, like Chinese jade—"

Then he leaned down and kissed her on the lips, with a gentle sweetness.

Automatically Holly had closed her eyes and when she opened them, Ad was smiling at her.

"Just a birthday kiss, Miss Lambeth. You know, everyone gets kissed on their birthday, don't you?" he asked in a low teasing voice. "Happy Birthday, Holly," he said, going out the door, "Happy New Year," he called over his shoulder as he went down the schoolhouse steps.

Holly stood there looking after him, not sure how she felt about the kiss or about the man who had kissed her.

PART 5

If suffering is life's teacher,
then let us learn courage, patience,
tenderness, pity, love and faith.

—Anonymous

Chapter 20

*A*fter New Year's, the weather turned bitterly cold. In the morning Holly had to crack a crust of ice off the top of the water in the rain barrel to get enough to bring inside to wash with and to boil for her coffee.

At night the wind whistled around the schoolhouse like a wild thing, crept in through the cracks and around the window frames. It was hard for her to keep the woodbox filled and to have a fire going to heat the classroom in daytime and her own rooms in the evening. Mostly she huddled, wrapped in a quilt, reading or writing her lesson plans; and then got into bed early to stay reasonably warm.

In the morning she would wake, trying to bolster enough grit to get up, teeth chattering and shivering, to start the fires in both stoves. Wearing a shawl, muffler, and gloves, she kept moving until her blood was circulating and it was time for the children to start arriving for school.

To add to Holly's general feeling of let-down during the second week of the New Year, when she went to the post office to pick up her mail, there was an official-looking envelope. Upon opening it she found it was from the District Superintendent of Schools informing her of the date of his visit to Riverbend to evaluate the progress of its pupils in comparison to the rest of the elementary schools of his district.

At first, this threw Holly into a complete panic. Although she had been pleased at the steady, if slow, progress of most of the children, she had suspected they might fall far below some of the other schools in the district. After all, the school had undergone the disruption of changing teachers. How long had they been exposed to the erratic tutelage of Larkin with his frequent absences? Even if he was present physically, due to his hidden drinking he had certainly not been in condition to control and teach.

Holly was well aware of her own inadequacy as a teacher. Even though she was making every effort to increase her own knowledge and skills she feared she would fall far short in the estimation of the District Superintendent. Therefore she began an intense campaign of readying her pupils for the scrutiny of Mr. Lanier and the examination in reading, spelling, and arithmetic he was sure to give them.

Teaching was hard-going after the excitement of the preparation and performance of the Christmas program followed by the ten-day holiday. The children seemed lethargic and uninterested in their lessons. To Holly's bewildered frustration, they seemed to have forgotten everything she had so laboriously taught them before the vacation. School days were narrowed to endless arithmetic drills and tedious spelling tests. At the end of each trying day, Holly felt exhausted.

The closer the date of his coming, the more nervous Holly became. Her prayers became desperate as her temper grew short. Her students paused, stumbled over the simplest words, and even the brightest among them seemed stumped at recitation of times tables they had rattled off with ease before. Daily spelling drills became routine and were greeted with moans each day.

It occurred to Holly that her reputation as a teacher might be at stake. But that was the least consideration. After all this was only a "way station" along her own path of life. Being Riverbend's teacher was not a career goal. It had simply been a means of escape from an unbearable situation. A straw she had grasped at for self-preservation.

Consideration of her own reputation paled beside the benefit and encouragement the children would receive by doing well in the District rolls. As one of the smallest and newest schools, Riverbend's status was in question.

Nerves frayed, Holly woke up on Monday the week of the superintendent's expected visit with a feeling of dread. She dragged herself out to the kitchen. While the water in the kettle boiled, she stared gloomily out the window. The scene did nothing to lift her spirits.

The sky was heavy, gray with clouds, the wind gusty. As she dressed, she heard the patter of rain and knew a rainy day meant the children would be inattentive, restive, and distracted.

As one by one they straggled in, Holly tried to be especially cheerful, promising that if everyone knew their times-tables and spelling words, she would read them another chapter of *Robin Hood,* a story they all particularly enjoyed, both the boys and the girls.

Outside, the wind was rising, hurtling rain in increasing violence against the schoolroom windows. The storm mounted during the early afternoon and, since some of the children had to walk long distances home, Holly decided to dismiss them early.

If Holly had known the storm would work to her advantage, she might have spent a more peaceful night. But she slept fitfully, awakened often by the wind shrieking around the edges of the schoolhouse and rattling the windowpanes. It was still raining hard when she awoke the next morning.

Only a few students showed up for school. These were mostly children who lived in town. The Brysons were the only ones from the outlying farms who came, and that was because their father delivered milk to customers in Riverbend. They told of ankle-deep mud on the roads that had become quagmires and were flooded in some places.

It rained steadily all through the day and throughout the week. On Thursday she received a letter from the District Superintendent stating that due to the weather and the impassable condition of the roads he would be unable to make his annual visit and would have to postpone it until spring. If she hadn't been so relieved Holly might have been angry. All that preparation, all the anguish, all the punishing, grinding repetition she had put the children through for nothing!

As it turned out, it hadn't been useless. Within a week Holly realized that every one of the children had benefited in some way from her insistence on their learning their lessons. Happily she sent away her order for the second volume of the *McGuffy Reader* to replace the ones they had all passed successfully.

Later, when discussing the entire matter with Vi, Holly complained, "And to think of all my prayers about the superintendent's visit going perfectly, and then it never even happened!"

Vi smiled. "Remember, Holly, God *always* answers prayers even if not the way *we* think He will." She paused significantly. "Who do you think is in control of the weather?"

One day, three weeks into the new school term, Holly sensed there was something indisputably wrong. She felt it almost from the moment she opened the school door and rang the bell. The children came in sluggishly, in a disorderly line, shoving and pushing. There seemed to be more confusion and quarreling than usual as they put down lunch buckets and slung their outer garments on the hooks at the back of the room. There was more than the usual amount of noise as they shuffled to their places, banged slates on desk tops, and dropped books.

Holly had difficulty getting the children's attention. The big boys were unusually disruptive during the geography lesson. Every time she turned her back to the classroom to point out something on the map, she would hear scuffling and whispering.

Beside herself as to what to do to get control of her pupils, Holly called an early lunch period. Since it was too cold for them to play outside, she read them aloud a chapter from *Robin Hood*. This time, however, it seemed to have lost its flavor. Even Molly Spencer, one of her best and brightest students, put her head down on her crossed arms on the desk during the reading.

Holly was really concerned as the wall clock inched to dismissal hour. When asked to erase the blackboard, Luke Healy moved without his typical energy, and Holly noticed he was flushed. Little Cissy McKay's eyes were glazed, and when Holly touched her cheek with her hand it felt like fire.

As Holly watched them straggle out the door and walk out of

the schoolyard, she was worried. Were these children all coming down with something?

Within forty-eight hours Holly's premonition came true. Only a handful of children showed up for school the next week. They each told of a brother or sister who was sick. Each day it seemed one or two other children failed to appear. By the end of the week it was known that the cause of these absences was the dread disease—smallpox.

Holly had been vaccinated as a child and so was in no danger of contagion from exposure to her pupils. Since vaccination had been prevalent in America for at least 150 years, Holly wondered why some of the Riverbend people had not been vaccinated. At first no one seemed unduly concerned. The parents Holly spoke to about it seemed more worried about the possibility of diphtheria which had taken its toll of Riverbend children in past years.

But the relative calm with which most people were taking the epidemic was soon altered when the number of deaths became known. First there had been two, then five, suddenly thirteen deaths were reported from the disease. Word spread quickly, rumors of rampant infection followed, and panic came in its wake. Riverbend was swept with a full-scale epidemic.

This change of attitude was further brought to the public concern when Ad printed a letter to the editor from Blaine in boldface type, outlined in black on the front page of the *Monitor* with an editorial admonition to the Town Council to take appropriate action for the protection of the community's health.

Holly read what Blaine had written, with growing alarm,

The present eruptive disease in the patients I am treating now is a far different type of smallpox than any I have seen before. There is no reason to panic if certain preventive, hygienic measures are taken. Homes of people already infected should keep a quarantine, and those not infected should avoid them. I have vaccination serum for those who have not been vaccinated and want to be vaccinated. In the houses where sickness is present, a dish or plate containing chloride of lime or other disinfectant should be placed.

The infected person should be kept quiet in bed, cooling drinks offered for fever, mild laxative given if required, liquids should be administered to patient as he can tolerate.

Meticulous cleanliness in the sickroom and in the care of the infected person keeps the disease from worsening. Linens, clothing, bedding, etc., should be washed and changed frequently. To prevent pitting of skin, the most effective remedy is to paint the face with collodion.

Under Mayor Morrison's leadership the council reacted promptly. They established a Board of Health to enforce precautions to contain the spread of the disease. School was suspended, all meetings were banned, yellow flags were placed on the gateposts or porches of all houses where there was infection. Someone suggested the idea of burning pitch pine in the streets to purify the air. Carbolic acid was recommended to disinfect buildings.

When it was realized that whole families were coming down with it and there was no one to care for the sick if the mother of the home was ill, an emergency "pest house" had to be found. The town itself was quarantined with citizens of Riverbend prohibited from traveling into other nearby counties.

The day the mayor's proclamation to close all public gathering places was posted, only five children had showed up for school. As Holly told the subdued little band there would be no school the next day, Suzie Briggs put her head in her hands and began to sob heartbrokenly. Holly was at her side in a minute. Kneeling down next to the child's crouched figure, she put her arms around the little girl's shaking shoulders and tried to soothe her, "As soon as everyone is well again, Suzie, we'll have school again."

Suzie kept on sobbing. Her older sister, May, fighting tears herself, told Holly, "Pa told us to come here, Teacher; said you'd take care of us. He's bad sick, and Ma hasn't moved from her bed all day yesterday."

A chilling realization clutched Holly. These children's parents were desperately sick, perhaps dying, or maybe even dead! They had nowhere to go, no one to take care of them. She would have to check it out but in the meantime—Holly got to her feet and saw the other children all standing staring at her with wide, frightened eyes. She looked from Joel to Cissy, who was clinging to him, to gangly Sam Durkin, looking as lost and scared as the younger ones. With cold certainty Holly knew what she had to do.

Thus, the schoolhouse was turned into a haven for the suddenly homeless as well as an infirmary as one after the other of the children, except Sam, came down with the smallpox. Fortunately, all but Cissy had light cases. The little girl, already weakened by malnutrition and neglect, suffered severely. Holly sent Sam for Blaine while, with the delirious Cissy in her arms, she paced agitatedly and prayed frantically.

At last, Blaine arrived, his coat stained with rain. "Thank God, you've come, Blaine; I think she's very ill." He looked as if he had not eaten nor slept in days. She was weak with relief that he was here and would know what to do.

He took the child out of Holly's arms and laid her gently down on the pallet of quilts Holly had made for her in her own bedroom. Holly hovered anxiously as he examined the little girl. Afterward he turned to Holly and said quietly, "All you can do is keep her as comfortable as possible, I'm afraid."

"What do you mean 'you're afraid'?" Holly whispered, feeling a rush of fear, the beginning of panic.

Blaine looked at Holly with sudden sympathy. Her wide eyes were shadowed with dark circles; she was pale and looked thinner. This woman, hardly more than a girl, had without warning been thrust into a crisis that demanded maturity, judgment, and emotional strength, as well as physical strength. "I mean that Cissy is very weak, Holly; I don't think she has enough strength to fight the infection—"

"Oh, no, Blaine!" Holly put her hand to her mouth.

"You've got to stay calm, Holly, be strong," he told her. "Those children in there are depending on you. I know you'll do fine. I've seen you in emergencies before. And I *know* you *are* strong, competent, brave—"

Holly shook her head, "No," she said. "You're wrong, Blaine. I'm not brave at all. I'm sickeningly frightened."

"That's what real bravery is," Blaine replied quietly. "To be afraid and to go on doing what has to be done, when there is nobody else but you to do it—in spite of how you feel. In wartime, men get medals for that kind of fear."

"Can't you stay longer, Blaine? Can't you do something for Cissy?" Holly pleaded.

"I'm sorry, Holly. Cissy is beyond help now. I can't stay, but I have other sick people I may be able to save."

She was torn between being selfless and selfish. What she really wanted was for Blaine to stay with her, give her the support she needed so badly, but she understood others needed him more. She also realized he was the only doctor in Riverbend and was taxed to the last ebb of his strength. He looked so weary and drawn, so sorrowful, that Holly longed to reach out, comfort him.

After Blaine drove away, Holly went back inside. Sam was standing at the door leading into the classroom, now an improvised dormitory of sick children. Sam, who had been one of the ringleaders of the trip to the saloon the day she had had to march in after them. What a miracle turn-around. He had been a staunch help during these troubled days.

Holly had to remind herself that Ad, too, had been an unexpected source of help. Vaccinated himself, he had no fear of infection and almost daily brought her boxes of needed groceries, medication, and extras.

"Take care of yourself, Holly," he'd told her sternly. "Don't play Florence Nightingale until you drop from exhaustion yourself. That won't do anyone any good." His eyes were concerned. "We don't want to lose you."

"What can I do to help, Miss Lambeth?" Sam asked in his gravely adolescent voice. Distractedly, Holly glanced at him and saw an unexpected understanding in the boy's eyes.

The Briggs girls were recovering and restless, Holly had noticed. They were finding it hard to lie quietly, which was imperative for them to do until all the eruptions had disappeared.

"Thank you, Sam. Maybe you could read to Suzie and May? That would help keep them still," she suggested.

"Yes'm." Sam grinned and started toward the bookshelves.

Holly went back into the bedroom, lifted Cissy, and wrapped her in a blanket; then holding her on her lap, she sat in the rocking chair and gently rocked her. From the other room she could hear Sam haltingly struggle to read *The Adventures in Sherwood Forest*. The child in her arms moaned faintly, and looking down at the once angelic, now blackened face of the little girl, Holly felt stinging tears cloud her eyes and run unchecked down her cheeks. For some reason the words "Suffer the little children . . ." came into Holly's mind. "Oh, dear God, why must these little ones suffer so?" She felt her heart was breaking.

She knew the little girl in her arms had in some way filled the place left lonely when Hetty had deprived her of being with Aurelia. But then Cissy had created her own special niche. After Holly's first week as her teacher, Cissy had never come empty-handed to school. It was only something she found along the way, a bunch of wild flowers clutched in her tiny, birdlike hand, or a pretty rock, or a handful of acorns. It didn't matter what it was, Holly thought, choked with grief—it was a gift of love. A gift that was given completely without any thought other than to be just that—an expression of love. "Unless you become as a little child . . ."—Cissy had taught her so much about love, real love, unconditional love, the only kind of love that really mattered.

Holly never knew how long she sat there rocking Cissy, humming the old familiar hymns of her childhood. Outside, the daylight faded, and the room slowly filled with shadows. She could hear the murmur of children's voices in the next room, and she thought she should really put Cissy down and go see about getting some kind of light supper for the recuperating patients. Cissy was very still, and Holly's arm had grown numb holding her head. Instinctively, Holly held her breath and, in a minute, realized that the little sufferer was no longer breathing.

Sometime later, Blaine returned. When she heard his buggy wheels, Holly threw a shawl around her shoulders and stepped out onto the porch. When he reached the top step, she told him, "Cissy's gone, Blaine; she died this afternoon."

Without a word, Blaine took Holly gently into his arms. She leaned against his shoulder, felt his hand stroke her hair, heard him murmuring her name. Holly let the tears come at last, and Blaine's embrace tightened. She felt the blessed comfort of his arms holding her, and from deep within her came an aching to stay within his embrace, draw from his strength—always. Words rushed up inside her, begging to be said. Words of love and need and longing. Holly had to bite her lip to keep from saying them. Finally, she gave a long shaky sigh and lifted her head.

"I haven't told Joel yet," she said. "I don't know how."

Blaine wiped her cheeks with his thumbs and said softly, "You'll find the right way. I trust you." Then Blaine took her arm, saying, "Come outside with me, Holly, there's something else you have to know." Blaine's voice sounded infinitely weary. Holly followed him to the porch, wondering what new tragedy he was about to tell her.

Blaine's voice was heavy. "I've just come from the McKay's cabin—Joel and Cissy's parents are dead, Holly."

"Oh, no, Blaine!"

"Maybe Cissy's better off. . . ." Blaine shook his head sadly.

Holly was too stunned to speak at first, then she whispered, "What will become of Joel?"

"I don't know."

"Why is life so hard?" she asked brokenly.

"I don't know that, either, Holly."

She searched his face for another answer but saw only the sorrow and shock in his eyes. With sudden insight Holly realized that Blaine was vulnerable to pain and unanswerable questions, too. Finally he said, "I have to go, Holly."

"Yes, I know," she said with difficulty.

"Try to get some rest. It won't do if *you* get sick," he said as he turned up his coat collar and went out into the rainy night.

Holly felt a tremendous ache to see him go. The truth she had denied so long to herself clearly surfaced as she watched him wearily mount into his buggy. She knew she loved Blaine whether or not her love would ever be returned.

The *Monitor* posted the number of cases and also repeated the information Blaine had given to the paper so people would be aware of the symptoms and know what to do if they or members of their families fell ill.

When it became necessary to clear out one of the older buildings in town as a place where victims with no one to care for them could be placed, this was also reported along with the news that some nurses had come from Portland to help in the emergency.

A dark pall seemed to settle over the town, streets were empty, business in the downtown stores of all kinds was practically nil, people only ventured out for the most basic supplies, afraid of contamination or infection from others about to succumb. Social life of every kind had totally ceased, there were no gatherings of any kind—not the sewing circle, quilting bees, or church meetings of the Missionary Society or Bible studies. Fear ran amok, no class of society was protected from this dread scourge. It struck rich and poor alike, and although it might be possible for the more affluent to nurse their sick at home, provide a few more comforts, the dreadful ravages of the disease itself knew no social barriers.

The stagecoach now only brought mail, and no longer did drivers linger at the Doggone Best or the Nugget to revive themselves. Instead, they made their stop as brief as possible in the place now known throughout the state as "plague town." Once the ban was posted on people from Riverbend leaving because of the fear of other counties in the area that they might spread the disease, there were few passengers on the stage.

The "pest houses" were crowded. Mops and pails smelling of chloride and alcohol could hardly contend with the peculiar smell of the illness itself. Makeshift beds of straw pallets were laid end on end beside cots; as the dead were lifted off and out, new cases were placed upon hastily cleaned ones.

The hillside cemetery was the only place in all Riverbend that saw daily activity. With gravediggers working round-the-clock, the Town Council allotted two new parcels of land for cemetery space, which had been previously earmarked for the expansion of business in town when the railroad came.

All day long on Main Street the steady sound of the hammering of nails on wood could be heard as Joe and Bill Slyder made coffins, stacking them and then unloading them onto carts almost as soon as they were finished.

There were now more obituary notices in the *Monitor* but fewer flowery eulogies written by relatives of their deceased, and funerals were quick and without many mourners outside the immediate families; sadly enough, fewer and fewer people showed up as whole families were stricken and perished.

The only light in the darkened *Monitor* office wavered as the solitary oil lamp on the editor's desk sputtered. Ad looked up, threw down his pen, and rubbed his eyes wearily. Then he reread what he had just written: "This is a town under siege. The smell of burning pitch through the night is a macabre reminder that people—children—are dying—"

He planned to dispatch this article in the morning to his former editor at the San Francisco newspaper where he used to be a reporter. How could he make anyone understand what it was like to live in a "plague town," to stir their compassion, their goodwill, to compel them to dig into their pockets and to send much needed medicine and supplies to this beleaguered community?

He ran his hand through his thick dark hair. His neck and shoulders ached; he straightened and stretched. Just then he heard a plaintive *meow*, and Chester leaped onto the pile of papers in front of him, his paws skidding a little, then made a dainty leap into Ad's lap. Absently, Ad's long fingers kneaded the soft fur of the tabby, who settled down with a contented purr.

A sizzling sound alerted Ad that the coffee pot he had set on top of the potbelly stove had boiled over, and he got to his feet, unceremoniously dumping Chester. The cat voiced an indignant yowl and marched off, tail switching, to find a more accommodating place to snooze.

Ad lifted the blue-speckled pot, stained by a dozen or more similar accidents of forgetfulness, but as he did, he burned his fingers and swore. He grabbed a greasy cloth hanging near the handpress mainly used to wipe the printer's devil's inky fingers, wrapped it around the pot handle, and poured himself a cup of the foaming brew. While waiting for it to cool so as not to scald his tongue as badly as he had his fingers, Ad stood morosely staring out into the darkened street. Ironically, on this Saturday night, when the saloons would usually have done a "land office" business, Main Street was deserted. The lights from the pitch fires mounted on hastily erected posts, cast an eerie illumination on the street where no one walked.

He hoped he had made the situation, the circumstances he had written about, real to the people who would read them. But how could he adequately convey the courage and selflessness of some, the humanness of the citizens of Riverbend during this crisis?

Ad's thoughts turned to his friend Blaine, who had worked tirelessly and without thought of his own health among the stricken people of this deadly plague. And Holly Lambeth—something uncharacteristically soft and tender touched Ad's heart thinking of how Holly had reacted during this time. Who would ever have dreamed she had the strength, stamina, and fortitude needed to care for those children? He had been wrong about Hollis Lambeth, and Ad wasn't usually quick to admit mistakes. In fact, he had always rather prided himself on having correct first impressions. But Holly had turned out to be no pampered Southern belle. She was—in Ad's opinion—the genuine article, a real heroine.

Holly woke in the gray, chilly dawn. She hadn't slept much. Not that she wasn't tired these nights; she just wasn't sleepy. It was more than physical. It was a feeling of exhausted weariness that came from some deep inner core of hopelessness and sadness. Cissy's death and Joel's heartbrokenness had made her aware of the uncertainty and fragility of life.

She lay in bed listening to the rain, knowing that it fell, too, on the new little grave on the hillside. She closed her eyes again, lying inert for a few minutes, unwilling to get up and face yet another terrible day, one more in an endless line of unendurable days. And yet, she had endured, she *had* survived. Was it that Blaine had expressed his faith in her that had kept her going more than her own determination? Why was his opinion of her so important?

At last, reluctantly, she pulled herself up, went over to the window, pushed back the curtain and saw that the day looked as gray and cheerless as she felt. Then all at once she saw someone swathed in a long cloak turning into the schoolyard, carrying two large baskets. There was something very familiar about that walk—the figure coming toward the schoolhouse.

Grabbing her shawl and wrapping it about her, Holly rushed to the door and stood barefoot and shivering in her nightgown as Vi mounted the steps. She looked up and smiled, "Thought you could use some help," she said.

"Oh, Vi, you better not come in here, we're *quarantined!*" Holly protested.

"That's all right. I've been vaccinated! My father was a pharmacist, you know, and he insisted on it. I've also had some experience nursing children."

"Oh, Vi, thank you!" cried Holly giving her friend a welcoming hug. "You're an answer to prayer. And I thought God wasn't listening!"

One night not long after Cissy's death, Holly was roused from an exhausted sleep by an insistent pounding on her door. She threw back the covers, struggled out of bed, flung her wrapper around her, and hurried to answer. An ashen-faced Ned, carrying Teddy and holding Aurelia by the hand, stood in the eerie light of a cold moon.

"Holly, I hate to bother you like this, but Hetty's real sick. I'm afraid it's the smallpox or maybe something worse. She's out of her head with fever, and I thought I better get the kids out of the house. I didn't know what else to do but bring them here. Then I've got to go for Doc."

"Of course, Ned," Holly said. "Here let me take Teddy. And Aurelia, honey, you come inside with me. They can stay here as long as they need to, Ned," she assured him.

"Thank you, Holly, I can't tell you—"

"Don't try, Ned. You just go on, find Blaine, and I hope—I pray Hetty's all right."

Looking at the calendar, a dazed and worn-out Holly suddenly realized that six weeks had passed. It was as though she had

214

been living in a long, dark tunnel. Most of the children were now in various stages of recovery. But this was almost harder than when they were feeling really sick. They were cranky, listless, homesick, as well as easily bored, easily upset. It was hard just keeping them amused and quiet until they were completely well or their families were recovered sufficiently to come to get them.

Vi went home, and one by one the other children were fetched home by grateful parents until there was no one left but—Joel.

As the last wagon with the last happily reunited child and parent drove out of the schoolyard, Holly saw Joel's small forlorn figure standing at the schoolroom window watching it leave.

The harsh reality of the little boy's fate gripped Holly. With a wrenching sensation she asked herself, *What was to become of Joel?*

Chapter 21

*B*y the end of February the epidemic had subsided sufficiently for the town to resume its normal activity. The
temporary infirmary, where the worst cases had been put and
for those who had no one at home to care for them, was closed.
Within another few weeks the Health Board, after enforcing all
the emergency mandates to prevent the further spread of smallpox, was dissolved.

Relatives had come to settle affairs, sell the property and
belongings of their family's victims of the deadly smallpox
scourge, and to take orphaned children with them when they
left. However, there were some who had no relatives; no one to
provide them with care or give them a home.

Joel McKay was one of those. He had remained at the schoolhouse with Holly, and no immediate action had been suggested
for his future. Through Geneva Healy, Holly found out that the
Town Council had already sent some of the children orphaned
early at the height of the epidemic to the orphanage at the
county seat. The word "orphanage" sent a cold shiver of alarm
through Holly's heart.

Joel in an *orphanage!* She could not imagine that lively,
inquisitive, precocious child institutionalized, regimented, and
made to conform to the necessary rules of a place already
crowded with too many children— no individualized attention,

no affectionate care. The thought of this little boy who had grown so dear to her in such a situation was too much for Holly.

School was not yet back in session on the March day when Ned had come to get Aurelia and Teddy. Joel was at the Healys', playing with their children, and Holly was alone. Although Hetty was still weak, she had recovered enough to want the children home. "I don't know how I can ever thank you, Holly," Ned said. "We are both very grateful. As soon as Hetty is able, I know she wants to thank you in person."

"Oh, Ned, I was just happy I could help," Holly reassured him as she hugged both the children good-bye.

In spite of Ned's assurances, she didn't count too much on hearing from Hetty, but it didn't bother her. Her mind was too preoccupied with another problem at the moment. What to do about Joel? She decided to go and talk to Vi about it. Vi would give her good advice.

Seated in Vi's sewing room, while Vi sat and continued to work at her treadle machine, Holly voiced all her jumbled thoughts. Finally, she sighed and said, "I can't just let him go to an orphanage, Vi. He's too special. He'd be lost there, I don't know what would happen to him."

"Lots of children grow up in an orphanage, Holly. They seem to survive. They're not starved or beaten, they're taught a trade. It might be the best thing for Joel. Anyway, what can you do about it? Ad had a piece in the paper yesterday about the children who had lost parents in the epidemic. They're now wards of the county, didn't you know? The Town Council decides what to do, where they go."

"No!" Holly exclaimed emphatically. "I can't possibly allow them to send Joel away! He's lived all his life here in Riverbend, all his friends are here—*I'm* here!"

Vi stopped pushing the treadle and held the wheel. "*You're* here? What do you mean, Holly?"

Holly stood up and started pacing back and forth, then looked out the window. It had begun to rain. She watched the rain pelting the old leaves on the oak tree in Vi's yard, and as they hit the window they ran down the glass pane in tiny rivulets. "I guess I mean I'm here for Joel," she said slowly, then turned around and faced Vi. "I could adopt Joel."

Vi's mouth parted in surprise. "You can't do that. You're not married; the Town Council would never place a child, especially a little boy, with a single woman."

"Why not, I'd like to know?" demanded Holly. "What about all the widows in the world who raise their children alone?"

"That's different."

"Why is it different? Most of the time they have to work to support their fatherless families. I work, I teach, and Joel would be right there with me all day."

Vi stared at her. "But I thought you were leaving in June to go back to Willow Springs. Do you mean if you got Joel, you'd stay here?"

Holly started pacing again. "I don't know. I mean, I hadn't thought that far ahead. But, I do know I'm going to try to adopt Joel." She halted, whirled around, and said, "Why aren't you supporting me, Vi? *You* brought up your daughter by yourself, didn't you?"

"It wasn't easy, Holly," Vi said quietly. "It was, in fact, very hard."

The two women stared at each other for a full minute without saying anything more. Then Vi said gently, "Let's go have a cup of tea, and I'll tell you how it was with me."

An hour later Holly walked back to the schoolhouse in the pouring rain under the umbrella Vi had lent her. The story that Vi had told her weighed heavily on her heart. It had made her admire her friend even more. It seems Vi had been the late child of middle-aged parents, was the proverbial "apple of their eye." They lived comfortably in a small town where her father, a pharmacist, was a well-respected pillar of the community and her mother a prominent church leader. Vi was given everything. When at a young age she had shown musical talent, she was given piano lessons; later she played the organ in church. Under all this loving care she had grown up in every way a model daughter.

Then the summer she was nineteen, Vi's whole life changed. A handsome pharmaceutical salesman with smooth manners, irresistible charm, came to town. Vi fell head over heels in love. Her parents were terrified of losing her and discouraged the romance. But dazzled and headstrong, Vi agreed to elope with the man. Only weeks later she found herself deserted in a San Francisco hotel with just a note of explanation that the man at least had the decency to leave for her. It revealed the sad truth that he was already married.

Vi was devastated, especially when soon she discovered she was pregnant. She could not return home because she knew it would break her parents' hearts, disgrace them. For days she walked the city streets dazed, depressed, desperate. Finally, she apprenticed herself to a dressmaker, who took a liking to her and when her pregnancy became advanced, offered to help Vi. This kind woman allowed Vi to continue working out of her home after the baby was born. Nearly a year later, she secretly contacted a friend in her hometown to get an idea of what the situation with her parents might be. To her sorrow she found out that her father had had a stroke and died and her mother was in fragile health and doctors felt she had not long to live. Vi knew if she made the decision to go home with her baby, that would be the last straw for her aging mother. It would be far better to let her die in some peace without ever knowing. So she wrote, saying that she was well and happy and would be home when she could. Her mother died without ever knowing the truth.

"I hated living in the city, and I didn't think it was a good place to raise a child," Vi told Holly. "By this time I had become an expert seamstress, so I knew I could make a living for us. So I packed Avesta and myself up and bought a stagecoach ticket to—"

"Riverbend—'the end of the line'!" Holly finished for her.

"Well, yes, that was almost the way I decided to come," Vi agreed. "I wanted to go somewhere where no one knew me, no one knew my story, where I could create a whole new life for myself and my daughter."

"And you did," Holly said. "So, why can't I?"

"Holly, I've just told you the bare facts of my story. I haven't told you what it's like to live with no family, no background, to have to be careful what you say, what you mention, or that you

219

might slip and name a town or a place that someone can connect with your past—I have made up a life for my daughter, too. I don't want *my* mistakes to ruin her life."

"How did you manage, Vi? I mean, the lonely nights, the times when you needed someone to turn to?"

"I had to build on a faith that I'd almost lost," Vi sighed. "I literally spent nights reading the Bible almost blindly, crying out for help." She paused. "Remember, when I told you to read until some verse or even just a line of Scripture quickens to you? As if it was meant for you? Well, finally it was one from Isaiah that spoke to my heart and that I came to lean on—Isaiah 54:4: 'Fear not, you will not be put to shame, for you will forget the shame of your youth and you shall not remember the reproach of your widowhood. For your Maker is your husband, the Lord of hosts is His name. . . .'" I just kept repeating those verses over and over."

Holly reached the schoolhouse and hurried up the porch steps, closed the umbrella, left it on the porch, and went inside. She was conscious of a new hope, a new determination. There must be a way to keep Joel, and she was going to find it. Almost from the first day of school she had felt a special bond between herself and the little boy. It had grown even stronger through the last few weeks, after the epidemic, certainly after Cissy's death and the death of his parents. Whatever she had to do to convince people that she was capable of bringing up a child, Holly was determined to do.

And if she couldn't—well, then she would take Joel home to Willow Springs. She felt certain that her mother and father would make him welcome as part of the family. Holly tried to imagine how a homecoming like that would be. Would there be as much gossip about her return as there had been before her leaving?

Holly's imagination took her no further. There was no use imagining circumstances that might never happen. She should concentrate on the positive. Take the first step, whatever that was, to adopt Joel, then worry about what to do next.

The first thing she had to do to reinforce her qualifications with the Council was to prove that she could offer Joel a stable home. For that she would have to apply to have her teaching contract renewed for another year. That would establish the fact that she would have a regular income and a permanent place to live.

It surprised Holly to discover that she had no qualms whatsoever about writing a letter of intent to teach at Riverbend for the coming year. She had no misgivings, no lingering regret that she wouldn't be returning to Willow Springs in June. It was the right thing to do. If there was a reason other than to ensure the granting of her petition to adopt Joel, she was not yet ready to admit it. It was her only purpose for wanting to remain in Riverbend, she told herself as she filled out the application to the School Board.

When Holly told the Healys what she intended to do, she asked Matt how she should go about petitioning the Town Council to grant the adoption and name her Joel's legal guardian.

Matt shook his head, warning her warily that nothing like that had ever come before the Council before. That did not deter Holly's resolve. She immediately followed his instructions as to how to place an item on the Council's agenda for decision at the weekly Town Council meeting. This was duly printed in the *Monitor* in the regular column as "News of Public Interest"— the usual procedure of publishing the business before the Council—in case anyone wanted to speak for or against the item.

On his way out to the schoolhouse, Ad felt strangely disoriented. He was still ambivalent about the decision he'd come to after a great deal of uncharacteristic self-debate. He left Main Street and turned onto the road leading out of the center of town, gave the horse its head, sat back in his saddle, and let his mind wander back to almost a year ago—to the first time he had set eyes on Holly Lambeth, just off the stagecoach, the evening she arrived in Riverbend.

He had known at first glance, *here* was a real lady. There had been an unmistakable aura of class about her from her quality clothes to the look of breeding and background about her, an air of independence and spirit that Ad particularly admired in a woman.

But for all her independent spirit and determination, Ad knew the odds could be stacked against her. No matter that it was now 1883, people in Riverbend had not all moved ahead with the times. In some places, the cities, for example, women were allowed all sorts of privileges once limited to men. Why there was even a woman reporter in the city room at the San Francisco newspaper where Ad had worked before coming here. Women owned their own businesses, negotiated their own contracts, managed their own property, bought and sold real estate. But here—Ad knew firsthand, some of the attitudes about a woman's "proper place" were still archaic. Unless there was a man—a husband—in the picture, Ad doubted that Holly's chance to adopt the little boy was very good.

He had come to admire Holly, her intelligence, the strength that she had shown during the epidemic, as much as he enjoyed her wit and her clever conversations. More than that, Ad knew he had come to care deeply for Holly. It was more than friendship if he allowed himself the truth. Maybe it wasn't love, but it was a deep affection that maybe eventually—who knows? Much as it went against Ad's long-held freedom, the kind of future he had always taken for granted, he could not let Holly face the possibility of losing Joel. If this step could help—even if it changed his life forever, which it certainly would, it would be worth it.

Ad turned his horse into the schoolyard, dismounted, and slung the reins over the hitching post. He brushed dust from his knees with his wide-brimmed hat, straightened his string tie, and checked his vest buttons, then marched toward the porch, took the steps two at a time, and knocked at the door.

When Holly came to the door, Ad was newly conscious of how attractive she was. Even with her rich brown hair slightly disheveled and a smudge of chalk on her cheek, she looked utterly charming.

Feeling suddenly awkward under her curiously direct gaze, he said, "Hello, Holly, I'd like to talk to you about something. But if you're busy, I could come back another time?"

"Do come in, Ad. I'm not really busy. Just the usual after-school cleanup, wiping blackboards, filling inkwells, and—what I have to do can wait. Come on in. What do you want to talk to me about?"

Ad twirled his hat absent-mindedly as he glanced around the schoolroom. He hadn't been in it since New Year's Day. He remembered how they had discussed what the coming year might hold for both of them. That seemed a long time ago, now. *A lot has happened since*, he thought, his eyes coming to rest again on Holly. He took a few steps around looking at everything: the children's pictures, the bunches of flowers in glass jars on the windowsills, a low tier of shelves filled with books behind the teacher's polished desk.

"Looks nice, Holly. You've sure done a lot, made some real changes," he commented, continuing to slowly circle the room.

"Thanks, Ad. The children help. It's fun," she said, giving a final swipe to the blackboard before wiping her hands on a cloth and folding it. "Why don't we go into my parlor, and I'll make us some tea? We can talk in there," she suggested, leading the way through the door into her own part of the building.

Here, too, Ad saw things he had never noticed before. Crisp curtains hung at the windows, some plants and flowers in a pretty bowl on the round table covered with a bright cloth. All the touches Holly had made to make it, well— cozy, homelike. An alarm sounded in his brain, and he shut it off quickly. Isn't that what women do? The "nesting instinct"?

Leaning against the doorframe, he watched Holly go about setting the kettle on the stove, getting down the tin canister of tea, and spooning out tea in careful measures into the teapot, enjoying the sheer gracefulness of her movements, Ad thought Holly looked especially pretty today.

She wore a simply styled dress the color of a robin's egg, its fitted bodice showing off a waist that Ad could surely span with both hands. Her hair was swept back and up from her neck, and here, too, the curls had escaped, making it hard to resist the temptation to run his finger the length of its slender column. Ironically, he wondered if perhaps Fate had ordained it that way to stiffen his resolve, the purpose of this visit?

"Cream and sugar?" Holly's question caught Ad off-guard, and he was brought abruptly back from the contemplation of her pretty neck to stammer, "Sugar, no cream."

"Tea's brewed," she announced and turned from the stove, her face flushed from the heat. Placing the teapot on the table, Holly motioned Ad to draw up a chair. "Now, what did you want to talk about?" Holly asked stirring her tea and fixing him with an interested look.

So, here it was, the moment that he had debated over and finally had come to the conclusion to act upon. But, not quite yet—

"I got an interesting letter the other day," he began, picking up his cup and studying the amber contents. "It seems I've won some kind of award."

"An award? How wonderful, Ad. What kind of award?"

"A rather nice one, and it has a bonus attached." Ad's voice betrayed a little of his own pride and excitement. "The series of articles I wrote about Riverbend during the smallpox epidemic and about how we survived it, about the extraordinary heroism of some of the people—" He let this sink in for a moment, gazing at Holly. "At any rate, it did have the effect of touching people and resulted in much of the help the community got—as you know, medical supplies came from the city, along with nurses and nuns to help with the sick." He shrugged. "Well, you know all this, but the main thing is that I've been offered a job. Not my old one but a better one, as a feature writer; they've even suggested a regular column, at a lot more money."

"Well, that's grand, Ad, I'm so happy for you."

"At least it means my exile is over."

"You mean you'll be leaving?"

"Yes. Of course, the job is in Monterey, down the peninsula from San Francisco. A smaller newspaper than the one where I worked before as a reporter in the city—but I'll have more clout and—" He halted. "But that's not really what I came to talk about, although I wanted to tell you that I would be going at the end of the month."

Holly leaned forward, her expression interested, slightly

regretful. "People here will miss you, Ad. Certainly at the paper—we *all* will."

"But you're leaving, too, aren't you, Holly? You only meant to stay until the end of the school year, right? Surely *you* never intended to stay in this backwater town."

"Well . . ." Her voice faded uncertainly.

"That's what I wanted to talk to you about—actually. Why don't we both leave—together?"

"*We?* Together?" It was a puzzled echo.

"Yes, you and I—and Joel," he finished slapping his hand on the table.

"Joel?"

"Look, Holly, I'm asking you to marry me. That way there'll be no problem about your keeping Joel. I mean, how can the Town Council refuse to let a married couple adopt a little boy?"

Holly's eyes opened wide, startled, then softened and warmed. For a moment Ad saw sudden hope leap into them.

"Ad, what a generous offer," she stammered. "I'm touched—flattered, actually." Ad shook his head as if to deny that, but she went on. "I realize what prompted you to make it and I cannot tell you how much it means to me that you—well, that you cared enough to do so. . . ."

Holly pushed back her chair, stood up, walked over to the window, and looked out. The last of the snow had melted; here and there tufts of new grass could be seen thrusting through the patches of brown earth, and the faintest hint of green buds were appearing on the trees. Both Vi and Blaine had told her that spring in Oregon was glorious.

If only Blaine had come to her with this proposal—*that* would have been easy. She had at last stopped denying her feelings for him. With Blaine, everything would be assured. She could happily stay in Riverbend, continue teaching, and together they could make an ideal home for Joel. *They* shared the same values, faith, the desire to make their lives meaningful, to count for something. Instead, it was Ad. Dear Ad. Her heart was deeply touched by his offer. It wasn't that she did not appreciate his motives. She did. But if she accepted it—on any basis—it would mean moving with him to California, starting all over in a new

225

place, in a new role, and with a man she couldn't give her wholehearted love to—couldn't, because that love belonged to someone else.

What Ad was offering was tempting. She knew what he said was true. If she were married, there would be no question of the Town Council's letting her adopt Joel. Alone—there was the risk of losing him.

After talking with Vi, Holly had felt strong and brave and sure, but now the doubts and uncertainty returned full force, disquieting that hard-earned confidence. Ad, who certainly had his "finger on the pulse" of things in this town, knew how things worked, understood the probable masculine viewpoint held by the members of the Town Council, knew what her chances were. Was it *because* he had weighed them and found them wanting in this that he had gallantly proposed marriage?

On the other hand, was Ad's proposal the answer she had been praying for? "God Will Provide." That reassurance of Scripture for every need came into her mind. Was a *husband* what God was providing?

"You don't have to give me your answer right away, you know, Holly," Ad said and his voice sounded both hesitant and a little offended. "Take your time and think about it. . . ." He paused, then said, "Holly, how often have you told me that you've worried about going back to Willow Springs? That you thought you might have changed too much to fit back into that pattern?" He let this sink in for a moment, then he demanded: "You want Joel, don't you? And you're not sure the Town Council will permit an unmarried woman to adopt a child, are you? What I'm offering you is the best possible answer, isn't it?"

"If that were all there were to it," Holly said slowly, then she turned from the window to face him again saying, "But, Ad, that *isn't* all—"

A glint of humor showed in his gray eyes as he said, "I felt there was a 'but' coming."

Holly smiled. "Yes, an important 'but'—"

Ad's expression was a mixture of chagrin and reproach as he answered for her, "You don't love me."

Holly hesitated. Her feelings for Ad were almost love. She

understood and appreciated what the offer he was making her cost a man like him, to whom marriage meant giving up his cherished freedom. Also, Adam was offering to take her away from a town that she had never wanted to come to in the first place, from people who held her destiny in their hands, people she was afraid had too narrow a vision so that they would rather see a little boy placed in an orphanage than with an unmarried woman he loved and trusted. Accepting Adam's offer would give her that chance.

But did Adam really love her? Her woman's instinct told her Adam found her attractive, intelligent, enjoyable to be with, amusing. . . . But more important, even than that, did *she* love him? Enough for marriage? No matter what the reason?

As she hesitated Adam told her, "You know a lot of marriages are based on a lot less than we have, Holly. We're good friends, aren't we?" Ad asked, then got to his feet. "There's no hurry. Think about it—"

"Vi would say—*pray* about it," Holly said softly.

At these words Holly saw that veil drop over Ad's eyes. It was the same silent closure she sensed in him whenever she brought up anything about God or prayer or faith. In that moment, Holly realized she did not really know how Ad felt about the important things of life—at least the things that were becoming more and more important to her.

A smile touched Ad's mouth. "Whatever—think, *pray*, make a list of the pros and cons of my—proposal."

Had he almost said *"proposition"?* Like a business contract? Holly wondered. Was this *that* kind of an arrangement to Ad? How did he *really* feel about her?

He picked up his hat and moved toward the door, saying, "Well, I better be heading back to town. I have a letter to write— replying to the editor at the Monterey paper, accepting the position they've offered me. They want me by the end of the month. When I go, I'd like you to go with me, Holly—and Joel, too, of course."

After Ad left, Holly had the urge to rush over to Vi's, tell her of Ad's proposal, and beg her advice. But something checked her.

No one could make this decision but she—with God's help. The rest of her life—and Joel's—depended on her choice. If she accepted Ad, Joel's adoption would be guaranteed. If not, his future would hang in the balance. It would be up to her to convince the Town Council that she, a single woman, was capable of raising a child—a male child—by herself.

Involuntarily, a deep shudder shook her. Her thoughts went back. He had said, "We're good friends, aren't we?" But what was that friendship based upon? She and Ad had been first drawn together by a mutual feeling—the bond of "exile mentality." In a way, Ad had always mentally had "his hand on the doorknob," he was always on his way out, he had never allowed himself to put down roots in Riverbend—or anywhere else, for that matter. He didn't want permanence or commitment. And Holly realized this was exactly what she *did* want.

Although Ad might provide for her earthly needs, a home, protection, allow her to have Joel—and they could go away together, to a new place, start a new life—was that all that was necessary? And even if Ad thought he wanted that now—was that only temporary? Would that last? Could Ad, in all sincerity, all honesty, promise lifelong fidelity? Was he willing to stand before God and make the vows for an enduring relationship: "for better or for worse, for richer or for poorer, in sickness and in health"? Was what he felt for her—affection, respect, *friendship*—enough? For both of them? For *her*?

Holly knew it was not. In her heart of hearts she knew what she really wanted in a marriage, in a husband. And she knew Adam was not the one who could fulfill that meeting of mind, soul, and spirit that she knew now was what she really yearned for in a relationship. And she knew that without it, she would never be satisfied. She and Adam would always be "unequally yoked." How could she commit her life to someone who tolerated but did not share her deepest beliefs?

The following week she sent Ad a note at the *Monitor* asking him to come out on Saturday.

She met him at the door. "Hello, Ad, let's go into the kitchen," she suggested, leading the way.

Ad looked wary as he came into the room. He dragged one of

the chairs out from the table, straddled it, leaned his arms on the back, and looked at Holly.

"I have a feeling the other boot's going to drop," he said with an attempt at humor. "As I remember, our last conversation ended with the word 'but.' I suppose I'm now going to hear the rest of the sentence. I believe I'd just suggested that you don't love me. Am I right?"

Holly said gently, "Ad, I *do* love you—*but*—," here she smiled a little, "it's not the kind of love I believe it takes to marry someone. It's different from that but just as real."

Ad scowled. "Are we talking about the same thing?"

"Maybe not, but I think so," Holly paused, then continued, "I know and *you* know, too, a marriage has to be built on strongly held mutual beliefs. On faith. Some common center." She chose her words delicately, before going on. "I realize you don't share some of the things that are basic to my life, things I didn't even realize meant so much to me as they do. The epidemic was a kind of turning point for me. This whole year has changed me—deeply. You were right when you reminded me that I might not be able to go back to Willow Springs. Maybe I've changed too much—but I can't marry you, either."

A silence fell between them. Holly's eyes blurred as she looked at Ad across the table where they had sat so often talking, discussing, arguing. Even as her tears distorted his physical image, Holly saw him more clearly than she had ever done before. They had both walked together through a time of testing, and both had seen the realities of life and death, and both of them had been changed by it. Holly saw in Adam the sterling qualities that his old aloof cynicism had hidden before. She knew him now for his true self— strong, caring, fearless in the face of the most terrible possibilities.

Ad stared at a point over Holly's head as if he could not look at her directly while he absorbed everything she had said. Then after a minute or so, he leveled his glance and really looked across the table at her. The woman he saw was a different person from the person he had seen when he first met Hollis Lambeth, newly arrived in Riverbend. He saw a face, more interesting than beautiful; those eyes he had always found so extraordinary—greenish, golden brown—now blazed with honesty. There was no flirtatiousness in them now, no awareness of her own charm, nor artifice in her manner. Here was a true lady, tested in the fire of trials she had never expected to encounter, a woman of gallantry and character.

With a sudden unforeseen wrenching of his heart, Ad found himself wishing that she *did* love him. After another minute he spoke, "I got a letter from the editor of the paper in Monterey. They want me sooner than I thought at first. In fact, they want me as soon as I can come. So . . . ," he said slowly, "since there's really nothing to keep me here now, I guess I'll write them back and then . . . go."

Ad got up and Holly walked with him to the door. He put out his hand, clasped her small one in both his, and looked long and deeply into that face he had come to admire—yes, love. Something good had come out of their meeting, knowing each other, for both of them. He would not have gone through life without having known her, unaware of what she stood for, heedless of what was meaningful to Hollis Lambeth.

"Sure you won't change your mind?" he asked, half-teasing-ly, half-seriously.

"No, I'm sure," she smiled back at him.

They stood there for a full moment looking at each other, then Ad said almost sadly, "I'll never forget you, Holly. That's a promise."

"Nor I you," she said softly, meaning it.

"Good-bye then. I hope things work out for you—about Joel, I mean," he said. He made a slight movement toward her, and for a minute she thought he would kiss her, but he just smoothed back his hair with one hand, put on his hat, and went down the steps and across the schoolyard, where he had left his horse.

As he mounted his horse, turned, and headed back to town, Ad felt a mixture of disappointment and relief. He understood Holly's reasoning. They *did* hold different values. Her life pattern was different from the one he had always followed, one of self-sufficiency, independence, uncommitted; he could never follow hers unquestioningly. And yet, he believed with a convinced certainty that hers was the better way. But to his regret it was not his, nor ever would be.

Seeing him ride away, Holly realized she *would* always remember Adam Corcoran—debonair, skeptical, soft-hearted, reckless, courageous, all the things that made him who he was— and made him unacceptable as a husband.

PART 6

End of the line!

Chapter 22

*J*ust as school was closing one afternoon, Matt Healy showed up. "Official business, Miss Lambeth," he said, handing her an envelope.

Upon opening it, Holly learned that the hearing on her petition to adopt Joel was scheduled for the next Town Council meeting, at which time they would consider and make a decision.

"What do you think, Matt, will they grant it?" she asked as she replaced the letter into its envelope.

"I couldn't say," Matt said, but his expression was doubtful. "There's never been such a thing come up since I've been on the Council. There's many would say it ain't fittin' for a—if you'll excuse the term—a spinster lady to raise a child. But then, on the other hand, seeing you're a teacher, used to children—well, I jest dunno."

Matt's ambiguous opinion did not do much to bolster Holly's optimism. However, she tried to distract herself by finishing up the year's work and issuing "promotion" certificates for the children to take home when school closed for the summer. As she filled in the names of Eliza and Annie Bates, Tom and Michael Healy onto the cards in her best swirly writing one afternoon, she could not help wonder who would be checking them over, planning lessons next fall when school reopened.

Holly put down her pen, stared pensively out the window. Her own plans were uncertain. It all depended on the decision rendered on Joel by the Town Council. If they didn't allow her to adopt Joel—she thrust the thought away. They *had* to. But if they *wouldn't*—the possibility persisted—what would she do?

Her mind suddenly in turmoil, Holly took up her pen again, determined to concentrate on the promotion cards, when she saw Ned's wagon coming into the schoolyard. But it wasn't Ned driving, it was Hetty! Holly dropped her pen with a sputter of ink and almost overturned the inkwell. She hadn't seen Hetty since before the epidemic. When Ned came to take Aurelia and Teddy home again, he said that Hetty was still very weak but recovering. Of course, that had been weeks ago. Now it was April. Why had Hetty come now?

Holly watched as Hetty got slowly down from the wagon seat. Holly hurried to open the schoolhouse door just as Hetty was coming up the steps. Under her arm Hetty was carrying something wrapped in brown paper. When she saw Holly, she halted; her hand went out to hold onto the railing as if for support. Hetty was pale but evidently unscarred by her attack of smallpox.

"Why, Hetty, hello. How are you feeling?" Holly greeted her, the surprise at seeing her cousin showing in her voice.

Hetty seemed to take a deep breath before she replied. "I wanted to come sooner but I wasn't up to it."

"Well, do come in." Holly realized Hetty had never seen her little apartment behind the classroom, had never come out to see her before. In fact, since the day of that awful confrontation she and Hetty had never been alone. She started to offer to make tea but then hesitated. Perhaps first, she had better wait to see what was the purpose of Hetty's visit.

Hetty entered the classroom and looked around. She saw the colorful posters, the pictures the children had drawn pinned on the walls, the old glass bottles they had made into vases to hold the wildflowers, the purple lupines, yellow daisies, and Queen Anne's lace they picked and brought in to Holly.

"It's very nice." Hetty nodded, then added a little awkwardly, "Some of the mothers I know have told me what a good job you've done here."

"Why, thank you, Hetty," Holly said genuinely pleased at the compliment. "Of course, I love the children, and I've found—of all things—that I love teaching!" she laughed.

"I thought you'd be good at it," was Hetty's unexpected comment.

It surprised Holly, remembering Hetty's negative response when she had announced her intention to apply for the school-teacher's job. Suppressing the impulse to remind her, instead she asked, "Could I offer you a cup of tea, Hetty?"

Hetty's mouth worked nervously. "I really can't stay, Holly. I left the children at the store and Ned's pretty busy, so I said I wouldn't be long—"

"You should have brought them. I would love to see them."

"Yes, I know. They begged to come with me when they knew where I was going, but I needed to talk to you—alone," Hetty said stiffly.

"Well, then, won't you sit down?" Holly suggested, thinking how odd it was to feel so ill at ease with your own cousin.

"Here, this is for you," Hetty said, thrusting the package toward Holly. "It's . . . actually, it's a 'thank you' for taking care of Aurelia and Teddy while I was sick." She was struggling to get the words out. "I don't know what I can say to tell you how much—I mean, after all I said and did—well, it was more than I should have expected for you to do for me—"

"Oh, Hetty, please!" Holly protested. "After all, we're *family*, aren't we?"

At this the tears rolled down Hetty's cheeks. "Well, I sure haven't acted like it," she burst out. "I just don't know how to say how sorry . . ."

"You don't have to, Hetty."

"Yes, I do, Holly. I was mean and acted so ugly to you. I guess I had a grudge or, oh, I don't know." She broke off abruptly and fumbled in her jacket pocket for a handkerchief and impatiently wiped her eyes. Then she pushed the paper-wrapped bundle again at Holly. "Here, take it. Open it."

Holly took it and fumbled a little as she untied the string and pushed aside the brown paper. Folded inside was a beautiful red-and-white quilt. Holly remembered seeing the bright-patterned calico pieces that made up the dozens of cartwheels on the diagonally stitched background months ago at Hetty's.

"Oh, Hetty, it's simply lovely!"

"It's the Star of Bethlehem design with twenty stars," Hetty explained. "Aurelia helped cut the diamond shapes to make into stars."

"Oh, it must have taken you hours to make it, Hetty! It's so beautifully done," Holly examined the tiny, exquisite stitches.

"It's the least I could do," Hetty said in her usual stiff way.

"Thank you, Hetty, it's something I'll always cherish."

"There's another thing I want to say, Holly. Ned and I have talked it over and agreed that if the Town Council doesn't approve your adopting the little McKay boy—we'll take him in. What I mean is, he can sleep at our house, and, of course, you can see him all you want and have him with you on the weekends or whenever—that is, if you think that would work out."

Holly was momentarily speechless then genuinely touched. "That's very generous of you and Ned, Hetty."

"Well, he's a nice little fellow, and it would be good for Teddy to have someone for a big brother," Hetty concluded, then started to the door. "I best be getting back."

"Next time bring Aurelia and Teddy, Hetty," Holly said as she followed her out to the door.

"Yes, I'll do that," Hetty promised and even managed a tight smile.

Then at the door, Hetty halted and turned back to face Holly. "There's something else, Holly . . ." she hesitated, ". . . I've had time to do a lot of thinking while I was sick. Time to go over things, things I didn't want to think about, look at—and what I saw—mostly in myself—well, it wasn't very nice." Hetty's inner struggle was apparent in her expression. "Jealousy is a very ugly thing. It's poison and if you let it, it goes all through you. I was deadly jealous of you, Holly. You were everything I wanted to be when we were girls. Then, by some miracle, Ned asked me to marry him and come out here with him. I jumped at the chance to escape from Willow Springs and all my unhappiness there."

Holly saw her swallow and she spontaneously put out her hand as if to stop the flow of words. But Hetty shook her head vigorously, "No, Holly, I have to say it. Then when Mama wrote and told me what had happened to you—I mean, about you and Jim—I was glad! Yes, glad. I'm shamed to admit it, but it's the truth. I gloated about it. I thought, *So something bad can happen to someone like Holly!*" Hetty bit her lower lip and hung her head for a minute before continuing. "When Mama asked me to let you come out here to stay until the gossip died down, I didn't want to do it. And when you came—everything that I remembered I hated about growing up in Willow Springs in the shadow of my pretty cousin hit me! I hoped you'd be so bored and dissatisfied here that you'd leave soon!"

"Hetty, you don't need to tell me all this."

"Yes, I do, Holly, it needs to be said. I've got to let all this poison out," Hetty rushed on, "but that didn't happen. Instead, you charmed everyone, made friends, created a place for yourself in Riverbend, *in spite of me!* And I resented *that*, too!" Hetty sighed deeply. "Well, I've learned my lesson, Holly. Besides hurting you, I've not only hurt myself but Ned and the children, too. And I just have to ask you to forgive me."

"Of course, I forgive you, Hetty," was all Holly could say. She was too moved by Hetty's obvious grief and remorse. She started to give Hetty a hug but wasn't sure whether to or not. It might be too soon. After all, Hetty had taken the first step toward reconciliation. Maybe she should wait, let her cousin set the pattern of their future relationship.

Hetty opened the door and started down the steps, out to the wagon and climbed in. She raised her hand in a wave before she picked up the reins and turned the horse around.

Standing at the door, Holly watched the wagon as it went down the road. Many things were going through her mind. She realized she had written Hetty off as troublesome, abrasive, and tiresome, never taking time to weigh the reasons that her cousin so often manifested these traits.

She understood so much more now about her cousin. Hadn't she gone through feelings of isolation, of being judged, rejected, disliked, and without friends, since she came to Riverbend? She could understand how having enough of those kinds of experiences could embitter someone. *Maybe it has to be that way,*

239

thought Holly. *A heart that has never known pain can't empathize with someone else's.*

Back in the house, Holly took the quilt to her bedroom and spread it on the bed, but the sides trailed to the floor on either side of the narrow bedstead. It was a quilt made for a larger bed, a double bed. It was the kind of a quilt that a young woman usually made for her hope chest or the kind that one received as a wedding present. Holly felt a little twinge of wistfulness.

Almost at the same moment she thought of Blaine.

Holly had not seen much of Blaine. Was he avoiding her? She'd spent an inordinate amount of time worrying why.

When the date of her appeal for Joel's adoption was set, Holly was told that there were several documents she would have to present to the Town Council with her application to become Joel's legal guardian. Along with a verification of her contract for another year as Riverbend's schoolteacher and a recommendation from Reverend Mobley that she attended church regularly and was of good moral character, would be a health certificate. This presented Holly with the perfect opportunity to stop by Blaine's office.

The night before her appointment, Holly washed her hair in fresh rainwater and soaked for a long time in a tub lavishly scented with rose oil. Afterward she sat for a long time brushing her hair in front of the mirror, her thoughts as dark as the gathering evening outside. Why, suddenly, did the optimism she had been feeling seem wrapped in a pall of melancholy?

Things were actually working out very well, much better than she could have hoped. Systematically she counted her blessings: She had a contract for the following year, she had supportive friends, there was the reconciliation with Hetty, the very real hope that her adoption of Joel would be granted—why then this sadness creeping over her?

Was it because Ad was gone? Did she have any lingering regret that she had not accepted his proposal, ensuring Joel's future with her? No, Holly had never been more sure that turning down Ad's offer was the right thing to do.

Then what was it? It was Blaine. Holly put down her brush and looked deeply into the eyes of the young woman in the mirror. Hadn't she matured, become self-reliant and responsible? Why, every time she saw or was near Blaine, did she become a fluttery schoolgirl?

Resolutely Holly reminded herself that Blaine had had a life before she had known him, before she ever came to Riverbend. A full, dedicated life. He was admired, trusted, respected; he did not seem to have a void in his life nor any need for someone to fill it. He was well-educated, widely traveled, had known personal loss, faced life-and-death challenges that she knew nothing of, had lived and known a whole existence of which she had no part, had a past that she had not shared.

Meeting such a man in this remote little town in Oregon had been such happenstance. Or—and here a little shiver trembled through Holly—was *anything* in life just happenstance or was there, as Vi believed, a plan, a Divine one, for everything—every meeting, every event, every person?

The next day as she got ready to go into town for her appointment with Blaine, Holly's hands shook as she pushed the pearl-headed hatpins firmly anchoring her bonnet on her head. Her hair was so shiny clean and silkily slippery that it defied her attempts to secure it neatly into a twisted coil. She wore a blue jacketed dress and a lighter blue blouse underneath with a ruffled jabot. It looked as though it might rain, so she carried her umbrella, recalling with a smile the first disastrous time she had set out for an appointment with Blaine.

Walking into his small waiting room, Holly was aware of its antiseptic smell, a clean, astringent odor that she always vaguely associated with him. On the desk to the right of the door was set a metal bell next to an open ledger, identified as "Patients Log," and a neatly printed sign that read, "Please sign your name and tap bell to let doctor know of your arrival."

After writing her name in the book, Holly gave the bell a tap then sat down, her hands clasped tightly over her small handbag in her lap. Almost immediately the door to the inner office opened, and Blaine looked out.

"Good morning, Holly!" he smiled. "I wish all my patients looked as much like they didn't need a doctor as *you* do!"

With a sudden little flash, Holly had a prescient vision of

241

what Blaine might look like in the years down the road. Traces of character were already forming around his eyes, the laughter lines would deepen, and there would be silver in the thick tawny hair. In that second a strange thought followed, *Will I know him then, will I share those years?*

Quickly Holly brought all her imaginings into subjection. In her most sedate manner she rose from the seat and said demurely, "Well, I certainly hope I'm well and healthy, Blaine. There's a great deal depending on it, you know."

"Well come into my examining room, and we'll soon find out. Although I've never been surer of my diagnosis," Blaine said heartily. He sensed her nervousness and was trying to reassure her. "Would you mind removing your jacket so I can listen to your heart and lungs?" he asked in a very professional manner.

Blaine took the jacket and hung it up on the coatrack; then indicated a small stool for her to sit down on, then put on his stethoscope. He listened to her heart and took her pulse. To her annoyance, both had accelerated the minute she had stepped into his office. Asking her to remove her bonnet, he poked some kind of instrument into her ears, checked her eyes, and had her open her mouth so he could look at her teeth and throat.

"My goodness, I feel like some kind of prize calf being readied for the county fair!" she exclaimed, flustered.

Blaine smiled as he folded up his stethoscope and returned it to his pocket. "Not at all. I give you a clean bill of health. You are as fine a specimen of healthy American womanhood as it has ever been my pleasure to see."

Blaine busied himself making notations on the certificate Holly had given him to fill out after the examination. Even as Blaine wrote the medical comments in professionally accurate terms in the appropriate spaces, he was keenly aware of Holly— the flawless skin of her softly curved cheek, the warm scent of her faintly reminiscent of summer roses . . .

Finally he handed her the certificate with a flourish. "There you go, Holly. With all the other good recommendations I'm sure you'll get, I feel very positive that the adoption will go through."

She drew on her gloves slowly, sighing and said, "I wish I felt that confident."

"Come on now, Holly, where's all that spunk? I don't think you've got anything to worry about. I *know* what my vote would be. Joel would be a very lucky little boy to get someone like you for a mother."

"Too bad *you're* not on the Town Council!" she declared.

"Everything's going to work out just fine. You'll see."

Holly got to her feet, and Blaine took her jacket down from the coatrack and helped her on with it. He followed her out to the reception room and opened the office door for her. At the door she held up the certificate. "Thanks, Blaine, for this. *And* your encouragement."

"Look, Holly . . . ," Blaine hesitated a second, then said, "May I take you to the meeting the day of the hearing?"

Holly was taken back by his offer. From the first, Blaine had not said very much about her plan. While everyone else had counseled, warned, advised, argued about it, Blaine had remained silent. Holly thought that perhaps he wasn't interested, or maybe he thought it a bad idea, or worse still, maybe he didn't really care about the outcome. She would have welcomed his opinion, wished he had come forward, made some suggestion. Of all the people in Riverbend, Blaine was the one with whom she most wanted to discuss it. Why not? She had been more hurt by this than she cared to admit.

But now she saw the genuine concern in his eyes, and it gave her a surge of strength and optimism. "Why, yes, Blaine, I'd like you to. Thank you very much."

Two weeks later, standing at the schoolhouse window, Holly waited anxiously for the sight of Blaine's shabby little buggy. Dressed in a simple olive green suit of light wool Vi had made for her, Holly checked her fob watch for the dozenth time, hoping nothing unexpected, some kind of emergency, would delay Blaine or, at the worst, prevent his coming to escort her to the meeting at Town Hall.

Joel was staying with the Healy family until the Council made its decision, and Holly missed him already. She had been awake half the night, worrying and praying about the meeting today. At dawn she got up, wrapped herself in a shawl, sat in the rocker by the bedroom window with the Bible in her lap, turning its pages, seeking comfort and guidance. Over and over she had returned to the book of Joshua, relating very much to *his* apprehension of what lay ahead. It *had* to be God's will for her to have Joel, she told herself. There were too many "coincidences" about their relationship for it *not* to be so!

Her nervousness began to abate. She felt curiously calm. Once before she had had to go before the Town Council to plead her case. She had won then, against all odds, and now the stakes were even higher. *This* time more than her own self-interest depended on the outcome: Joel's life, his future, his bright little mind, his eagerness to learn, his outgoing personality, and his loving heart—all the things Holly saw in him that no one else had seen or cared about. Why wasn't it obvious to everyone that this homeless orphan would be better off with her than placed in an orphanage in another county? Why couldn't a single woman raise a child? Vi Dodd had.

Holly's hands twisted tensely. She wouldn't let Joel go to someone else, to a farm family who might use him as another field hand, consider him just an extra mouth to feed. She was determined to fight for Joel as she had never fought for anything in her life before. And if she lost, if the Council refused her request to adopt him—what then? She pressed her lips into a straight line. Holly dared not think of the alternative that had already presented itself to her rebellious spirit.

Just then she saw Blaine's gig pull into the yard. She hurried out ready to climb into it before he had a chance to get out and help her.

"Fortified to face the gladiators?" he greeted her, trying to lighten her mood.

"Yes," was all she could manage to say. She was too preoccupied, mentally rehearsing her speech, hoping it had the right mixture of conviction and appeal.

They were almost to the edge of town when Blaine looked over at her and remarked, "That's a mighty pretty hat."

Surprised, she touched the brim with one hand and said, "You noticed?"

"Of course, I noticed," Blaine said, then added quietly, "don't you know I notice *everything* about you, Holly?"

Suddenly, spending considerable time putting new ribbons on her bonnet seemed suddenly worth the effort. Breathlessly, Holly realized Blaine was looking at her the way she had always hoped he would. She started to reply, but they were too near town and there wasn't time. They turned into Main Street, and Blaine drew up in front of the Town Hall. He pulled on the brake, then got out and came around to the other side of the buggy to help her down.

"Good luck, Holly. I know you'll do a good job,"

"Aren't you coming in with me?" she asked.

"This is *your* moment, Holly. You're going in there as an independent, capable woman. You don't need me or anyone to make your case for you. Remember Larkin and the Renner boy and the day you walked boldly into the Doggone Best—you didn't need anyone then and you don't need anyone now. Nobody can forget what you did during the epidemic. Just stand up and be yourself, Holly. That's all you need to do." Blaine helped her down, held both her hands in a strong clasp for a single second.

Holly looked up into his face, a face she knew now that she loved. She longed to say, "You're wrong, Blaine, I need *you!*" But she couldn't. Not after what he'd said, not after what he believed about her. She swallowed her fear, straightened her shoulders, and started up the Town Hall steps, repeating under her breath the words she had read and memorized the night before from Joshua: "Be strong and of good courage, I will not leave you nor forsake you. Do not be afraid, nor be dismayed, for the Lord your God is with you wherever you go."

If Holly had been made to relate word by word what took place in the council meeting that day, she would have found it impossible to do. She recalled her name being called to address the members with her petition; she remembered Vi squeezing her hand for encouragement; then the next thing she knew, she was standing at the podium, clearing her voice to speak.

Others in that crowded meeting hall that day *did* remember the sight of the slender young woman, becomingly yet conservatively dressed, whose voice shook a little as she began but grew stronger as she went on, "Even though I do not have a husband, a protector, a provider, I feel that as Riverbend's schoolteacher, with the salary and living quarters allotted me, I will be able to give Joel McKay a stable home. More than that, I love him dearly. We have been through things together that many a mother has not experienced with a son born to her. I comforted him at the death of his own parents. I have nursed him through the sickness that took his younger sister, and I shared his grief. We have grown closer through these trials. If I am given the privilege of rearing him, I feel I can best help him learn and develop the abilities I see in him. Since he's been one of my pupils, I've become aware that he *is* extremely bright. Now, that I've had the opportunity of observing him more closely, I am convinced Joel McKay has the potential of becoming a fine man, a benefit to this community. With your help and the help of those other citizens of Riverbend who are sympathetic and supportive of my appeal to adopt Joel, I believe he will have a far better life with me than being made a ward of the county and sent to the orphanage. I have submitted the personal character references you required, and I earnestly ask you to grant my petition for legal adoption of the minor child, Joel McKay."

Mayor Morrison had to gavel down the spontaneous applause that erupted as Holly resumed her seat. When quiet was restored, the Mayor said gruffly, "The council will take a fifteen-minute recess to consider Miss Lambeth's petition. When we return, we will announce our decision."

Holly felt as though she were reliving the time she had applied to become schoolteacher, only this anxiety was more acute. It was hard to believe that had been nearly a year ago. She had arrived in Riverbend feeling as though she were about to serve a penal sentence. All she had hoped for then was to endure it long enough to let the gossip about her and Jim

Mercer's broken engagement die down. Now that seemed almost unimportant except as the reason she had come to Oregon in the first place.

Holly sat stiffly in her chair, hardly conscious of the people who came up to shake her hand or pat her shoulder and wish her well. Her mind was locked into that inner room where Joel's fate and hers was being decided. She couldn't even pray. No words came to her to plead except, "Help! Lord. Please, Lord."

Finally, a nudge from Vi alerted her that the members were taking their places on the platform. The mayor moved to center stage and, shuffling some papers, declared, "As you all know, the case brought before this membership was an unusual one, and under most circumstances such a petition would not even have been considered. However, since Miss Lambeth is known to us all, has established her name and reputation in Riverbend, and is held in high esteem by all who know her, we hereby grant an affirmative response to her appeal to adopt the minor child Joel McKay."

"You've won, Holly, you've won!" cried Vi, hugging her.

Relief made Holly weak, as the realization broke through her tension; joy filled her heart bringing both tears and laughter.

Caught up in the excitement, Holly felt dazed, astonished, still unable to believe that it had really happened. People she did not even recognize came up to congratulate her. Then, suddenly, Holly looked around—searching for the one face that was missing. Blaine! Where was Blaine?

The following week was the last week of school. After the rest of the children had left for the day, Joel helped Holly tidy up the classroom. Both he and Holly were finding it hard to believe that what they had hoped and prayed for had really come true.

"And will I be your little boy forever and ever after?" he asked her now as he had a dozen times since the hearing.

"Yes, Joel, and my *big* boy and my grown son and my great strong manly son when I am an old, old lady!" Holly told him, laughing and hugging him and tousling his hair.

"You'll never be old!" he declared, then added anxiously, "Will you?"

"Not for a long, long time," she laughed.

Holly had not told Joel that she had been offered a contract for another year to teach, because she was unsure of what she was going to do. Even that fact astonished her. Six months ago the thought that she would not be heading home in June never entered her mind. She had not yet written her family about the adoption. This presented another puzzling problem. Of course, she felt sure the Lambeth family would have welcomed Joel with the proverbial open arms. But Holly knew what her mother's and other female relatives' private reaction would be—a single woman with an adopted child would have a difficult time finding a husband!

"May I go now?" Joel's voice broke in on her thoughts. "Uncle Ned said I should come and work at the store after school today. He has lots of boxes to put away."

"Yes, go ahead, Joel. We're about finished here," Holly said. Good old Ned, he had been her staunch support right from the start and had taken Joel under his wing immediately. Holly was grateful, too, that the long breech with Hetty was finally healed. Although they were still careful with each other and would probably never be close—at least not like Holly and Vi were, there was now peace about their relationship, past and present.

After Joel left, Holly was so preoccupied she did not hear buggy wheels outside nor the sound of footsteps on the porch. The schoolroom door was open because the weather was mild, but it wasn't until he said her name that she looked up and saw Blaine in the doorway.

"Holly, may I come in?"

She was on her knees in the front of the low shelf, straightening books that the Primary pupils used.

"Of course, Blaine," she said and sat back on her heels, dust-cloth in hand. "What brings you out here this time of day?"

He pulled up one of the wooden stools and sat down.

"Business."

"Business?"

"Yes, serious business."

"What kind of *serious* business?"

"The *most* serious business there is."

"And what is *that?*" Holly, smiled, knowing that Blaine enjoyed conundrums and word games.

"Love."

"Love?" Holly gasped.

Blaine chuckled, "You have a most annoying habit of repeating everything I say."

"Well, you say the most *amazing* things!"

"Yes, love is amazing, and it is also serious business," he paused. "I love you, Holly, and I'm not sure what to do about it."

Holly blinked, tried to absorb what Blaine had said.

"I guess I've known I was falling in love with you over the last year. I certainly respected you. Admired you. I respect you for your courage, your honesty, your independence," his smile broadened, "your sense of fun, your generosity, and your sweetness—"

Blushing, Holly got to her feet and Blaine stood, too. Twisting the dustcloth nervously, Holly moved to a safe distance, distractedly dusting the top of the teacher's desk. "You make me sound like a paragon of virtue!"

"Well, of course I do. Doesn't every man think the woman he loves is perfect?" He moved steadily toward her. She took a few steps backward, bumped into the blackboard and found herself trapped. "When I realized I really loved you—maybe it was the day of the picnic or the night out at the Renner's farm or maybe at the Christmas party or during the epidemic—who knows when it was? I just *knew.*"

"But you never said anything, you never spoke about—"

"What could I say? I thought that maybe Adam was in the picture. And then when he left town and you decided to petition for Joel's adoption as a single woman, I realized you weren't planning to marry Adam. I began to think there might be a chance for me. But I didn't want to say anything *before* the hearing for fear *you* might think I was just doing it to make the adoption possible."

Holly thought of Adam and his proposal. She glanced up at Blaine. She stared at him in disbelief. "But it *would* have—"

"Yes, but then *you* wouldn't have known you were able to do it on your own."

The meaning of what he was saying finally penetrated. Blaine cared, *really* cared, wanted her to have the confidence, the justifiable pride of accomplishing that alone, *wanted* her to have that victory for herself.

"But you could have said something—," she faltered.

Blaine plunged his hands into his pockets and stared over her head out the window. "I couldn't. I know the kind of background you come from. I recognized it the moment I met you. Maybe because I come from the same kind. I know what a family like yours expects of a husband, and it isn't the life of a country doctor in a frontier town." Blaine shook his head.

"I don't even know why I came out here today. I probably shouldn't have. I just kept thinking that school is ending and that you'd probably be leaving, and I might never see you again. I guess I thought I couldn't let you go without at least . . ."

"At least what?"

"Telling you how I feel. But what do I have to offer you? A doctor's life doesn't belong to him or his family, it belongs to his patients. Any time, any hour of night or day—it isn't much of a life to offer a woman. The truth is I didn't dare hope that you could love me. Didn't dare ask you—"

"Oh, *ask* me! *Please* ask me, Blaine!" the words were out of her mouth before she realized she had said them.

His expression showed the joyous shock. "Holly! You mean it?"

"I never meant anything more," she said softly.

He held out his arms and she went into them. Holly felt his strength enfold, envelop her. She felt infinitely safe, unconditionally loved. For a long time they stood, just holding each other, heartbeat against heartbeat. Then slowly Holly raised her face, looked into Blaine's eyes, and knew that at last she had found what she had been looking for all her life. Commitment, purpose, and a love that would last forever.